CONJURED DEFENSE

J. C. JACKSON

SHADOW PHOENIX PUBLISHING

Conjured Defense

J.C. Jackson

Copyright © 2019 J.C. Jackson

Published by Shadow Phoenix Publishing LLC

ISBN-13: 978-1732283534, 978-1-7322835-5-8

Cover designed by J. Caleb Design

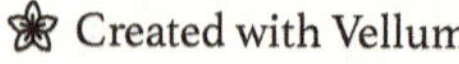 Created with Vellum

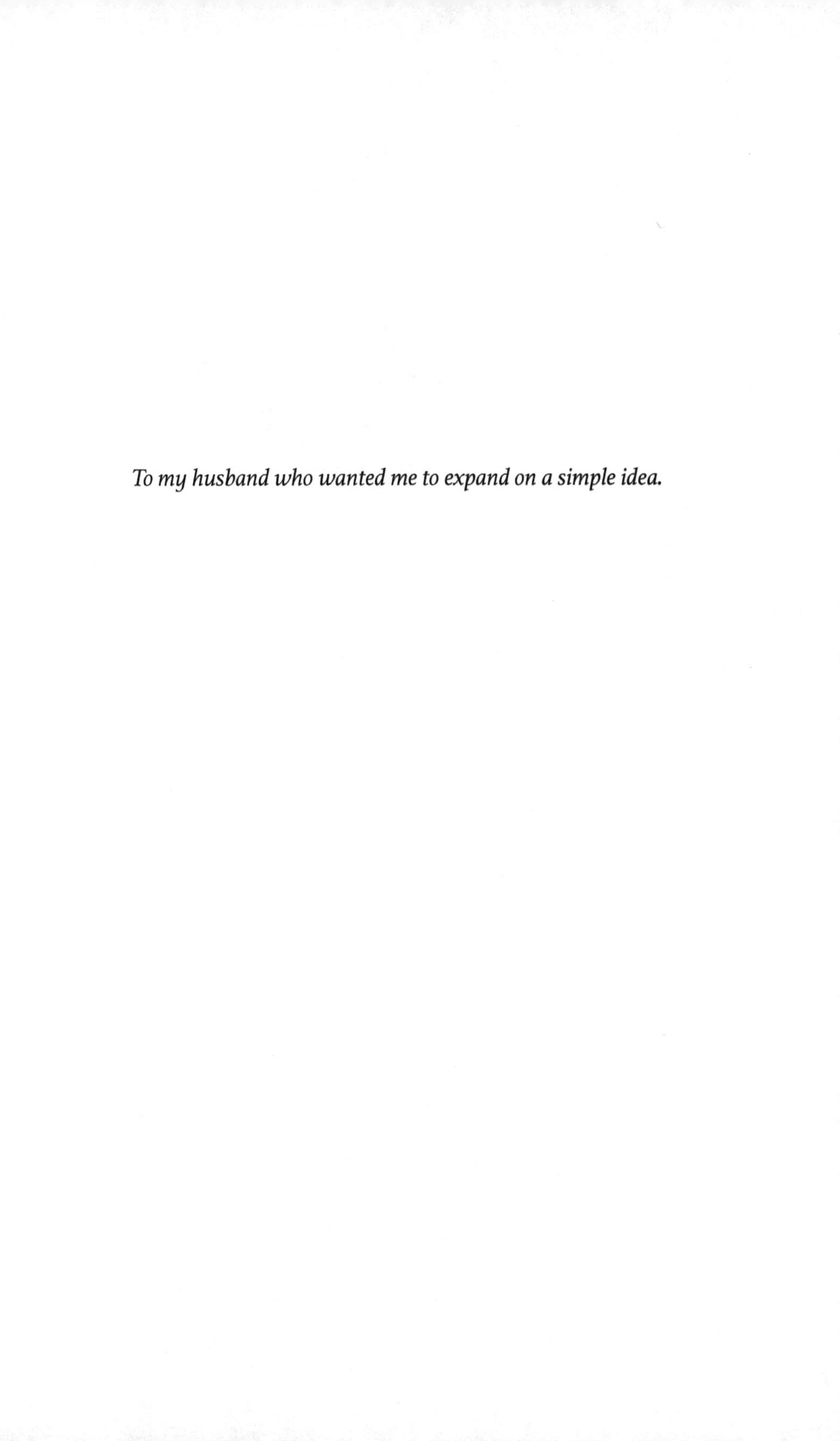

To my husband who wanted me to expand on a simple idea.

THE ICY AIR cut through the thick layers of clothing I wore. I always seemed to end up in these types of situations in the cold. I hated being cold.

I took a deep breath to bring myself back to the problem at hand. I watched silently from my hiding spot as those who hunted me stood below. If they kept with their previous pattern, they would soon pass, following one of my false trails. My window of time to meet up with my partner on the other side of town grew shorter each time I stopped like this.

Once they cleared out, I tucked my loose dark auburn strands under the hood and behind my long Elven ear before I dropped back down to the ground to continue. The snow made it difficult to hide my movements so I stuck to more public roads, keeping my invisibility spell up, hoping the new footprints would be overlooked among the other traffic.

In the distance I spotted two people wearing Terran Intelligence Organization coats. I fell in line behind an Elven woman, following her footsteps. I brought my scarf up over my nose and mouth, holding my breath as they approached. My invisibility spell would not hide the condensation.

"Gods, can't anyone get eyes on this girl?" one of the men complained.

"It's like she's a ghost. I'm starting to think Ketayl isn't even out here. She'd be the smart one of us if she decided to stay inside somewhere warm."

"Shouldn't we check the side streets and alleys? I'd assume she'd travel there than risk being spotted on the main road."

"She's an arcane caster. I have no idea what she's capable of. Besides, the teams scouting those areas haven't had any luck either."

If they were becoming this lax about searching for me, it was to my benefit, but I still could not let down my guard. My luck there would be someone more observant waiting closer to my destination.

I looked for some cover. I needed a break from using my invisibility spell.

Glancing down the alleys as I went, I spotted one which appeared to have what I needed. Checking to make sure the path was empty as far as I could see, I darted down it, kicking the snow off my boots as soon as I hit clear pavement.

I quickly ran a trail into the nearest doorway before I carefully backed out and continued down the covered alley as soon as I stopped leaving a trail. Using a quick flight spell, I got myself up onto the roof top patio area of the restaurant I passed.

Taking a moment to survey my surroundings, I heard commotion below.

"She must have come this way."

"Those could be anyone's footprints. They probably belong to someone who works here."

Keeping my invisibility spell in place, I peered over the edge, but the two were out of my sight under the overhang.

I backed away and sighed. There might not be any rest here.

"Should we check it out?"

"Let's ask if they've seen her. Otherwise I see no reason to search the place."

I rolled my eyes and moved farther onto the patio. I needed to rest.

Shivering, I huddled down in a corner of the bar where I would be out of sight of anyone inside and anyone possibly looking for me from a higher vantage point. Then I released my spell. I just needed a few minutes to recover and then I could keep going.

I moved my coat so I could check my watch. Frowning at my

empty wrist, I forgot I left it behind since the battery died a couple of days ago. How much time did I have left?

Why did it have to be so cold? And why did I have to go through this so soon after Silver and I returned from Ghost Forest? We had not even been back a full week.

My thoughts were interrupted by voices below. "How in the Hells has no one seen her?"

"Do you think we should ambush her at the meeting point?"

"We need to catch her and get the information she carries before then. Can't involve her partner - both of them would be more trouble than we can handle."

"At this rate we won't catch her at all."

"Fine. Let's search toward the meeting point. Doesn't sound like anyone else is having luck either."

I sighed. *Great. Just great.* Now I was going to have to expend even more arcane energy to get past them. I doubted they were the only ones considering ambushing me near the meeting point.

How was I supposed get past all of these people?

I ran through scenarios in my head, searching for the best solution. Preferably something without conflict.

Closing my eyes for a moment, I stretched my senses out, hoping there was a pocket of concentrated arcane energy in the area. After a few moments, I located one near the meeting point. It should be enough to give me a boost. The hard part was getting over there.

If only I could teleport, but I could not risk running myself so low on arcane energy. Not with so many looking for me.

The cold kept me from resting too long. I put my invisibility spell back up and continued.

The main road swarmed with TIO agents. I paused, unsure if I should attempt my previous method of getting by them.

No, I would never be able to hold my breath long enough and I needed to move fast. I went back down the alley, quickly navigating between buildings, dropping my spell. It sounded like they had given up checking the back alleys for me.

The town's smaller size made it harder to hide, but it still contained enough narrow channels between the buildings I could get past the agents on the main street. Turning a corner, I slid to a stop at a wooden fence.

"I think she came this way. The tracks look fresh."

I turned in time to see two agents come around the corner.

The Human man grinned. "Looks like we scored."

With wide eyes, I took a step back as the two approached. My chest tightened and my breath came faster. I could not get caught. I needed to get out of here. I looked around frantically, continuing to back away from them until my back hit the fence.

I held out my hands, putting up my shield spell to give me more time to think.

The man who had spoken walked into the shield and bounced off, making my spell show its hexagonal pattern momentarily.

"What in the Hells?"

His partner laughed at him. "Caster, remember?"

"It's cheating is what it is."

The fence. I needed to get over the fence. They had not called in my location. I should meet no one on the other side.

Using a quick flight spell, I got over the fence, but my hood caught and tore on the fence. I fell and landed hard on the ground. My thick clothing and the snow provided little padding.

As soon as I heard the agents curse and climb the fence, I threw up my invisibility spell and created an illusion of myself running down the alley.

I sighed in relief as they chased my illusion before I climbed back over the fence and continued on, releasing my spells. At least those two were easy to distract. It would not be long before they were back though.

I swung back toward the more populated streets. I put up my invisibility spell again and worked to create false trails for a few minutes before hiding my tracks in others.

Commotion sounded behind me. Agents came out of the alleys, looking frustrated. Their new hunts began as they followed my false trails.

I needed to stay calm and move carefully. *Only a couple more blocks.*

Silver leaned back against a long, fully enclosed, black truck. His braid fell over his right shoulder as it always did and he wore his armored jacket. The cold did not seem to phase him.

I scrunched up my nose at him. I already missed my hood.

As I got closer, my partner pulled out his phone and looked at it, but I caught his eyes glancing up around him. What he saw was out of my current view.

My guess was some of those agents planned to ambush me at the meeting point. I concerned myself more with what Silver's reaction might be. I did not want anyone to get hurt.

I took my time approaching, careful of my foot placement so I did not draw attention while soaking up the arcane energy from the concentrated pocket. Silver's eyes flicked up in my direction when I stood across the street from him. Then he looked both left and right.

I stopped and turned anyway, in case there were agents behind me. There were, but none coming in my direction. They focused their attention on the alleys and in the opposite direction.

Why were there so many people?

Silver pushed himself fully back to his feet, shoved his phone back into his pocket, and got in the truck. Had I missed my window to get out of here?

One street. I needed to cross one street and I could leave this frozen hunt.

I pulled my scarf up over my nose and mouth before I moved a little closer to my goal, pausing to see who was on the street. Both sides of the cross street held agents all looking toward the truck Silver was in.

So close to getting out of here. I wished I had a way to communicate with my partner. There had to be something I could do to turn their attention elsewhere.

I glanced back down the street behind me and considered my earlier distraction. How far could I get them to chase an illusion? How fast could I get in the vehicle so I remained unseen?

Even with being in the pocket of concentrated arcane energy, I would run myself low getting out of here. At least I would not need to teleport far.

I created an illusion of myself again, peeking out an alley down the right hand side of the street. Immediately it was spotted and I directed it toward myself and then back down the main part of the street.

Agents yelled, calling out my illusion's location. Others whose attention had been in the opposite direction turned and helped with the chase.

My illusion turned down the alley with the fence. As soon as the last of the agents I spotted on the roads passed me, I teleported the short distance into the back of the truck, landing hard.

I heard Silver turn. "Ketayl?"

"Go." I released all of my spells and stayed put. I shivered and hoped my partner thought to turn the heat up.

I watched the buildings start to move slowly.

Several seconds passed before my partner asked, "You okay?"

I sniffled. "Cold. Running low. I'll stay back here where I'm out of sight and the windows are dark."

"Just rest. I'll get us home."

I listened to the sound of the heater blowing, having no energy for conversation and thankfully Silver seemed to understand that.

THE SOUND of the back hatch of the truck opening startled me. I picked my head up to look out the window. Where were we?

Silver stood at the back. He folded his arms. "You certainly took your time. I thought I was going to have to leave."

I rolled my eyes and scooted out of the back, which was awkward with the heavy winter garments. "The snow made it difficult." I glanced around at the underground parking garage we were in. He got us back to the main office as promised.

"What happened to your coat?" Silver examined where I had torn the hood from the collar.

"I got caught on a fence."

My partner shook his head.

Shivering, I rubbed my arms. It was cold in here.

"Come on. Let's get you warmed up." Silver put his arm around my shoulders, gently guiding me toward the exit.

The ride up the elevator was silent. My partner escorted me to a conference room. He went to the side and poured a hot drink.

"Sorry you had to wait so long," I said quietly, rubbing my arms.

"I would have waited past the designated time if needed. I didn't like the idea of you being out in the cold like that."

"We wanted to give them a chance," a male voice said. "Looks like we might have to make it harder for you next time."

Startled for the second time, I spun on my heel. Rorek stood there with his arms crossed. The Dwarven man was the one who organized this training exercise.

Rorek stroked his long brown beard. "You made some of the best trackers in the business act like rookies. Not an easy feat. Granted, they haven't been put up against an arcane caster like you before."

I rolled my eyes and sat down, huddling into my large, thick coat. "Can we do this when it's warmer next time?" I asked.

"Then they'll never catch you," Rorek said with a smile.

I shook my head.

Silver put a steaming mug down on the table next to me. He reached for the zipper of my coat.

I batted his hands away. Apparently this exercise put him in over-protective big brother mode. "Leave it alone. I'm cold."

"Ketayl..." Silver sighed. "You'll warm up faster if you take it off in here."

I grumbled at my partner, but let him help me out of the heavy garments. Then I drank the tea he made for me.

"You're always so cranky when you're cold." My partner smirked at me.

"I can't wait for them to get back and we review how close you passed some of them," Rorek commented as he moved around the room, turning equipment on. "Not to mention they weren't supposed to ambush you at the meeting point."

I closed my eyes and clamped my mouth shut before I said something I would regret. I just wanted to get back to my work. I needed to get back to finding if there were any other necromancers out there.

"Do you have her things?" Silver asked.

"Oh, right!" Rorek said.

I opened my eyes as Rorek rushed to get the box he made me deposit my phone and other personal items in before the exercise started. I was grateful to have my boots back. The big heavy ones loaned to me hurt my feet.

I dug my phone out and glanced at my missed notifications. Sitting up straight, I almost knocked my mug over. "I've got to go. Lockonis messaged me hours ago."

"I'm sure she remembered you were doing the training simulation today," Silver said. "Just relax and warm up."

I shook my head, downing the rest of the hot drink faster than was wise and cringed as it burned my throat.

"You don't want to stay and listen to them whine?" Rorek asked.

"Probably better if I don't. Let me know if there's something I can do better next time." I shoved my feet into my boots and left.

2

"Hey, Ket, I was wondering when you'd get back. How do you feel about being a test subject?" Lockonis asked with a broad smile as I entered what the cyber team lovingly called the "dungeon". The only illumination in the room came from the many screens mounted to the walls and on their desks.

My stride slowed as I eyed the fiery red-headed Elven woman. "I... uh..." I looked back at the door I came through, wondering if I should leave. I clearly remembered the last thing I tested for her and I hoped I never needed to test the arcane restraint again.

"Relax, I've been wanting the big guy to give it a try, but he's stubborn." Lockonis signaled me over.

If she was attempting to get Vince, the director of the TIO, to try something, it could not be that bad. She led me to a desk in the back, past the cursing Gnome woman with pink pigtails, to a Halfling hidden in a mostly-dark corner office. He worked on some electronics under a desk lamp and sat surrounded by gadgets of all shapes and sizes.

"Tonky, you got the stuff ready for Ket?"

"Yeah, just give me a moment."

"I'll leave her with you then." Lockonis patted my shoulder and left.

I rubbed my shoulder to get rid of the sensation. She could have at least told me why she called me down here instead of leaving me to worry about what she wanted me to test.

Something sizzled and smoke rose from the board he held. I took a step back. The acrid smell gave me little hope.

He fanned the smoke with his hand for a moment before turning to me with a broad smile. "Ready to try out some new toys?"

"I guess?" Not that I needed any more to deal with.

"Give me your phone," Tonky said with his hand out.

Reluctantly I dug it out of my pocket and relinquished it. A new device was deposited in its place. I examined the watch-looking thing curiously. Its square blank face was far bigger than my last watch.

"I left most of the settings on default so adjust them to your liking. I'll forward information to you about it." The watch dinged a second later with a message from Tonky.

I fussed with putting the watch on, toying with it while he gathered items from around his desk. What was the purpose of this?

He held a small, open cardboard box out to me. "Figured it was easier to pack everything together. The charging cables are in there as well and some other accessories Lockonis ordered. Any questions?"

I bit my lower lip and examined the device attached to my wrist. "Um..."

"Hey, if you have any, you know where to find me. Just toying with it should get you a feel for the operation. If you don't like dictating your messages, you may prefer to still respond from your phone. Oh, your phone." He jumped and spun on his chair to reach for it, but picked up the one sitting next to it.

I must have been too distracted to have noticed him plug it into his computer. He checked a couple of things before handing it to me.

Tonky smiled at me. "You're all set."

"The other one is mine," I said softly.

"Upgrade. Transferred all your settings and files from the old one."

I turned the new device over. "Oh. Thank you."

"Anytime. And if it's after hours, you know where I live." Tonky smirked.

He was my next door neighbor.

I bowed and left.

Lockonis stopped me before I could escape the dungeon. "All set?"

I looked down at the box in my hands. "I think so. Is this really necessary?"

"Yes, and for reasons you'll probably not like."

I shifted the small box to my hip, my lips forming a thin line. I could always forget the device like I used to forget my phone all the time.

"First, we're rolling out the watches to team leads to see how effective they are. Second, I want to track your heart rate through it and see if we can't get more data about what is going on with your arcane capabilities. Expect some intense training sessions."

I sighed. I might not like it, but even I could admit I would be highly interested to see if there was something which could give us a better picture.

"And lastly, in the event you decide you want to get chased by a bunch of magically-controlled werewolves again, it can be tracked."

I doubted the particular scenario in question would happen again and I loathed the idea of being able to be tracked. Something in her statement caught my attention. "You weren't able to follow me?"

Lockonis shook her head. "You flitted into my range a couple of times, but until you were on your way back, I had no idea. Glad I made you go on active communications. Pretended I could so no one got too nervous and messed up your plan."

"Oh."

"Anywho, I wanted to get your thoughts on..." Lockonis stopped when my watch dinged repeatedly as if it was an emergency.

Both of us looked down as I turned my wrist up to read it. The short message from Vince said: "My office. NOW."

"Guess the big guy is making use of the priority system. I'll go with you."

I worried about what I would encounter as both of us ran.

WE ENCOUNTERED Silver en route who was headed in the same direction. He smirked and reached for my box. I glared at him and held onto it tighter. Could he pick a better time to be childish?

Fletch, Vince's assistant, tilted his head toward the door to the office when we entered. He continued typing nonstop.

I suddenly got a sense of deja vu. This time, however, I could not hesitate and think too much about what I would encounter as Lockonis strode right in and Silver walked right behind me.

"Wasn't expecting you," Vince said flatly as he watched Lockonis take a seat at the small conference table in his office. He pointed to us and the chairs in front of his desk.

She shrugged. "I was in the area when the alert went off."

Vince sighed and turned his attention to us as we took our seats. "I need the two of you for an assignment."

"Related?" Lockonis asked.

"Not likely," Vince said. He picked up a remote and pointed it at the screen mounted to the wall behind us. "There's been an incident at a Naval Command research facility and since it involves not only civilian contractors, but also a handful of arcane and divine casters, I can't think of a better team to send out. As well as the incident involves a prototype system merging magic with technology and I only know of two people who are familiar enough to send."

"That is a dilemma," Lockonis mused. The smirk on her face showed her amusement. "And how convenient we're both in this room."

"You're staying home, Lockonis."

Silver and I were the only mixed arcane and divine team I knew of within the Terran Intelligence Organization. That there existed teams within other organizations piqued my interest. Perhaps it could give me insight on how to better work with the paladin next to me.

Vince's words to Lockonis meant I was the next logical choice as someone who was familiar with mixing technology and magic. The only other choice.

As I turned to look at the screen, I caught my partner toying with his braid - he flipped the tail back and forth. He contemplated something.

"There's been a push within the Navy to decommission the battleships and move toward more specialized vessels. Especially smaller and faster ones."

I bit my lower lip to suppress grinning at the opportunity before me. I had missed my chance to look at the defense system on the ship in Ocean's Edge during the Brown case where I first met Silver. I had hoped for another chance to take a look at it.

"Spelltech is working to create a new combined system to keep the battleships in service. Currently, the battleships employ a conjured defense system typically run by an arcane caster. The new system would employ both arcane and divine casters and includes offensive capabilities to augment the existing cannons and guns."

Now Vince completely had my attention. A system like that sounded both powerful and delicate at the same time. Though I wondered how close it bordered on merging the two types of magical energy together. That gray area concerned me and would be the reason to send both myself and Silver.

"There was an incident with a test run. No deaths, but there is growing unrest between the Navy and Spelltech regarding if it was a malfunction or sabotage."

"The Jeweled Coast, huh? And Sandpoint at that. I hear it's gorgeous this time of year," Lockonis commented. "We don't have a branch in the area so there'll be no local support. Just the two of them?"

"I see no reason to send a bigger team," Vince said flatly.

"I was just asking. No need to get testy. I'll get gear bags prepped."

"If you want in on this so badly, you can coordinate with them from here," Vince shot at Lockonis. Then he turned back to us. "You'll have to send any evidence you can't process yourselves back. High priority. There'll be a Shrike ready to take you to Great Tree in two hours. Go."

WHILE I TRAILED BEHIND SILVER, I looked up the weather for Sandpoint. It was on the other side of the equator which meant they would be in summer. A new system merging technology and magic *and* it was warm? I could not hold back a grin. This would hopefully turn out to be a good, simple trip.

With the information we had, I doubted it needed more than another pair of eyes on the system to figure out what happened. Granted, if it was sabotage then it would likely fall to us to figure out who and why.

"You seem excited for this. Also looks like you picked up some new gear," Silver said with a teasing tone.

"Lockonis wants me to test the watch and apparently I was due for an upgrade."

"What else you got?" Silver fell in line beside me and reached for my box again.

I tightened my hold and glared up at him. "Go get packed. We don't have a lot of time."

Silver grabbed my arm and pulled me down a different hall than the way I needed to go.

"What are you doing?" I tried to stop and pull away, but stumbled forward.

"You need to go to the armory and stop avoiding Coburn."

"I have no reason to... hey!"

Silver pilfered my box and took off down the hall. I had to run to attempt to keep up with his jog. *Childish pain in my...*

By the time he slowed down so I could catch up we stood outside the armory. I took my box out from under his arm while he opened the door and turned to leave.

Silver picked me up with one arm around my waist and pulled me inside. We had been over why I avoided coming down here. I still had not come up with how to explain my broken staff.

"Put me down! This can wait until we get back." I struggled to get out of his hold, mentally cursing his strength.

"You're not going unarmed."

"I won't be unarmed." I doubted my partner forgot about my casting abilities.

Silver turned and set me down so I faced the counter a Dwarf stood behind with his arms crossed. My staff laid there between us. How had it gotten down here?

Coburn stroked his beard, looking at the staff. "At least you broke the internals while it was open so it was still serviceable."

"I, uh..." I wrung my hands.

He put something black on the counter. "Let's see if this one can handle what you've got." Coburn smiled. "Lockonis told me months ago about what happened. Never thought about a caster using it never mind the way you did."

I stepped forward and picked up the shrunken staff already tucked into its new holster. "Thank you."

Coburn waved me off. "And let me know if you have any problems with this one. I've got some ideas for improvement, but I haven't figured out how to keep it as light as these two."

Silver stepped up next to me. "Can I get my gear? We're headed out."

"Yeah, absolutely. Let me go grab it." Coburn disappeared around a corner.

My partner smirked down at me. "See, nothing to worry about."

I sighed and added the staff to my box. "I should get going. I'll meet you in the hangar."

Silver opened his mouth to say something and then closed it for a moment before he said, "Alright."

Taking my leave, I hurried to my quarters. I hoped this time might be a little better. Silver finally stopped treating me like I was his boss.

The excitement from earlier drained away as I thought about the potential problems we faced. I needed to focus right now. I could think through all the scenarios on the flight there.

3

"ARE you sure you're okay with talking to Naval Command?" I asked while I reviewed the information Lockonis sent about our loaner vehicle and where we were staying. I trailed behind Silver through the airport being slowed down by the weight of my gear bag and luggage. At least I thought to change for the weather we flew into.

Now where was the bus we needed to take to get our loaner vehicle? I scanned the signs overhead to get my bearings.

"What in the Hells are you doing here?" an angry voice shouted from nearby. It sounded like it came from around the corner.

I struggled to keep up with Silver who decided he wanted to check out what was happening. He was not slowed down by what he carried.

"You're here to plead your case before they even have a chance to review our reports."

"I ain't here to sway them," a Dwarven man in a Navy uniform argued with a Human man.

I stepped up alongside where Silver stood watching them around the corner. I asked, "Do you think they're here for us?"

He snorted. "I know they are. Should we confront them or just leave?"

I glanced at Silver. Neither of us wore anything to label us as part of the TIO, though his armored jacket would stand out. "I'm more inclined to leave. They shouldn't be here and I'd rather choose the time and place of our first meeting."

"Sounds like a plan. Where are we going again?"

I pointed at the buses outside the doors on the opposite side from where we were. "We have to get over there."

"We'll have to deal with them now if we go past them."

People walked by from where they came from their own flights. "Maybe not. Wait until the crowd gets a little thicker and we'll join as part of the group."

"Is that how you escaped everyone in Mystic Port?"

"No." And I had no plans of telling him how I managed it.

Silver smirked down at me. "Something tells me you've done this before."

"Maybe."

More people came down to head around to collect their luggage and we merged in with them. The two continued to argue, but with all the commotion, it was hard to hear them.

Silver took my free hand in his and kissed the back of it, grinning broadly. "M'lady."

I quickly pulled my hand away from him. "Don't you start that again," I shot at him. I swore I would never understand what went on in his head.

With no further issue, we got past the two arguing and had taken the bus to the correct location. Now we waited at the counter for our loaner vehicle. The clerk had gone to the back for something when Silver asked, "Do you have the information of where we're staying?"

I nodded. "It looks like it's pretty close to the base. I'm going to find out if there's a conference room we can use to set up for the first meeting."

"Uncommon ground," Silver noted.

"Seems only fair."

As soon as the woman came back, Silver grabbed the keys and took off before I could finish filling out the paperwork.

"Hey!"

"I'm driving."

"*You're such a pain,*" I muttered in my dialect of common, knowing he would not be able to understand me.

"In regular common, please."

WHILE SILVER WENT to get himself coffee, I sat and read through the case file on my tablet, idly toying with the badge hanging around my neck with one hand. The representatives from both Naval Command and Spelltech would be arriving shortly.

I perked my head up when I heard the door open. It was about time Silver got back.

The Dwarven Naval officer from the airport entered and I forced a smile, shifting uncomfortably. I had been hoping to not face either one alone and had also wished it was neither of the two from the airport.

He smiled at me and reached across the table. "I'm Commander Jonim Stormrider with Naval Command. Jonim is fine - I don't stand on ceremony when I don't have to."

Before I could take his hand, the door slammed open and I jumped at the sound. The Human man who had been at the airport stomped in.

The representative from Spelltech looked me over. "Where's your boss?" he demanded.

I rubbed the bridge of my nose in an effort to head off the oncoming headache these two would likely give me. Certainly not everyone was this aggressive, or at least I hoped. Though hope was fading fast.

This may be the one time the title I hated came in handy. I opened my mouth to tell him she was back at the main office when Silver strode in.

"About time. How long were you planning to make us wait?" The Human man continued his demands.

Even Jonim seemed confused by his behavior. "Jake, take it easy, we just got here. Ain't even asked them their names yet. And since I know his lack of manners as of late, this is Jacob Martin, the owner of Spelltech."

Silver turned to me and I shrugged. He took a sip of coffee before he said, "I'm Silver Blaise with the TIO and this is my partner, Ketayl."

Jake crossed his arms and tried to stare my partner down. His lack of height in comparison made it comical. "Well, all you have to do is tell these hard heads our project was sabotaged and we can be done."

My partner nodded over to me. "That's for her to decide."

I put my tablet down and sat forward. "A decision will be made after a full investigation. The more both of your organizations cooperate, the faster this can go."

"She's not serious, is she?" Jake asked, looking at Jonim, "We already came to the conclusion it was sabotaged. Likely by the military who doesn't want this project to succeed. And what do TIO agents know about a system like this which incorporates magic and technology?"

Jonim balled up his fists. "Dammit, Jake, get your head out of your ass for one second and..."

"Enough!" A hint of my power made it into my voice, causing an echo and both men stilled. A smirk appeared on my partner's face for a moment.

Silver sat down next to me. "We might know more than you think. At least she will. I'm just the divine side of the equation."

Jonim stroked his beard. "You're saying you're both casters?"

I nodded.

"And you're arcane?" the Dwarf pointed at me.

I nodded again.

"And the two of you work together regularly?" This Commander seemed a bit slow to get the idea.

"Pretty well at that," Silver commented. "I take it the divine and arcane casters don't get along?"

"Like Orcs and Trolls," Jonim confirmed.

This could prove problematic. Jake glared at Jonim.

"Can you describe what happened exactly?" Silver asked. I was content to let my partner talk.

The two looked at each other and then Jonim spoke. "We were running a test on the defensive side to see if we could figure out why the casters keep hitting resistance. Normally the energy being put in is amplified to create the shields around the ships which is why those can be operated by a single caster, but at this rate we'd need a shipfull of casters to get the output, defeating the purpose."

Jake sighed. "Look, I can admit when I've been rude. Jonim has actually been the one of the few who is supportive of us."

I glanced up at Silver. Had Jake come in confrontational because of his assumption we would be biased?

Jonim continued, "Things were moving along as usual. As soon as the poor bastard started syncing sparks flew. The damage is minor, but the casters don't see it that way and of course not Spelltech. I know enough about the system to admit it shouldn't have been able to do that."

"I'm still uncertain if it has anything to do with the shielding we have between the two systems, but it shouldn't affect the output." Jake sat back with his arms crossed and stared at the ceiling.

I raised an eyebrow, uncertain of the comment he made. "What materials are you using for the shielding?" I asked.

"I know you're curious, but we should focus on what happened," Silver chided.

"It could have something to do with it," I argued.

Jake watched us, the grin in his expression had me concerned. Was he planning something? "It's a silicon composite."

"That could be a problem - silicon is a crystalline substance," I pointed out.

"And you can store information or spells in that," Silver concluded with a sigh. "I've seen you copy enough files to the computer to get a rough idea of how it works."

I shrugged. "There could have been a build up of energy, but I'm not ruling out that something was done to the system."

Jake sat forward. "Wait, are you telling me you work with mixing magic and technology?"

I nodded.

Jonim laughed. "Told you the TIO wouldn't send just anyone."

Silver took hold of the conversation again. "We decided it would be best if we divided our investigation. I'll be working with Naval Command and Ketayl will be handling Spelltech."

"Perfect," Jake said, his smile giving me the chills. Suddenly I wanted to be the one working with Naval Command. The chance to look at the system and perhaps test it myself kept me from backing away.

"Is the system still operational?" I asked.

"Mostly," Jonim said. "Either system can be routed to the other console. The defense station took some damage, but nothing that can't be fixed once we're given the go ahead."

"This is in the event something happens to one of the casters. Theoretically one caster could operate both systems, but it obviously wouldn't be ideal. Just enough for them to get out of the fight," Jake added.

My gaze shifted up to Silver who had taken the moment to drink his coffee. He stopped the motion. "Don't even think about it. It sounds like it would cause a great deal of strain on the caster. Emergency situations are one thing. You already pointed out a problem with the shielding material."

I frowned. "Yeah, but I know how to work around that."

Silver rolled his eyes. "No testing the system without me present."

"Fine." Overprotective big brother indeed.

SILVER DROPPED me off at the warehouse Spelltech operated out of. It sat next to the water with large, metal shipping containers stacked nearby. A vessel much smaller than a battleship, but still large to me, was docked nearby with yellow tape around the bottom of the ramp to board. It must be where the prototype was installed. That they got to this stage proved the military thought their project worthy of serious consideration.

Either that or Spelltech sank a lot of money into this gamble. It would explain Jake's aggressive and protective behavior.

I pulled myself from the view of the water and hiked up my gear bag, heading for the nearby door. I could enjoy the warm weather when this was over.

Jake greeted me as soon as I entered the building. "So good of you to come so early. Let me give you the tour."

I stepped away as he reached to put an arm around me. "Let's keep this professional," I said flatly.

He jerked his hand back as if my words had burnt him. "Oh, um, of course."

Then the tour began. The way he spoke gave me the chills. He would alternate between speaking slowly and deliberately to suddenly being excited and repeating himself. I needed to stay focused on finding the truth.

As time passed, I wondered if this tour would give me any insight or simply be a waste of my time. Perhaps I could find someone else I could approach if I had questions.

"What is this?" a male voice asked. A Human man wearing robes from the Arcane College strode over to us. "Not satisfied with my incredible capabilities? She's not going to be able to operate your system at all."

I took note of the embroidery on the collar and the length of his sleeves. He looked like a Magister. I folded my arms to keep from shifting uncomfortably.

"Agent Ketayl is here with the TIO and you will give her your full cooperation in this investigation," Jake barked back.

The Magister glared at me for a moment. "You will address me as Magister Murkell."

"Gerard, don't you have anything better to do?" Jake asked, rolling his eyes.

The Magister huffed and stormed off.

Jake turned back to me with that creepy smile of his. "To be truthful, he's had the hardest time with the system. I've asked the Arcane College for someone else, preferably of higher rank, but my requests have fallen on deaf ears."

"I'm not surprised," I muttered looking around. There was nothing here I could see to be of use in this investigation.

"I take it you've had dealings with them before."

"You have no idea." I refused to admit to much else.

"I never did ask what your rank is. It seems to be an important thing for arcane casters."

I shrugged. "Not everyone finds it important. Currently I don't have one."

"You certainly are interesting. Let's continue."

I followed Jake around the facility. There were other projects in progress, but none of them were anywhere near the stage the dual-magic system was.

What caught my attention was a dozen or so Spelltech employees working with an obvious lack of Naval personnel. Something felt off about all of this. I needed to dig further into this company: history, financials, backgrounds... something to piece together how a company with seemingly nothing to show got to this point.

Finally we came to an office loaded with papers and boxes.

He pushed his way into the room. "Anything regarding the system you might want will be in here."

I walked as much as I could around the cramped room. "Can I get a look at the schematics?" A computer sat almost completely buried by a mound of plans.

"Once you sign an agreement to not discuss what you see here."

I glared at Jake. "No. I'm not here to steal your system. It also defeats the purpose as the case file will be reviewed by myself, Silver, and our superiors."

"Right, right. Sorry, habit." Jake shrank back.

"Besides, I've got my own projects to concern myself with," I said to give him some peace of mind.

"That's right - you like to tinker also."

"I guess you could say that. I've created a few things the TIO uses. Nothing world shattering," I said idly while looking around. *How does anyone find anything in here?*

Jake appeared to be lost in thought. "But you create things they find useful enough to implement. Perhaps I should petition them."

I kept my mouth shut. I doubted Lockonis would agree. None of what Spelltech currently worked on here would be of interest to the TIO as far as I could tell and likely she would find him as unpleasant to deal with as I did. She would just be more vocal about it.

Not to mention the concern I had about his motives. He incorporated both arcane and divine in all of his projects with no notable success using either. It would not be too far of a step to go into attempting to combine them. I needed to discuss this with Silver later.

"I'm afraid I haven't had the time to get this all organized. I don't trust anyone else to do it properly."

"Is it available digitally?"

"Most of it." Jake pulled a set of plans threatening the screen on the desk. "This is... not the right one." He dug through the pile again, thankfully moving them to another pile in the office. "Ah, here we go. This is the current version of the prototype docked outside."

I looked around the room. It would be cumbersome to hold the large papers and there was no clear flat surface to roll them out in here. I stepped toward the door - I remembered seeing a table nearby.

"Oh, those don't leave the office."

I raised an eyebrow at the man. "There's no place to lay them out in here. I'm taking them to a nearby table to look at."

"Oh, uh, good point."

I raised an eyebrow at the man. *Why do I get the feeling he is going to be uncooperative?*

Jake followed far too closely on my heels for my liking. He looked around nervously while I rolled out the plans and stood on the other side of the table as if to block them from the rest of the room.

"I'm curious as to the security you have for your work. The door to the office was unlocked," I said.

"Everyone knows not to go in there. And I've got a camera set up monitoring it."

I resisted the urge to roll my eyes. There was more security on the door to my quarters than he had for his sensitive files.

I scanned a couple of pages, noting interesting choices made in the design. "It's certainly unique. Where was the failure?"

"That's just the thing - I haven't been allowed on-board. Perhaps you would like to take a look at the actual prototype?"

Now I was the key to get him back on-board. I folded my arms and frowned.

I noticed Silver enter. He spotted us and strode over. Either he was quick or I lost a lot of time with Jake's tour.

Jake turned to see who I looked at and shifted nervously as Silver stepped up next to me. "Got anything?"

"More questions. We'll need to take this onto the prototype to narrow down the problem area," I said.

"Sure, yeah, whatever you want. Let me carry that for you," Jake said swiftly and rolled up the plans. He hustled ahead of us.

I stayed a distance back and Silver kept pace with me. "Got anything interesting from Naval Command?"

My partner nodded. "We can compare notes later."

Our guide hesitated as we approached the guards. Silver and I both showed our badges at the same time and the soldiers nodded, signaling us through.

Jake got caught getting under the yellow tape. I ducked under with little issue and Silver simply jumped it. He led us through the small vessel to a room I would guess was roughly in the middle of the ship, but only a level down from the main deck.

Most of the room appeared to be in pristine condition. The only damage surrounded the station to the back corner. The center station appeared untouched. The defense system was offset? I had seen it on the schematics, but gave it little thought over how the power was transferred. I wondered briefly about the layout.

Stepping under the shattered screen above the damaged station, I looked up, trying to get an idea of what could have caused this. The station itself bore black marks primarily around the grips.

"This is the defense station?" Silver asked.

Jake shifted from foot to foot. "Yes."

"Why is it off to the side?" my partner asked.

"We gave room priority to the offense station. The screens you see mounted will show a full view of what's going on around the ship. The defense caster doesn't need that information," Jake said sharply. I noted the tone difference he took with my partner.

"Not unless they have to take over offensive operations also," I commented. "I take it you don't employ a zonal shielding system."

"We simplified the defense system. If the situation has gotten that bad, they might take a couple of shots, but their priority will be on defense to get out of the situation. Besides, you probably don't understand how needlessly complex the zonal shielding system is."

"I've done research on the topic," I said.

Jake's statement meant he was more interested in offense. I wondered what Naval Command thought of the lack of zonal shielding.

"Oh, well, you know, it doesn't matter which type of caster sits in the chair, but we thought it would be better to have an arcane and a divine caster pair so the roles would be easily defined. Otherwise it's just a type of energy," Jake explained.

I looked up at Silver and he raised an eyebrow at me. My thoughts on Jake's oversimplification would have to wait.

Jake eyed us carefully. "You two weren't put together just for this. You work too well together. At least a dozen arguments break out between the casters I have everyday."

"No," I admitted. I thought we already established this yesterday.

That greasy smile I hated graced his face again. "So how do you do it? I'd love to find something to fix this problem."

Silver explained, "They've got to respect each other's differences. The opposition is a taught behavior. I have my strengths and Ketayl has hers - we balance each other out."

Jake frowned. "And here I was hoping there was some secret you could share."

"People aren't machines," I said, getting into the defense station so I could climb up on the chair to see better. The damage above me looked out of place given where the feedback occurred.

I was still too short and a little too far over - I would need to be outside of the station to get at it directly from below.

"Ketayl," Silver said softly and waved me back.

I hopped down the from chair to see what he wanted. He turned me around and then picked me up and put me on his shoulders before I could protest. He stepped over to where I wanted to be. It put me just high enough to reach the burnt panel.

"Warn me next time," I grumbled at him.

I more felt his shoulders shake in laughter under me than heard him.

As I tugged on the panel Jake said, "The screens have nothing to do with the system. The wiring for the stations runs under the floor."

"Then why is it burnt out?" Silver asked while I pried the panel loose.

I could make out Jake opening and closing his mouth a few times out of the corner of my eye.

Finally I pried it free once Silver put his hands under my feet so I could get more leverage.

"We... we assumed the panel took damage from the screen burning out," Jake said.

"Isn't the camera network separate from the system?" I was fairly certain I saw it on the schematics.

"It... yes... Look, it was chaos and this is the first time I've been able to get back on-board since it happened. The Navy has kept this place guarded."

"Can I get a boost?" I asked, looking down at Silver.

My partner got his hands under my feet. I grabbed the panel to steady myself and stood up. Suddenly I had to duck as Silver pushed me higher. I glared down at him as he settled my feet on his shoulders and held onto my ankles.

"You really need to warn me," I shot at him.

Silver smirked up at me. "I can't help myself."

I shook my head and got back in the ceiling.

"I heard you guys came on-board," Jonim said from below.

I backed out enough to nod at him. "Does anyone have a hand-light I can borrow?" I would have asked for mine, but I did not want anyone other than Silver in my gear bag and I currently stood on top of him.

Jonim dug in his pocket and pulled out a small one, disconnecting it from his keys. Silver took it and handed it up to me. "Thanks."

After a minute of trying to make sense of what happened, Silver asked, "What do you see?"

"A lot of burnt out wires. If the system's network is below the floor, it doesn't make sense for there to be damage up here. Not unless something was crossed somehow."

"See, sabotage," Jake said sharply.

I backed out and tossed the handlight down to Jonim. "I wouldn't rule out malfunction yet. I'm not forming any conclusions until we figure out how this happened."

Now how to get back down? I tentatively let go of the panel and balanced on Silver's shoulders. My attempt ended when he decided to drop me, catching me on the way down.

"Hi there. Ready to be short again?" Silver grinned broadly.

I rolled my eyes and pushed myself out of his hold. *Child.*

"There's been no preliminary investigation?" I asked.

"No," Jonim said. "We shut it down, locked it up, and contacted the TIO. There's too much at stake to not have an objective third party take over the entire investigation."

Which meant between the two of us, we would have to track this down. "I'm going to enlist Sparks' help. He'll be able to analyze the images we send. This is a lot to go through for just the two of us."

Silver opened his mouth to say something, but was cut off.

"You said this wouldn't go beyond the two of you and your superiors," Jake said, his temper noticeably rising.

Jonim physically stepped between us and Spelltech's owner. "Jake, I'll have you removed if I have to. Be grateful the TIO didn't send a full team to dismantle this project. My superiors have been wanting to do just that."

"Right, right. Sorry." Jake paced, biting the tip of his thumb.

I made my way over to the offense station to get an idea of what a functional station should look like. "It would probably be best to find out how the system operates so we know when we find something out of place."

"I'll leave instructions with the guards that the TIO can have full access to the ship. Whatever you need, just let us know," Jonim said.

I envied Silver getting to deal with the Navy. They sounded far more cooperative and professional than Spelltech.

Stepping into the offense station, I barely brushed one of the grips with my hand when suddenly I was everywhere at once outside of the ship. I could clearly see the dock and the ocean. I turned my head slightly and the view matched.

What caught my attention more was a sense of relief. My control over my power was not needed here. I could breathe.

"Ketayl?" Silver's grip on my shoulder pulled me back out and I moved my hand away from the grip.

"I... I'm sorry," I stuttered. "I didn't know the system was active."

"It's never not active," Jake said proudly. "It's in an always ready mode so there's no time wasted needing to power it up."

The need to touch the grip again became too strong and I reached for it only for Silver to grab my hand.

"No, not with the reaction you just had," he said softly.

"Aye, ain't seen another caster sync so well and certainly not anywhere near as quickly," Jonim commented. "Most have a hard time getting the screens on let alone firing the whole thing up."

"We need her to test the system fully. I knew it worked," Jake said excitedly.

The man shifted moods faster than I could keep up with.

"I thought you said the screens were a separate system," Silver said.

"They are," Jake said emphatically. "Look, they're designed to come on when the system activates. There's no magical energy being diverted to them. They operate off power from the ship."

"It's one of the initial sensors to get tripped. We've used it as a base for tests," Jonim explained further.

Silver's hand on my shoulder drew my attention. "Ketayl, I think we need to take time and compare notes. That way we can formulate a plan of action."

I sighed. Formulating a plan would save us time from simply running in circles. I signaled for the others to lead the way out. I paused before I stepped away from the offense station. I still needed to touch it again. A quick second would be fine. Just one more moment of being able to breathe.

My hand was grabbed and I was roughly pulled away. "No," Silver hissed.

"Sorry, it's just..." I shook my head and walked ahead of my partner. He needed to be a barrier between me and the system. I wondered how he would react to it.

4

THE RIDE back to the hotel was silent. Occasionally I would hear a faint creak from Silver's fingerless leather gloves as his grip tightened on the steering wheel. *How am I going to explain my actions without sounding crazy?*

He opened the door to the hotel room and held it for me. As soon as I entered, I went to the large windows to put some space between us. This room was smaller than others we had previously stayed in so there was not as much space as I would have liked. I immediately turned my attention to the small ship with the prototype on-board. I had not noticed we could see it from here before.

Even from here I felt drawn to it. I wanted that perfect moment of being completely balanced without having to fight for it.

I blinked when the curtain was drawn in front of me. "I know you're upset, but you don't have to be rude," I snapped at him.

"It's also rude to ignore someone," Silver growled.

I tilted my head to the side. "What do you mean? You didn't say anything."

"Ketayl, you've been staring out the window for the past five minutes. You heard nothing I said?"

I shook my head and bit my lower lip, trying to figure out how I lost time. I swore it had only been seconds.

Silver dropped to sit on the edge of his bed. "I don't like this. You barely brushed the damn thing and now it's as if you're obsessed with the system. What happened? What draws you to that machine?"

I sighed and took a seat next to him. "I'm not sure how to explain it. At least not without sounding crazy."

"Then sound crazy."

I glanced at him out of the corner of my eye. His rigid back told me he was still angry, but those blue eyes intently staring at me were full of concern.

"I think I connected differently than intended. I should have needed the screens to see outside and it felt like I was everywhere outside the ship at once. Maybe because I wasn't prepared for it I couldn't stop it? Because I'm an Arcanist? I don't know."

"That doesn't explain why you kept wanting to touch it."

I bit my lower lip and thought through the experience, searching for the right words. "I can't explain the irresistible urge to touch it again. Not in a way that makes sense."

"Try me." Silver snaked his hand under my hair to rub the back of my neck.

It pulled me fully from the draw of the system and my mind was able to focus again. I had not even noticed how clouded I still was.

Silver knelt down in front of me. He kept his hand on the back of my neck. "What just happened?"

It was as if he dissipated some spell I had not realized I was under. Even with the curtain drawn part of me still felt compelled to touch the system again, but now it was gone.

"What's going on? Ketayl, talk to me."

"I don't feel drawn to the system anymore."

He breathed a sigh of relief. "Okay, maybe now we can get somewhere. You were scaring me there. At least we know how to get you back if you ever have to touch it again."

"Was it that bad?" I bit my lower lip. The last thing I needed was more questions from the people we were dealing with.

"I'm the only one who knew something was wrong. The others didn't seem to notice anything unusual, but we've been working and living together long enough I know when something is off."

"Sorry."

"I don't want an apology, I want to know what happened. Your control is normally far better. Tell me how you felt when you touched it."

"Peace?" I shook my head. "Relief - a brief moment I didn't feel like I had to fight to keep myself balanced and maintain control." I took a shuddering breath and a couple of tears rolled down my face as I thought about it.

My internal battle had become second nature to handle on a day-to-day basis, but for a split second I got the chance to breathe. A chance I would likely never have again.

Rough fingers brushed the tear away. "Promise me you won't go on-board without me. In fact, I don't want us to split up if we can help it. Jake concerns me."

I backed away from Silver if only to give myself some breathing room. "I'm not arguing, but why?"

"There are multiple reports showing his behavior becoming increasingly neurotic the more setbacks Spelltech has. The Navy is considering pulling their support from Spelltech not only because of the setbacks, but also because of his behavior. He's been downright abusive on occasion to the personnel at the base."

At least I was not the only one who thought something was wrong when dealing with him. "What happened when I touched the grip?"

"The whole system activated. The lights dimmed when the screens kicked on and the entire station lit up. And frankly, I haven't seen your eyes do that color-changing thing since you broke the barrier on your reserves. It wasn't just the gray this time - it was your entire eye it covered."

I sat there staring at Silver. They stated the others had barely managed to get past the first set of sensors. All I had done was accidentally brush the grip.

How had I manage it? I should not have been able to do more than feel a thrum from the system without actively engaging it.

"We can figure out what happened with you later when we start reviewing the files," Silver said, breaking my train of thought.

I nodded, stood up, and moved away from Silver, going to my gear bag to get my tablet. "I want to delve further into the company. He gave me a tour of the facilities and the dual-magic system isn't the only thing they're working on, but nothing else is even close to operational."

"He seemed protective of the plans for the system."

I folded my arms, thinking through the encounter. "And yet the office is left unlocked. Jake claims there are cameras and everyone knows not to go in. The place is such a disaster even he had a hard time putting his hands on the most current plans."

Silver stroked the small patch of hair on his chin. "Anything digital?"

"Some apparently. I haven't gotten into the system."

My partner sighed loudly. "This is going to take a long time."

I typed up a message to Lockonis requesting Sparky's assistance. "I think we need to start with reviewing the footage and then interview the people involved with the test when the accident occurred. Preferably privately. That way when we start digging through Spelltech's files we can narrow down what we're looking for."

"Agreed. How long do you think it would take you to transfer the files to your tablet?"

His question made me pause and look up at him. "This one is faster than my last one, but it would still take about as long as it took me to copy the files to the computer we first used in Ghost Forest."

"Too long then. To a gem?"

I crossed my arms and tilted my head, trying to figure out what he was getting at. "Depends on what you want copied."

"Anything useful to us. I don't want to have to fight with Jake every time we need something. Jonim is about the only person willing to deal with him and he has other duties he needs to attend to."

Biting my lower lip, I thought it over. "A few seconds at most. I could do it without him noticing, but I don't have anything to copy to."

Silver grinned broadly. "Sounds like we need to go shopping."

"Wait. No. There's got to be something we have here that we can use." I needed to dissuade Silver of this idea.

"Oh come on. You never let me buy you anything," Silver said, pouting.

I rolled my eyes, my watch vibrated on my wrist. I looked down at it and paused for a moment before rubbing my fingers on the material the band was made out of. "This is silicon. I can use my watchband."

Silver frowned. "You like to ruin my fun."

I FINGERED my watchband while we waited, staring at the gray material. My partner sat across from me. He insisted we stop for something to eat.

"Something wrong?"

"I'm worried we're crossing a line we shouldn't with this plan," I said.

Silver shook his head. "We have a right to the files pertaining to the investigation which Jake has been borderline impeding. Not to mention I'm certain you'll be able to organize it better."

"Taking it to a computer I could. It's a little harder in this format."

"Stop worrying so much and enjoy this moment of reprieve."

I wanted the other moment of reprieve I had earlier when I brushed the grip at the offense station. Silver was right to worry, even after being away from the system and seemingly broken its hold, I still longed for that moment again.

My watch buzzed with a message from Sparky stating he was ready for anything we might need. I dug my phone out of my pocket to reply, asking him if he could get a full background on Spelltech and its owner.

"Not supposed to be working right now," Silver chided.

"Sparks messaged me and I want him to get started on pulling information."

Silver snorted. "Don't give him a reason to go hang out with the cyber team. He's been wanting any excuse to go hang out with his Gnome friend."

I shook my head. He and Sparky still had a very odd friendship that I could not comprehend.

"I'm thinking once we finish here, we head back to the base and see if we can't get the footage from the accident and find out where everyone involved is," Silver suggested.

I nodded. "Probably see if we can get a hold of any reports filed. I'd also like to take a look at footage from other tests. See if there was something out of the ordinary."

"Well, they did say they were only operating the defense station this time."

"Doesn't mean it's the only time they've singled out a system to test. There's got to be a pattern to how they run them."

Silver stared at me for a moment. "Are you backing the idea it was sabotage?"

"No," I shot back. "It would help rule it out if something was out of place. There's a chance of negligence."

He stroked the small patch of hair on his chin. "They're so busy pointing fingers I don't think the idea crossed their minds."

"Jake employs a dozen or so people, but I don't know if any of them work on the ship system. The people I saw were all busy with other projects."

Silver frowned. "And it sounded like he rotated through Naval personnel fairly regularly. He complained they were incompetent if he didn't drive them to request a transfer first."

"Hard to get anything accomplished if you keep rotating through people. It could lead to accidental negligence, but honestly, it should only be the casters doing anything with the system itself. The most anyone else is doing is either recording or directing them through the test."

"What about maintenance, repairs, or changes to the system to try and drive better performance out of it?" he asked.

I shrugged. "I guess I'll be spending a lot of time going through the files in that office."

"We, remember. We need to stick together."

I dropped my gaze to the table. I had initially been excited about this assignment because I would get a chance to look at a new technology, but now I feared it to some degree. Namely in how I could not fully shake this feeling of being drawn to the system. Silver called it an obsession and I started to agree with the assessment.

"How good of a look did you get at the plans?"

I perked my head up at his question. "Enough to get a rough idea of how the system operates. Why?"

"We probably shouldn't have this discussion in public."

I glanced around. The few other patrons here were preoccupied with their drinks, their food, or their company. There still could be an unwanted listener.

"Has Kitteren said anything about how things are going in Ghost Forest?"

"About the same I think. She didn't say much in her last message. I can only imagine she's not too thrilled to be stuck doing so much paperwork."

Silver laughed and shook his head. Our conversation put on hold about the case. My mind did not stop working on piecing together what I had seen so far.

———

"ALRIGHT, OUT WITH IT," Silver said as soon as we were back in our loaner vehicle. "You were churning something over in your head all through dinner."

I bit my lower lip. "I was thinking of the projects Spelltech has going on. All of them incorporate using arcane and divine casters somehow."

"What's Jake's magic background? I didn't sense a divine presence."

"Nor is there an arcane one," I confirmed.

My partner glanced at me quickly. "Trying to use both without being proficient in either?"

"Is it even possible? I think he might be simplifying the two types of magic a little too much. I'm not sure how his projects even work without having some sort of magical background."

Silver flicked the end of his braid back and forth as he drove. "I think toying with something he doesn't understand would be more accurate. He didn't even know about his shielding materials doing the opposite of what he wants."

"It's not common knowledge."

My partner tossed me a look. "This isn't a common project."

"True, but…"

"Is it more rare than I'm assuming?"

I nodded. "Most people outside of the Arcane College didn't know how to store spells or information until I brought it to the TIO. Even then I found out about silicon when I learned the computer systems."

"A good thing we have you then. Should you have shared it with him?"

I shrugged. "There's little he could do with what I've said so far outside of change his shielding material, which would be a lot of work if I remember the diagrams right. Remind me I do want to check and see if there's residual arcane energy in the shielding."

Silver tugged lightly on his braid with one hand. "I should probably check for divine also. That might have caused a problem if they're using the stations interchangeably."

"Are they?" I could not recall it in any of the reports we had seen so far.

"Sounds like they might have considered the idea at the very least."

I took a deep breath and let it out slowly. They could have just as easily blown themselves up.

No sooner had we passed the gate to the base when I felt a pull on my senses and sat up straighter. Something was barely there - just enough to be noticed and I felt the strong desire to go touch the system again.

Silver pulled over roughly and threw the vehicle into park. "What's going on?" His fingers got under my hair to rub the back of my neck.

His touch dampened the effect enough so I could focus. "I'm good. Let's go."

"No, you're not," Silver argued. "Is that *thing* still affecting you?"

I stared at my hands in my lap, unsure of how to deal with Silver's rising anger. "It caught my attention is all. I'll know to expect it now."

My partner hesitantly pulled away and we continued to the Naval offices. I followed him, staying close by his side. The pull got stronger the closer we got to the ship and I refused to chance a repeat of earlier. Once I knew what to expect, I could handle it. At least I kept telling myself that.

Silver spoke with the person at the front desk who directed us to someone else.

The computer lab was staffed by a Human man who smiled broadly when he saw Silver. "How can I help you?" I caught the name Colbernoux on his uniform.

Silver flipped the end of his braid back and forth. "We want to review the footage and any reports from the accident with the proto-type dual-magic project on the ship."

"Absolutely. Let me get you set up and into the project file." He led us to a computer at the back. "Hope this station isn't too out of the way. Some of the others get picky about their spots. This one no one ever bothers with because it's in the corner and they usually want to chat while they're here."

"This is fine," Silver replied. He put his hand on my back and pushed me toward the chair.

Taking a seat, I made a face at the screen. Silver would want me to be the one navigating.

The man helping us looked at us confused for a moment before reaching over my shoulder to get us to where we needed to be.

I leaned away so he would not accidentally touch me, but it put me precariously close to touching Silver.

"This is the file you want. If you need anything else, let me know. You can just shout for Aris - most people do."

Silver pulled a chair over once he left. "He's a little odd," he whispered.

I had already begun pulling up the particular files we wanted to look at first. "What do you mean?"

"Maybe later. Let's focus on this so we can get get out of here."

Pulling up the video first, I shifted my chair so both of us could sit in front of the screen. There was no audio, but at least the footage was from more than one angle. The four cameras started as soon as someone entered the room.

Jonim was the first in followed by a pair arguing. I grabbed the tablet from my bag to match the faces in the video to the files. One arcane and one divine caster. A Spelltech employee entered with a tablet in hand and stood behind the defense station.

"What is it?" Silver asked.

"They brought in an arcane and a divine caster for this test. It doesn't make much sense if they're only testing one of the stations."

"Didn't they say they were trying to figure out the best combination? What's the affiliation of the divine caster?"

I scrolled through the information on my tablet. Silver reached over and paused the video before dropping his chin on my shoulder. I moved slightly to get him off, but he apparently had gotten comfortable. At least it dampened the effects of the system and I could focus better.

"A priest affiliated with a church devoted to the God of Magic," Silver commented, reading my screen. "I guess that makes sense, though I thought most of them were purists about not mixing magic with anything else. Typically they don't like arcane casters either."

I tried to turn and look at him, but could not with how we were situated. "Aren't you considered an oddity?"

"Yes, and happier for it. Okay, back to work." He reached over and resumed playback.

We sat through more time of the two arguing. Jonim kept trying to break it up. I tilted my head, seeing something which made little sense. "I wonder why Jake isn't here?"

"Maybe he normally doesn't. We'll have to check other tests. He could also be monitoring the system from elsewhere."

I shrugged. Given his personality, I thought he would be right there expecting a miracle to happen.

Finally the test began and the divine caster took a seat at the defense station. No sooner had his hands touched the grips than sparks rained down on him from above and the station around him lit up with bolts of electricity dancing across its surface. Parts of the station exploded, throwing shards.

The caster was thrown back against the chair, tearing his hands from the grips. The arcane caster ran to the door, frantically trying to yank it open, the person recording data from the test hid behind the chair, and Jonim moved to help the unconscious caster.

The room went dark for a few seconds before the emergency lighting kicked in. At that point everything we needed to see was done.

"Odd Jonim never mentioned he was there," Silver said.

I crossed my arms and sat back. "We'll have to ask him why. I wish I had the programs here so I could get a closer look at sections of the footage."

"Let's see if I can't at least do something toward that." Silver grinned and got up, heading to the other side of the room where Aris sat at his station.

I rolled my eyes and pulled up the reports associated with the incident. Jonim's was thorough - documenting not only what happened, but also the argument between the casters. However, that particular piece of information was unimportant.

I switched over to the notepad program on my tablet and jotted down who we needed to talk to. I hoped to corner Jonim away from Jake.

Curiosity overrode my need to keep working on this puzzle and I turned to see what Silver was doing. I stretched a bit in my chair to see over the other stations. My partner leaned against the wall, chatting with Aris, idly flicking the tail of his braid back and forth. A smile graced his features as they talked.

What happened to finding out if we could get copies of these files? I still had not figured out how to pull digital files with a spell.

Even if we got the files, I still did not have access to the programs I needed. I would have to send it to Sparky. I cringed at the thought of how much work I would be sending him, knowing what his normal workload looked like.

Right now, I needed to focus, which was difficult with the constant pull from the system. I brought up a video of a previous test and sure enough, Jake was there running around frantically - yelling at everyone in the room. They were testing both systems though.

Digging through the project file further, I found a spreadsheet someone kept of the tests and a description of each with corresponding dates and times. *Perfect.*

Until I found out they never tested a single station like this before. Frowning, I sat back in the chair, crossing my arms. I began to wonder if testing the one station might have unbalanced the system.

No. Unless there was something drastically different about the offense station, I would have caused a repeat of the incident. The rough principal of the design simply converted the type of energy into the particular system it was being supplied to. Both stations acted the same way until you got to the finer controls.

Though the caster at the defense station in the prototype became no more than a power supply. I knew the current defense systems in use created zonal shields which could be moved and stacked to protect a particular side. Unless they planned to implement it in a later stage.

But then the current design made no sense. The defense station would need to be centered just as much as the offense station or both would need their own views of the exterior. Though I did not need the screens.

I ran a hand over my hair and tugged on my bangs in frustration. Just one more time with the system and I would have a better grasp on this.

"Don't do that - your hair is so pretty." I turned to find Aris standing behind me with a smile on his face. Silver stood next to him. "So I hear you want a copy of the project file. I've gotten the go ahead from my superiors. How do you want it?"

I shifted so I was not twisted awkwardly to look at the two of them. "Can we get it encrypted and sent in a message?"

"Standard military encryption okay?"

"Yeah," I said moving out of the way.

Aris brought up a mail screen. "Here, just plug in the address and I'll take care of the rest."

I slid the keyboard over and started typing. I referenced my phone to make sure I spelled Sparky's actual name correctly.

"You're having it go to Sparky?" Silver asked.

I bit my lower lip for a moment. "He's got access to the programs needed and he can update the case file far more easily than we can."

"Good point," my partner conceded.

I stepped away when I was done and let Aris do his part. On my tablet, I typed up a set of instructions for Sparky. I hated piling more work on him, but we were limited in what we could do here.

Now that there was nothing to distract me, I felt the pull of the system again. It was still faint, but enough to make me long for that moment of balance. Just a moment of what it must feel like to be normal.

"Ketayl?" Silver asked softly, jarring me from my thoughts.

I shook my head. "Sorry, I think the time difference is messing with me." It was the first excuse I could think of. Admitting the system still affected me would only worry Silver and slow down our work.

"Maybe we should call it an early night. Think I can make good on drinks another time, Aris?"

Our assistant stood up and looked at my partner. "Yeah, I'm good whenever. You know how to find me. Oh, and it's sent. Just got a confirmation of receipt so whoever it went to has it."

I bowed. "Thank you."

"Hey, come back and visit anytime." The look Aris gave Silver confused me, but I figured it had something to do with their conversation earlier.

5

I LAID in bed staring at the ceiling. Silver still rested, but I only managed maybe an hour. I listened to his soft breathing from the other bed, but it had not helped lull me back into a resting state. The gentle rain had not helped either.

Silver opened the curtain before we went to bed because if I rested longer than him, he would not wake me when he needed to view the sunrise. Not that it mattered really. When we lived together in the house in Ghost Forest for a couple of months, I would often sit with him for his morning rituals. The quiet and stillness brought a measure of peace and balance, but not nearly at the level the system had in that all too brief moment.

Sliding out of my bed, I padded as quietly as I could around where Silver rested and stood at the window, looking out at the ship through the rain. Would actually testing the system make this worse or would I feel more complete?

Maybe it was less about the system itself and more I had a chance to stretch my power out. No, that made no sense.

I touched the window with my fingertips. Usually I found the rain calming. Especially summer rain, but then I could sit on my balcony or at least open a window. I rested my forehead next to my fingers, soaking in the coolness of the window. What I needed to do was not give Silver reason to worry.

And yet here I was up in the middle of the night. I should go back to bed and at least pretend to be resting. I turned to find Silver sitting up, staring at me.

I bit my lower lip and hurried to think of a reason for being up.

He signaled for me to come sit next to him on his bed. Hesitantly I did so, staying as much on the edge as possible. Rough fingers dug at the knots in my shoulders and neck, releasing the tension built up. At the same time, the siren's song of the system dampened. How he was able to do it, I did not know, but hopefully it was enough so I could get some rest.

"Uneasy resting in a new place?" Silver asked quietly.

"Yeah, I guess." It was as good of a reason as any and one he knew my pattern of. Unless I was exhausted then I cared little where I rested. I drifted as he worked out the tension.

"Hopefully we won't be here too long. You should take some time off to readjust when we get back."

I took a deep breath and reminded myself I withheld the truth for his sake. If he worried too much about what went on with me, he would be unable to focus fully on the task at hand.

I still disliked doing it.

"I'D LIKE to see if we can talk to Jonim away from Jake," I told Silver as we got ready for the day.

"That might not be as easy as you think. I'll see about arranging a meeting. It looks like we may have to split up after all just to cover more ground."

I frowned at his statement. I would leave it to Silver to handle. Dealing with Jake could be an issue, but one I figured I could handle. "What is the status of the divine caster involved?"

"Still in the infirmary, but he's able to talk. How willing could be another story."

I raised an eyebrow at my partner.

"Apparently he hasn't wanted to talk to anyone. Nothing outside of what he needs for medical attention anyway."

What we saw was traumatic, but not to the point of silence. Perhaps something different happened which we were unable to see on the video.

"Okay, what?"

I came out of my thoughts. "Hm?"

Silver knelt down in front of where I sat on the edge of my bed. "You're a few too many steps ahead of me right now. What are you thinking?"

I bit my lower lip and debated if I should say something. He already knew I was theorizing. "I'm not even sure it's a possibility, but what if he ended up connecting to the system the same way I did?"

"You didn't cause it to explode the second you touched it."

"Could be something with the defense part. I'll have to check the records and see if he tested the defense station before. I think I saw his name on the list, which would cancel out my theory."

Silver sat back on his heels. "Not necessarily. Not if they made an adjustment from a previous test."

"I'll see what kind of headway I can make with the files in Jake's office." With any luck, I would be left alone to work.

"Have you heard back from Sparky yet?"

I pulled my watch off of the charger, noting there was a request for a call from the Halfling. "Do you want to start a call to him? I think he has something."

"Video?"

"Yeah."

Silver got his tablet and started the call while I tied the end of my hair off. I stepped up to see over his shoulder, getting my watch on.

"About damn time," Sparky said the moment the call connected. "Oh, hey, um, hi boss."

I knew his outburst was toward Silver. I asked, "What do you have?"

"What don't I have. The guy you wanted me to look into is a nutcase."

"Tell us something we haven't already figured out," Silver said.

Sparky rolled his eyes before picking up a tablet. "Okay, so Spell-tech is a relatively new company. Jacob Martin was originally an archaeologist until he started it a few years ago."

"That's quite the career change," Silver noted.

"Yeah, no kidding. Especially when his focus was on Atlantis."

"What?" I leaned forward. "Are you sure?"

Sparky nodded. "Yeah, I spent last night reading through some of the papers he published. I haven't really delved into the topic, but from what I could gather, even among others interested in the subject, he was considered pretty out there."

I glanced over at Silver. This just might have fallen into our domain. I got the sense of it when I saw he was attempting to use both types of magic.

"I've got records of him stating he found some ancient Atlantian book and about that time is when he started claiming there used to be only one type of magical energy, but it had been split into the arcane and the divine."

"So how did he manage to get into weapons research and a military contract?" Silver asked.

Sparky shrugged. "A good song and dance? Your guess is as good as mine. I'm still digging, but his financials are weird. Tonkey is helping to make sense of it. Actually got a few of the cyber team helping. This one caught their attention."

"I take it Lockonis knows then," I commented.

"Of course I do," Lockonis said and smiled at us as she walked into view of the camera. "Realized when we started digging up info for Sparky that we were potentially dealing with a much larger issue and you were going to need more help."

I nodded and remained silent. We could not let Jake know there were even more people working on this.

"We'll keep following this lead on this end. Send us the information you can, but focus on figuring out what happened. Any chance you have an idea yet?"

"No," I said quickly, cutting off anything Silver might say about what happened yesterday. "I've got to go over the plans and figure out why sections which shouldn't be connected also burned out. Spelltech hasn't been forthcoming with information."

"Okay, we'll be in touch. For now, I want you to keep yourselves ready for anything." Lockonis reached forward and ended the call.

Silver turned and looked at me. "You didn't want to tell her about your reaction the to system yesterday?"

I stepped away from my partner. "No. It was an isolated incident."

A growl emanated from my partner. "Only because you haven't been exposed again and I know not only does Jake want you to test the system, but you want a chance at it also. What happens then?"

"You figured out how to break it," I reminded him, hoping it would calm him down.

"And if that doesn't work? What then?"

I ran my hand over my hair, tugging on my bangs in frustration. "We'll figure it out. It may be something as simple as I was unprepared and can back out of the system on my own. I just need to know how."

"Would you stop risking yourself for once?!"

His angry outburst made me stop. I stared at him with wide eyes. "Sorry."

"Just... Let's be smart about this, okay?" Silver held out the holster with my shrunken staff.

I sighed and took it, setting about putting it on over my calf-length pants. "Yeah." Truth be told, what happened to him a few months ago still haunted me. I could not handle the thought of losing him. It was easier for me to take the risks.

Silver took a deep breath and let it out before he said, "Okay, let's find some breakfast and get started for the day."

6

SILVER HELD the door to the infirmary open for me. I already had my tablet out to take notes. I only hoped Priest Mason Holland could provide insight into what happened. Something that was not visible in the video.

The dark-haired Human man sat on a bed with his arms crossed, glaring us down. Silver previously stated he had been uncooperative thus far. I hoped we could convince him we were here to help.

"I've heard about the two of you," Mason said sharply. He turned to my partner. "If you're the divine caster then that means she's the one who twists the purity of magic."

I stopped short and looked to Silver to make sure I heard correctly. His jaw was set and he glared down at the man. The creak of his leather fingerless gloves sounded far louder than it should have been.

We did not have time for this. Ignoring the comment, I said, "We're here to ask you about the accident."

"I'm not talking to someone who defiles what the God of Magic has blessed," Mason spat. "Just like this forsaken project. Leave now - I won't tolerate your presence any longer, heretic."

What had I done? Silver held up his hand for me to be silent. Now I was completely lost as to what was going on.

"Ketayl, could you step outside please?" My partner's words were clipped, his focus on Mason.

I looked back and forth between the men and debated if I should listen to Silver or not. Not understanding his intent, I chose not to fight him on this. "Um, yeah. Let me know if you need something."

The door barely made a click as I left. I stood there, staring at the closed door for a minute before I started pacing outside of the infirmary. *That pompous, self-centered... ugh!*

I resisted the urge to throw my hands up. I tugged on the ends of my bangs instead.

What part of we were here to help did he not understand? Could he not put aside his bias just long enough to let us do our work? And why did Silver ask me to leave? What happened to working together?

Were we going to have the same issue with the others? If so, how would I handle the Magister?

Looking up information on the Magister would keep me distracted and more importantly where Silver expected to find me.

Once I calmed, I could feel the pull of the system again. How was a machine doing this?

Dropping down into a nearby chair, I dug out my tablet and searched for the name in the records I originally brought with me from the Arcane College when I transferred.

I would be missing the last few years, but I could get a rough idea of who I would be dealing with. Gerard Murkell, where was he? Finally I found his record.

He was awarded Magister a couple of years before I left. He went out on a couple of assignments, but had been recalled from each for misconduct.

That he managed so much in only a couple of very short assignments either impressed or disgusted me - I could not decide which. I wished I had more updated records, but these would have to suffice.

No real focus on study. Made effort only when he was coming up on being removed for not advancing. There was nothing here I found useful. Though his lack of ambition in the arcane arts explained why he struggled with the system.

I switched over to the case file. Sparky should have updated it with the new information we sent by now. Once I found it, I pulled up the spreadsheet again. What other tests had Mason Holland taken part in?

"Please don't tell me there's been another accident," Jonim said. I looked up to find him coming down the hall.

"Oh, no. Silver's doing an interview. Priest Holland took offense that I'm an arcane caster," I said, keeping my voice as even as possible.

"Not surprised. Mason is one of the more aggressive ones. Guess I should wait my turn." Jonim sat down across from me.

Now seemed a good of time as any. "We were hoping to have a chance to talk with you about the accident since you were there."

"I knew the two of you would come looking for me soon enough. Hoped to catch you at the airport. I didn't want to say anything in front of Jake since you've seen how he can get."

I raised an eyebrow at the admission. "Is there a place we can talk privately?"

"Yeah, my office is good. Do you want to wait for your partner?"

Glancing at the door, I thought it over. "If you don't mind. He's been in there a while and I'd go check, but I don't feel like taking insults again right now."

Jonim smiled softly. "Alright, besides, I want to have it out with the bastard anyway and you gave me one more thing to come down on him for."

He disappeared through the infirmary door leaving me alone again with the siren's call.

I needed to focus. Maybe read through what they uncovered so far regarding Spelltech?

Sparky had done me one better and included copies of the papers Jake authored. This could make for an interesting read. Settling further down in the chair, I hoped to gain some insight into the archaeologist turned weapons developer.

I browsed the titles and chose one which sounded appropriate for the particular system being developed. About the time I got fed up with Jake repeating himself and started skimming for new information, Silver and Jonim came out of the infirmary.

My partner appeared relieved when he saw me. What happened in there? I figured that conversation would have to wait.

"I know I shouldn't be the one doing it, but sorry about Mason's attitude. He'll probably still be a stuck up bastard, but he knows not to impede your investigation," Jonim said.

"Actually, you might get an apology out of him. I came down

pretty hard on him," Silver added. "I just wouldn't go in there right now looking for it."

Is that why he asked me to step out? I was both touched and annoyed at the gesture. I nodded and put my tablet in my bag, waiting for Jonim to lead the way. His office was a couple of buildings over. The thought crossed my mind that Jonim was possibly being too helpful, but I would wait and see where things went.

Taking a seat, Jonim settled behind his desk and looked back and forth between us. "Like I said before, I ain't trying to impede your investigation, but I didn't want to say anything in front of Jake."

"Because of how he reacts to things, correct?" I asked.

Jonim sighed. "Yeah. As much as it might look like it, Jake and I ain't friends. Frankly, I only tolerate him because it's my job."

"Does he know you were at the test?" Silver asked.

Jonim snorted. "He better. He asked me to fill-in for him. Had some important appointment he couldn't miss or something. I might sit in normally if I've got the time because the military obviously has interest in the project, but ain't seen him miss one yet."

I jotted down what he said on my tablet. That saved us time in reviewing footage from previous tests.

"Anything out of the ordinary outside of that?" Silver asked.

"Just that we were testing only the defense part of the system. Seeing if there was something that could help figure out why they've been struggling with the offense part."

"Makes sense to some extent," I noted. "Spelltech treats both parts of the system similarly."

"I take it no changes were made to the system since the previous test then." I was glad Silver was here. He was better with people.

"No. Or at least there shouldn't have been," Jonim said.

Silver stroked the small patch of hair on his chin. "Why bring both an arcane and a divine caster if only one system was being tested?"

Jonim shrugged. "Beats me why Jake ordered it. I assumed he wanted to see who could get more out of it. And I can't help but notice you're a bit better armed after yesterday."

I glanced down at the holster attached to my thigh and then at Silver. He was the one who insisted I wear it.

"A hopefully unnecessary precaution. Besides, she needs to break the holster in," my partner explained.

I rolled my eyes.

"Have there been any odd reportings from the casters testing the system?" Silver asked.

"Odd as in how?" Jonim asked.

I kept my eyes down and silently pleaded for Silver to stop.

"Any type of feedback. Something beyond what would be expected in operating the system."

"Not that I'm aware of. Most of them complain it's like trying to push through a wall. You got something else though, lass, I'm sure of it. You barely touched one of the grips and the system fired up like it never has before. Great it works. Not so great you're the only one to manage it."

I refused to look up.

"Why is that a negative?" Silver asked.

Jonim took a deep breath. "Because it means we're really limited on who can operate it. That's not going to work for the higher-ups."

"Good point," Silver noted.

"Would anyone have wanted to hurt Mason specifically?" I asked. I had to change the subject. I needed to keep Silver from bringing up what I experienced.

"Not to that extent. They have no idea who might be testing what and when until they're called on."

I frowned.

"But likely Jake knows," Silver said.

"Sabotage his own project? The man might be a bit crazy, but he'd be insane to do it. It's his brain child - I can't imagine him doing anything of the sort. Not to mention what benefit would there be?"

I shrugged. "Just exploring all avenues."

"Did you have to come up with another theory?" Silver whined as we left the building.

I signaled him aside and dropped my voice. "Look, I just don't want them finding out everything that happened yesterday. I mean, I don't even understand it myself. Hells, I don't even know what the eye-color changing thing is."

My partner eyed me for a moment. "You don't?"

"It's not like I can see it."

Silver glanced around for a moment before pulling me closer against the building. "Before when it happened, it was just the gray part of your eyes that continuously shifted colors. Yesterday the effect covered your entire eye. They didn't see it because your back was to them."

I let out a sigh of relief.

"It doesn't mean I'm not still worried. Ketayl, you've been distracted since you touched the system."

Mentally I cursed - I thought it went unnoticed. "Just a lot to think about. So many possibilities and I'm no closer to an answer than when we arrived."

Silver stared at me for a minute before backing away. Lying to him hurt, but what was my other option?

"Have you thought about the fact it'll happen again when you test the system?" His back was to me.

I bit my lower lip. "Yes, but I plan on being better prepared next time. We should finish our interviews and then start in on the files." I wanted this conversation over and strode toward where we parked our loaner vehicle.

My feet halted when I saw the rear tire on the driver's side was flat. First getting insulted by Mason and now this. Today was not going well.

Silver went over and knelt down next to the tire, examining the problem. He pulled his phone out and a business card.

"What's going on?" I asked.

"It's been slashed. I'm calling Jonim." Silver stood up and took a few steps away once he put the phone to his ear.

I sighed and pulled my camera out, taking pictures of the tire. Was this targeted or simply someone wanting to cause damage? The rental stickers in the back driver's side window and the temporary tag in the front would easily mark it as a visiting vehicle.

While we waited for Jonim to come out, I pulled out my tablet and the cable to connect it to my camera to upload the images to the case file. Should I inform Lockonis?

Jonim arrived with a couple of other officers. "You two okay?"

"Yeah," Silver said, "Just found this little surprise when we got here. Figured I'd wait to have you guys look at it before changing it."

"Appreciate it. Actually, we can have it pulled into the garage to be dealt with and better looked at." Jonim stroked his beard.

"You want a full investigation, sir?" one of the men with him asked.

"Yes. Ain't dumb enough to think this a coincidence. No one else in the area has been touched and they ain't the only visitor."

Once the files uploaded, I packed the camera away and examined the images I took. "I'll have Sparks look at these, but I'm thinking a knife with a serrated edge was used."

Jonim stroked his beard. "It not be a common type of knife around here. We don't host combat units." He signaled for the men with him to begin and then for us to follow him. "I can set you up with one of our fleet vehicles if you would like."

"We can walk for now," Silver said.

I mentally groaned at the thought. Spelltech's warehouse was on the other side of the base.

"Alright, I'll check in on you folks later and see if you need anything." Jonim returned to the others.

I sighed and hefted my bag up on my shoulder. "Is this area under video surveillance?"

Jonim stopped and turned. "Yeah, planned on pulling the footage myself, why?"

"Can we get a copy?" I asked.

The Commander nodded. "Yeah, don't see a problem with that. I'll forward it to you when I get it."

"Thank you." I looked up at Silver. "We should get going."

7

"WHAT ARE YOU READING?" Silver asked. We had taken a break from sorting through the mountains of papers and plans stacked all over the office. We ended up creating a file system to some extent while we slogged through.

"One of the papers Jake wrote when he was an archaeologist. It might have something to do with the system."

Silver put his hand on my tablet, pushing it down. "Take a break."

"I'm fine." I needed to stay busy being this close to the system.

"No, you're not. Why don't we go see how they're doing with fixing the tire and then get something to eat?"

His plan would put some distance between me and the system. "Yeah, okay."

"We can compare notes since it's a long walk."

We reached the door before we were stopped. "Ketayl! Good, I caught you before you left." Jake was out of breath from running across the warehouse. "I'd like to have you fully test the system."

I heard the faint creaking sound of Silver's fingerless gloves. If he was clenching his fists, then I was about to have a different problem on my hands.

"Now isn't a good time," I said quickly, resisting the strong desire to jump at the opportunity. "Besides, I haven't seen anything resembling a manual so I know how to navigate it. I'd like to read over the documentation on the system first."

I bit the inside of my cheek to keep from going over there to test the system now without any precautions.

Jake gave me that creepy smile of his. "Oh, absolutely, I can pull the information together for you."

"The offense system can also be operated by a divine caster, correct?" I glanced up at Silver.

My partner raised an eyebrow at me, his face softened slightly.

"Yes, yes. The system is built to handle either type of energy."

I turned back to Jake. "Then it couldn't hurt to have another data set to work with, correct?"

Finally he looked at my partner. "Oh, of course. How rude of me. I got so wrapped up in what happened yesterday I didn't even think about that."

"But first we'll want to look over and make sure there's nothing wrong with the system per your specifications," I added. "For now, we need to get something to eat before coming back to the reason we're here." I pleaded to whichever deity would listen that my words were enough to ease Silver's concern. The system pulled harder at my resistance and I clenched my teeth at the strain.

Once we got some distance between us and Spelltech's warehouse, Silver commented, "That was some smooth talking. I thought for certain you would jump at the chance."

"I didn't turn him down," I pointed out. And with how strong the pull was, it had been difficult to say the least.

"No, but thanks for taking the precautions you did."

I felt a little better about being able to keep Silver's concern at bay.

"So how much did you manage to get copied?" he asked.

"Everything I put my hands on." Which was much of the room since I spent quite a bit of time sorting information. Anything divine I gave to Silver to look over.

He grinned broadly. "Are you planning to take it to your tablet later?"

"It'll make it a lot easier to sort through and access."

We were about halfway back to Jonim's building when Silver suddenly slammed into me and we fell to the side against a nearby building. I twisted in the fall - the side of my hip against the pavement and the back of my shoulder, neck, and head against the metal siding of the building. The instant headache made everything go out of focus.

I tried to push Silver off of me until I realized his actions kept us from being hit by a speeding vehicle. This day continued getting worse and it was only noon.

"You okay?" Suddenly Silver's face was too close to mine.

I had no room to back away. "Yeah, but you're heavy."

He gave a quick laugh and stood up, taking me with him. I rubbed the back of my head. I hit the building harder than I thought.

I winced when he touched my head. Others were running over to us.

"We should go to the infirmary to get you looked at," Silver said quietly.

I shook my head and immediately regretted the decision as the world spun too quickly. I grabbed Silver for support.

"You two okay?" a female Dwarf asked. She wore a Navy uniform. "I swear they never should have let some of these morons pass the drivin' test."

"I am, but she needs to get to the infirmary," Silver said.

"I'm fine," I shot back. Overprotective big brother was out and I was going to have a fight on my hands.

Others gathered around and I shifted uneasily being one of the subjects of attention. The dizziness would not let up. Actually, it had gotten worse.

The female Dwarf got into my vision. "I think not, lass. You likely have a concussion. Watched you hit the building pretty hard, but hey, it's better than getting hit by a car."

I gripped Silver's forearm tightly to remain upright. Usually dizziness began to fade by now. "We should get going." Moving would help.

Vehicles began showing up nearby. They seemed to be in a hurry.

"Ketayl, no, you need to get looked at. Do you remember anything about the last five minutes?"

"We nearly got run over." I moved to stand up and then wondered when I sat down. Silver's grip on my shoulder held me in place.

"Lass, that was over 10 minutes ago. You faded out there and stopped responding."

I touched the back of my head and felt something wet. Bringing my hand forward, my fingers were covered in blood. When had this happened? I could not remember hitting my head so hard.

Thinking on it, I could not remember what the car even looked like. I turned my attention up at Silver, confused, but had a hard time focusing.

People in medical uniforms hurried over to us. There were others in Navy uniforms. Why was it so hard to concentrate?

I SAT FROWNING at the wall in the infirmary while the doctor on duty tried to see how badly I hurt my head. There were a couple of other scrapes and bruises, but nothing I would complain about.

What confused me is why Silver had not simply used his power to deal with it. Of all the times for him to listen to me about not using his power on me, he chose now.

I kept my silence while Silver and the doctor documented my injuries. My partner stepped away as his phone rang. The sound echoed loudly in my ears and I cringed.

At least it was one less person poking and prodding at me for the moment. They had been holding my hair up to see how bad the cut was, but with as much hair as I had, they were having a hard time locating it.

"Yes ma'am. One moment." I watched Silver out of the corner of my eye as he fiddled with his phone before holding it up as if taking a picture.

I turned my attention to the floor. I was exhausted and hungry. Neither I wanted to admit to. I had to get this case finished.

Jonim entered the infirmary and folded his arms, waiting to the side. I would be stuck here for a bit, but Silver could handle him as soon as he got off his call.

I entertained the idea of going back to the hotel and hiding from the rest of the day. Insults, a slashed tire, almost getting run over - I could not take much more today.

No, there was work to be done. Though I was about ready to accept the cold, wintry conditions back at the main office. Maybe I could get a day or two here after we were done to enjoy the summer weather.

I heard the door open again. "By the Gods, what happened?" Jake asked far too loudly and I cringed, covering my ears.

"Out," Silver said sharply. His volume hurt as well.

"Let them be. We can talk outside," Jonim said at a much lower level.

The sound of the door opening and closing was almost drowned out by the pounding in my head. What was going on?

"Hey," Silver said softly, pulling my hands away from my ears. "Just a little longer and then I can heal this, okay?"

"Healing a concussion isn't the same as cuts and bruises. I'd recommend just letting her rest and recover on her own," the doctor said. "Though this is a bad one."

"I've had plenty of practice healing concussions," Silver retorted.

"I leave it to her to decide then. For now let's find the cut. I want to run another scan to make sure there isn't anything else we missed."

Mason watched us from his bed on the other side of the room. At least he did not feel the need to throw insults while I sat here with two men combing through my hair.

I hissed when a gloved hand touched a particular sensitive spot.

"Sorry," Silver said gently. "I think I found it."

"Alright, let's get it cleaned up so we can see how bad it is," the doctor said.

I kept my squirming and noises to a minimum while they cleaned the area and documented the damage. Why did we have to go through all of this? It was taking time away from what I needed to get done. What was it I needed to get done right now?

I struggled through the fog clouding my mind trying to remember what it was we had been doing. Where were we headed when we nearly got run over?

While they worked, I attempted to stay focused. Even during the scan I disconnected from the world and Silver would have to prod me to turn for the doctor.

Again I sat on one of the beds in the infirmary. I was unsure when I got back here, but no one poked and prodded me. Losing track of time bothered me though.

"Only with her consent," I heard the doctor say, bringing me back to the present for a moment.

"Ketayl." Suddenly Silver was in front of me. "Can you focus for a moment?"

"Can try," I said, my words a bit slurred. I made no promises.

He brushed my bangs back. The callouses on his fingers distracted me by the familiar comfort.

"Ketayl."

I blinked and forced myself to return to what was going on. "What?"

"Will you let me use my power to heal you? I'm familiar with how to handle concussions."

"Since when do you ask?" This was strange. He never asked - he just did it.

"I know, but this time I need your consent."

"Oh, okay."

"Good enough for me. I was about to make a few calls since I wasn't sure she could consent," the doctor said. "And I couldn't tell you how long it would be before her symptoms let up."

Silver put his hands on either side of my head and rested his forehead against mine. I went to back away, but he held me still. A sense of peace washed over me and I stopped pulling back. Slowly the pain faded and the fog lifted. Until he stepped away, I was content to stay there.

Then the world slammed back into place. "What time is it? Where's my gear bag? I've..."

"Easy, Ketayl," Silver said gently. "I knew you'd bounce back pretty quick, but you're still going to need to take time before we get back to work."

I crossed my arms and glared up at him.

My partner laughed and patted me on the head before stepping away to talk with the doctor.

Mason stared at me. I sighed and braced myself for what was to come.

He got up and came over. "Hey, about earlier, sorry."

I tilted my head at him, not understanding.

"Never thought I'd see the day when a divine and an arcane caster could get along never mind what the two of you have."

"We're an oddity," I admitted. "He used to be part of a church who had a number of mage parishioners and my family is mostly divine casters."

"So you were both used to the other side then. I'm afraid my earlier reaction to you was more what would be expected out of me rather than my true thoughts on the matter. If I ever get off of this forsaken assignment, I plan on to expanding my horizons. Also if I ever get out of this infirmary." Mason laughed lightly, looking at his gauze-wrapped hands.

I tilted my head, curious. "You don't want to be working on this?"

He shook his head. "The others at my church pulled seniority so I got stuck with it when the request came in. They also probably figured out I'm a little too curious for their orthodox views. I mean, this project is an interesting concept, but I don't see it working out."

I bit my lower lip for a moment. "I'll admit I've seen plenty of flaws in the design, but nothing that should have caused what happened to you."

"So you think it was sabotage?"

I shook my head. "I won't know until we get a closer look at the system. There are still too many possibilities to rule out."

Silence fell between us for a bit.

"Your buddy there is pretty scary when he's mad," Mason said quietly.

"You should see it when you piss her off," Silver said as he came back into my little section of the infirmary.

I glared up at him.

"Ready to get out of here?" Silver asked me.

"Yeah." Silver put his arm around me as I slid off of the bed. "I can manage on my own," I shot at him.

"You're always so cranky when you've been hurt. Let's get you cleaned up and then get something to eat."

I clenched my teeth. He could eat his words.

Mason laughed quietly. "You two are something else. Guess I better get back to bed before I get yelled at."

Why was Mason still here? His injuries were not severe. I doubted the answer to that question would lead to anything useful.

8

AT LEAST WHEN Silver said he wanted to get some physical training time in, he did not make me join him. While he worked out, I sat on the side of the training room trying to concentrate enough to get some reading done at least.

I remained unsure if my problem was a residual effect or the content I was attempting to understand.

Reading through Jake's papers tested my patience. I could read boring, dry, arcane theory books all day long, but the way he composed his papers drove me mad. I resisted the urge to pull out the pencil for my tablet and strike through all of the unnecessary repetition and filler words.

Taking a momentary break, I watched Silver, with a heavily loaded barbell across his shoulders, squat down and stand back up. Likely he chose this course of action both to keep me from being too active and so he could think through what we had found so far.

Glancing at my watch, I itched to pull out the plans I copied earlier and go through them thoroughly, but here was not the place. Not when Jake had no idea I made copies.

Come to think of it, I had not seen Jake since he burst into the infirmary. Or Jonim for that matter.

I stared at Silver's bare back. I could understand why Jonim had shown up, but why Jake? It was still a struggle to piece together information from that time period. Had he been carrying something?

I ran a hand through my bangs and tugged on the ends in frustration. I was grateful Silver got us out of the way, but his own strength caused a different set of problems.

"See something you like?" Silver asked teasingly as he walked over.

"What?"

"You were staring at me."

I turned away from him, embarrassed I went so deep into my own thoughts, I had not realized I appeared to have been staring. "No, I wasn't. I'm trying to remember what happened, but I can't."

Silver knelt down in front of me. "Hey, don't force it. It may come back, it may not. It doesn't matter - there were enough witnesses and security footage to make up for it."

When I realized I stared at the sun pendant on his necklace, I forced myself to look away. It was a weird habit I had when he was shirtless.

"Reached any conclusions yet?" I asked, changing the subject.

"No. We'll need to compare notes, but I'd rather you took it easy until tomorrow."

"It's already early evening. We've wasted a lot of time."

A large, rough hand touched my cheek gently, turning me to face him. "Ketayl, no. Your lack of memory may not be a concern in what happened, but pushing yourself right now could complicate matters. The damage may be healed, but your body isn't fully recovered."

I sighed and sat back. I knew what Silver would do if I ignored him when he was like this. He had rearranged my schedule more than once while we were in Ghost Forest to make sure I took time off when he thought I was overworked.

Picking up my tablet, I decided to continue reading. Silver would eventually get the hint and go back to his workout.

"What are you reading?"

Or not. "I'm trying to get through one of Jake's papers again. I'm tempted to edit them just so I can figure out what he's saying."

"Why not? Unless you're planning on giving him a copy I don't see the issue."

I stared at my partner. "Am I supposed to be working or not?"

"I need you to keep it light. That sounds pretty simple and not overly taxing. Well, it might be depending on how bad it is."

I bit my lower lip for a moment. "Pretty bad."

"But it's not you putting together a complex puzzle. Use this time to get the pieces you'll need before you start going after the big picture. And you better believe you'll be getting a full night's sleep tonight. Especially after you were up last night."

"Saying I am and it actually happening are two different things," I muttered.

Silver grinned broadly. "I know how to make sure it happens."

I rolled my eyes. This man was impossible.

THE NEXT MORNING, we were back in Jake's office with a couple of extra soldiers for security. Jonim insisted on them and Lockonis backed him up. We had no other support here.

Through all of this, Jake remained suspiciously absent given his burst into the infirmary the day before. I stood over a table we managed to clear with the latest plans rolled out. Was there anything to connect the defense part of the system to the screens in the room? By the looks of it, the defense station should not even turn them on.

Which in one regard made sense since that person only supplied power to form a single, uniform shield around the vessel though they could turn emitters off. They had no reason to need a view of the outside.

Silver stood over my shoulder. "You have something?"

"A lack of something. The defense system isn't designed to trigger the activation of the screens."

"Isn't it supposed to be able to take over in case something happens to the offense station?"

"In theory. Either these aren't the most recent plans or..." I shifted the pages to make sure others bore the same corresponding revision date in the corner.

"Someone's lying."

I blew a sharp breath through my bangs. "I doubt he forgot."

Silver stroked the small patch of hair on his chin. "What about the offense system? Maybe the trigger was excluded from the plans?"

I shrugged, it was a possibility. I pulled out the pages for the offensive part of the system just as Jake came in. I shifted uncomfortably when I saw the giant smile plastered to his face.

"I'm so glad to see you're back on your feet after yesterday," Jake said, his tone odd, but I was unable to place why. "I have the documentation you asked for." He held out a thick binder.

I bowed taking it.

"Did they ever find out who was so careless?" Jake asked.

Then I placed it - he sounded fake.

"No," Silver answered, the word clipped. "You said previously the system triggers the screens in the room, correct?"

"Oh, yes, yes. Either station," Jake said.

"Can you point out where for the defense station?" I took the other pages and moved away so he could see.

"Oh heavens, it's not on these. It's on the plans for the camera network. Both stations use a single trigger. Seemed silly to include it here. I haven't gotten the brightest people to help build this and they would have put it in twice or worse, three times. I'm fairly certain they're the reason we've had so many problems."

The truth or something to distract us? "Where are those plans?" I asked.

"Um..." Jake looked around the office.

"Never mind, I'll find them," I said. "Actually, can we get onto your computer system? I assume these were created digitally."

"Oh, of course, of course. Let me get you logged in. I should have thought of that." Jake quickly shuffled over to the computer in the room.

When Spelltech's owner had his back to us, I turned to Silver and tugged on my bangs. I hoped he understood I was at the end of my patience with this man.

"So when do you think you'll be able to test the system?" Jake asked.

I sighed. I knew the request was coming. While I remembered what being synced with the system was like, the blow to my head seemed to have fully disconnected the pull it had on me.

"We need to check the system first to make sure there isn't a repeat and she needs time to go over the documentation," Silver answered.

I put what I had in my hands down. It was as good of a time as any to play this card. "I'm curious as to what gave you inspiration for this design."

"I, uh..." Jake glanced at Silver. "I guess I've always been fascinated by tales of Atlantis and the technology they were rumored to have developed. It's certainly 'outside the box' as they say and I think there's much we can learn."

A very practiced answer.

"Atlantis is certainly an interesting subject," I noted and returned to what I had been doing. At least the people who theorized on it were more credible than the people who believed Terra was flat and Earth was a mirrored copy on the other side of a coin.

"Do you also study it?" I refused to look up at Jake - his tone was both excited and greasy. "I have written several papers on the subject. Perhaps you would like to take a look? When you have a chance of course. Getting this settled is top priority, I understand."

I remained silent about my brief attempts at reading said papers.

"Let's get this solved first and then we can talk," I replied. "Speaking of, we really should get back to work."

"Oh, yes, yes, of course. Excuse me. Let me know if you need anything."

As soon as the door closed and Jake had gotten a distance away Silver mused, "You strung him along."

"It wasn't my intent. I had been hoping for something more than his pitch. It feels like there's still something missing in these plans. The system shouldn't work at all without an amplifier, but I don't see one or even a reference to it."

"Just don't ever do that to me, okay?"

I raised an eyebrow at my partner. "I don't understand."

"I want you to always be straightforward with me. Truthful would be nice also."

Putting my hands on my hips, I tilted my head, still lost. "What are you getting at?"

Silver scrunched up his face in anger. "Don't pull that crap with me, Ketayl. I know the damn system was still messing with you yesterday. You claimed to be distracted by the case, but you haven't shown the same behavior as you did before we almost got run over."

I looked down at the plans before me. "Guess the blow to the head reset everything," I muttered.

"Yeah, well I don't want that being the only option to break you out of it fully."

I sighed. This was not the time to fight. "I'm sorry. I didn't want you to worry, okay? We've got a lot to do and I was working through it. It's completely gone."

He folded his arms and stared at me.

"Seriously, no problems with it since." Getting him to believe me after lying to him was going to be harder than I hoped.

"And what of when you go to test the system?"

I sighed. "Give me a chance to read about it and come up with a solution. It could be as simple as I didn't back out of the system correctly."

Silver made a disgruntled noise but said nothing further.

I moved away from him and sat down at the computer, concealed from outside the office by the mountains of paper. Putting my head in my hands, I hid my face with my long bangs. Why was his approval or disapproval so important? We were here for a job and I had done what I thought best.

Everything had run so smoothly while we were in Ghost Forest but now...

"Ketayl," Silver said softly, his hand on my shoulder, "we'll figure this out. Just don't lock me out, okay? Let me help."

I took a deep breath before refocusing on the screen before me. "Yeah."

"How fast do you think you can learn how to use the system?"

I turned to look at Silver. What was he getting at? "I've got a good handle on how the system should function and the layout of the control panels at the stations, but not the individual power flows and where the triggers engage for the screens."

"Do you think you'd be able to match it to the system on board after lunch?"

"Maybe. It depends how complex the power flow is compared to what I've read about the defense system currently in use by the Navy. I'm starting to wish I had Holly's photographic memory."

"Yours is pretty good," Silver said. "Spend as much time as you need going over it. We can go over the binder at lunch and plan from there."

I looked back at how thick the binder was. "I'm not sure we can get through all of it over lunch."

Silver leaned over and kissed my cheek before moving away. "You're amazing at parsing information quickly. We'll get it figured out."

I touched the spot his lips had been. What was that for? "Are you saying you want me to test the system this afternoon?"

"I'd rather go first if you don't mind. We can physically look over as much of the system as possible and decide then. If there's something you think is missing on the plans, it likely isn't going to be easily accessible and searching for it through the system makes some sort of sense."

"Hope neither of us blows it up. Jake won't be pleased."

"Not our problem." Silver grinned.

"Will be if one or both of us gets hurt," I reminded him.

"Just start reading. I'm getting bored."

And a bored Silver was never a good thing.

9

WHILE SILVER DROVE, I read through the binder. Not a manual, but instead the reports from the tests, which included each caster's experience. Possibly better than a manual. I copied each page while I read.

"You're going through it pretty quick," Silver noted.

"It's all reports from the casters. I guess an actual manual doesn't exist, but this could be more insightful."

"Anything so far about how to back out of the system safely?"

I hesitated before answering. "No, but I've got early tests here and so far no one has managed to trigger the camera network."

"Perhaps skip ahead?"

I nodded and slowly made my way back to more current tests, copying information as I went. I skimmed the pages, looking for at least a mention of the camera network or the screens.

About three quarters of the way through the binder, I finally found one. It was the current arcane caster from the EAC. There was nothing about backing out of the system though.

Maybe he had not gotten far enough to matter. Should I go to the end and work my way backward?

No, I should finish copying the information and then start narrowing down what I was looking for. I flipped through the pages faster, working my way toward the end, catching keywords as I went.

"You don't have to go that fast," Silver said as he pulled into the parking lot of a restaurant.

I turned my attention out of the vehicle. I knew we had been in the car for a while, but we were nowhere near the base. "Where are we?"

"I thought I'd take us a distance from the base to give us time to go through the information and this place came recommended."

"Oh. I think I'm going to have to go backwards through the reports. I'm hoping someone has gotten far enough into the system to have an idea of how to back out of it."

"Jake wouldn't know?"

I shook my head. "I wouldn't expect him to. He's not a caster at all, which makes this project all the more strange for him to be involved in."

"But he has a fascination with Atlantis which inspired the design."

"That's putting it mildly," I muttered as we got out of the vehicle. I hugged the binder to my chest. "I think there's plenty of evidence to point out he doesn't understand his own design."

I waited until we were seated before delving into the information again.

"Ketayl, at least figure out what you want to eat first."

His words made me pause and I looked up at him in confusion. Once we had moved into the temporary house in Ghost Forest, we went out to eat little and usually always to the same place. And then I always got the same thing. "Sorry, I forgot."

He laughed lightly. "I miss Ghost Forest. I wonder how everyone is doing."

"Kitteren and Rathal are still out there - you could always call one of them," I said idly as I looked over the menu. I missed Ghost Forest also. It had become home even though it was far colder than I cared for.

"Speaking of Kitteren, have you talked to her?"

"I sent her a message telling her I was headed out on assignment," I said idly as I looked over the menu.

"Ketayl..."

I sighed. "She's been pretty busy with taking over the branch. It just works out that now we're both busy. I'll message her later."

Silence fell between us and I folded the menu and put it aside once I made a decision before returning to the binder. There were reports on the accident, which I planned to read later, but I needed something now about what it was like to actively be engaging the system.

I only paused reading long enough to place my order and then returned to the best report I had found so far. The one which seemed to have made the most progress, but even then the caster had not gotten far past activating the screens. Not a mention of needing to back out of the system.

I frowned - this was going to make convincing my partner to let me test it next to impossible. I might have to find my own way back out.

"Nothing?" Silver asked.

I shook my head and put the binder aside. "Unless there's information in a different report, there's not a mention of needing to back out of the system."

"Have you considered you had a different experience because you're an Arcanist?"

I took in a sharp breath at his use of the term. I still hated it despite my more positive experiences with it over the past few years. "It should operate under the same principles."

"Except that all of these casters, myself included, have to invoke our power. You're constantly connected to yours. I suppose it would be similar to the fact the system is always active," Silver argued, flicking his braid back and forth in thought.

I tapped my finger on my glass of water and considered the concept. "If that's the case then only another Arcanist or... is there a divine equivalent?"

Silver shrugged. He had not even known Arcanists existed until he met me and his world view seemed to have been as narrow as mine once was.

"Either way it makes the system useless for military application," I concluded.

"Not completely useless, but certainly not ideal." Silver pulled my hand off of the glass and kissed the back of my fingers. "I don't want you using the system, but I won't break the agreement with Jake. I will do everything within my power to get you out."

I made a face of annoyance at him and pulled my hand away. "Let's hope it doesn't come to that. I'd rather avoid the lingering effects." There was no pull from the system, but a pure desire for just one more moment of being able to breathe. The thought alone frightened me. How easy would it be to go in and not want to leave?

"Yeah, I don't want to deal with you having another concussion. Not to mention I'm sure if Kitteren ever finds out I caused it, she'll have my hide."

I shook my head. "It was an accident and I don't plan on telling her."

"Thanks."

The server arriving with our food paused the conversation. An awkward silence followed.

"Name?" Silver asked.

"What?"

"What your name would have been?"

I rolled my eyes. "Name?" He asked when we had lulls like this and we ended up having the same conversation every time.

"Not until you tell me yours."

I had little hope of him actually answering who he was romantically interested in, but I asked every time anyway. Silver simply grinned broadly at me from across the table. Shaking my head, I returned to my food. At least he stopped fighting me about testing the system.

I SCOOTED FARTHER under the defense station. Unfortunately, I ended up with examining the low areas. We already went over the offense station and found no issues we could determine.

My grip slipped while pulling on a panel - I wore gloves both as part of procedure and in hope they would be enough of a barrier to keep me from accidentally activating the system. Trying again and getting it free, I shined my handlight up into the wiring. "It's pretty damaged in here. Looks like most of the wiring is burnt out if not all of it."

"Given the footage, I expected that," Silver replied from above me. He straddled my legs and went over the control panel.

Our escorts remained outside, not seeing any danger to us as we were the only ones on the ship at the moment. They chatted softly between themselves. Though I was certain as soon as Jake caught wind we came aboard, he would be here pestering us.

"I might have to get under the floor. We should see if there's a ladder also so I can get into the ceiling again. It's going to take a while to trace both systems back to the source," I said, "There's a chance it started at or before the trigger. Wherever that is."

"Let me worry about the high stuff. It doesn't look like there was anything off on the console. Not that there's much here to tamper with."

I slid out so I could look at him which put me mostly underneath him. It was awkward being at this angle. "Do you want to test to see if this station is still active?"

"And risk shorting it out again? No. Let's keep searching," my partner said. Then he turned his attention down to me and grinned mischievously.

I rolled my eyes and went back to the wiring I had been examining. What he found amusing, I knew not nor had I cared to find out.

Twisting, I removed another panel, following more burnt out wiring into the floor. I thought about skipping sections so I could find the end faster. Which direction from here?

"There you two are!" Jake said loudly.

I jumped and slammed my head on the underside of the console. "Ow..."

Large hands grabbed my hips and pulled me out from under the console. "You okay?" Silver asked.

I rubbed my head. "Yeah." This trip had been a couple of blows to the head too many.

Jonim stood with him and our escorts stood at full attention outside the door. "Jake here is saying the two of you are willing to test the system."

I glanced up at Silver, still nursing the sore spot on the back of my head.

"We will at some point, but we haven't fully determined the offense system won't suffer from the same problem," I said. I needed to push off connecting with the system again. I worried I would lose myself to it.

"It won't," Jake said quickly. "The offense station is much more heavily shielded."

I wanted to remind him his material of choice was the opposite of what he needed, but remained silent. If I could get my hands on the shielding, I could see if it overloaded.

"Do you want to give it a shot? It's not an official test and won't take up too much of our time," Silver suggested. "Might give us an idea of what to look for."

Now he was pushing for it? Or perhaps he simply wanted to get rid of Jake. I signaled for him to go ahead.

"So what's the general procedure here?" Silver asked as he sat down at the offense station, pulling his rubber gloves off, but leaving on the fingerless leather gloves he normally wore. "She read the reports, I didn't."

"Most of them extend their power into the system, reaching as far as they can. A couple tried to ram it," Jonim said.

My partner turned to me as he reached for the grips. His hands hovered over them. I nodded. Then he grabbed them fully, but nothing happened. Several seconds later the screens turned on and the main lights dimmed. A set of blue ambient lights came on.

Jake bounced excitedly and hurried to look over Silver's shoulder at the station. "He's gotten farther than anyone else."

Then everything shifted back to the way it was and my partner took his hands off the grips. "I had a lot of resistance in there. I couldn't get past a certain point."

"Same thing everyone else said," Jonim noted.

"Mind if I try ramming it?" Silver asked.

"I don't see a problem with it," Jonim replied and looked at Jake.

Spelltech's owner crossed his arms and appeared to be lost in thought. "It could break through whatever wall they've been running into. There might be a break-in period I hadn't realized it would need."

Silver grabbed the grips again and everything came on again in quick succession. Jake appeared overly thrilled at his progress.

"I don't think the higher-ups are going to like a break-in period," Jonim commented.

Jake waved him off.

Everything switched back to normal. My partner shook his head. "Felt like I was close, but without another to measure against, it's hard to tell."

"It was farther than your first attempt. Ramming it seems to have better success. I can certainly take this going forward," Jake said emphatically.

Silver came and stood over me. "The same?" I asked quietly.

"No."

"Stay close?" Suddenly I was afraid. I wanted to feel the sensation of being balanced again, but continued to worry I would lose myself to it.

"Intend to. Hold back and ease into the system. I don't think you'll have the same problem I did given your natural predisposition."

"Natural predisposition?" Jake asked, getting into my personal space.

I backed away quickly and Silver moved to stand between us. Why was I shying away from what I was? Did he have to know?

It would be unscientific to withhold the information, but his project so far had been anything but.

"Please, you must explain. I need to know if I must look for a different type of caster," Jake pleaded.

"Jake," Jonim said, "Need I remind you that you promised the system would work with any caster? While the information may provide insight, you would still have to figure out how to get it to work for someone like Silver here."

"Right, right. Shall we make sure the last time wasn't a fluke?"

Silver turned and put his hand on the side of my face. "You okay to do this?"

I stared at the station, still afraid, but wanting to know. Needing that single moment to breathe. That moment to feel normal even while I was essentially out of body. Realizing I had not answered, I nodded, slowly making my way toward the station.

Taking a seat, I reached for the grips before Jake stopped me. "Your gloves. It needs skin contact."

I glanced at Silver. "Just wanted to see if the gloves would stop it as a precaution for while we worked."

"Oh, right, right."

I hesitantly touched it with a finger and felt a thrum of power under it. No other connection though.

Sitting back I pulled my gloves off, handing them to Silver. He took my hand in his and I wondered why Jake said nothing about the fingerless gloves he wore.

Taking a deep breath, I pulled my power as tightly into myself as I could. I struggled to keep it contained like this, but it was the best option. I grabbed the grips quickly, unsure of how long I would be able to maintain the hold and it mattered none because I immediately returned to where I was yesterday with a view of the outside no matter where I turned.

The brief moment of perfect balance was broken as I struggled to get air, afraid I might be stuck. I needed to calm down and back out. How?

And why could I see outside without the screens?

I heard a faint voice, but nothing understandable over the sound of the water. I thought I heard my name, but it was as if the wind whispered it.

The longer I wandered searching for a way out the more my panic rose. Even being perfectly balanced could not stop it. A moment of calm washed over me before it was taken away by the ocean.

I reached for the disappearing calm, but it was too far gone. My breathing became faster as I realized I was stuck. And it was not because I lost myself to the system.

Comfort came through again, but not strong enough to override my panic. It stayed though and pulled at me. It felt familiar. *Silver?*

The pull became stronger and I held on to it, hoping it would be enough to draw me out. I made sluggish progress at first and then suddenly slammed back to the system's control room.

Feeling lips on mine, I pulled back and swung with an open palm. The sting of my hand told me I connected before my sight returned.

"I'm not sure I entirely deserved that," Silver said after a moment, rubbing his cheek.

I still labored to get enough air, scared and unsure of what happened. I kicked at the floor, plastering myself to the back of the chair and as far away from the grips as possible.

"You have to tell me what happened!" Jake said excitedly. "No one has ever gotten the system fully operational."

"Back off!" Silver barked.

Jonim moved forward and pulled Jake back. "Give her time. It looks like this 'natural predisposition' of hers caused a different set of problems."

I held onto the sides of the chair and looked frantically around the room. I was where I should be. Why could I not calm down? Was it Silver who kissed me? Why would he?

My chair spun away from the console and Silver got down in my vision. "Hey, focus on me."

I followed his breathing, slowly calming down. His hands wiped at my face.

"We need to run a full test with her. Targets, everything," Jake said excitedly.

Silver looked over my shoulder. "No. No more tests. You have no idea how difficult it was to pull her out of the system." He sounded angry.

"Hey, let's all calm down and we'll review what happened before deciding anything," Jonim jumped in.

"Can you give us a few minutes?" Silver shot at them.

"What? How can you...?" Jake started.

"Let's go," Jonim said. Shortly after I heard the door open and then close several seconds later.

My partner held my head so I stayed looking at him. "It's just us. It's okay. I'm sorry I kissed you against your will, but I couldn't pull you back without a stronger connection."

I let out a shuddering breath. I needed to process everything, but I felt a lingering effect on my lips still. I could not hold the flood of tears back any longer.

Silver pulled me from the chair and we sat together on the floor. I had no idea how long we were there before I calmed down enough to talk.

"Ketayl, talk to me. What happened?"

"I couldn't ease in. I held my power in as much as possible and... I was stuck. I couldn't find a way out. I didn't want to stay."

"They said you immediately synced to the system at about 95 percent. Could you hear us?"

I shook my head. "Heard a voice, but no words. I thought I heard my name, but it was so faint."

"Who'd it sound like?"

Who? I had not paid attention at the time. Closing my eyes, I recalled the voice. Male, familiar. "You," I answered.

His arms tightened around me and he stuck his nose in my hair. Normally I would gripe at him for his actions, but I was still too shaken to push away the comfort.

Silver's phone rang. I moved away from him so he could stand up and get it out of his pocket. "Blaise," he answered, walking away.

I shakily got to my feet and dug for a fresh pair of gloves. Suddenly Silver's hand appeared over mine and he shook his head.

Once I pulled my hands away, he moved back to the other side of the room. "Yes, ma'am. You'll have my full report as soon as I have a chance to write it."

I sat on the floor near our bags, still unstable. I guessed by the snippet of conversation I heard he spoke with Lockonis. Her timing was all too good.

Pulling my knees to my chest, I buried my face.

"I've got to go," Silver said as I heard his footsteps coming back my way. I looked up in time to see him pull the phone away from his head and end the call. He knelt down in front of me. "No more today, okay?"

I nodded. I could not think straight to argue with him.

"Does the system still have some sort of hold on you?"

I shook my head. The connection I had the last time was absent. "Maybe more to do with whatever you did."

"Speaking of, did you really have to slap me that hard?"

The heat rose in my cheeks and I buried my face again. "Sorry. I reacted. Didn't know what was going on."

"Fair enough." Silver reached into his gear bag and pulled out his tablet. "Do you think you'd be up for a video call? Lockonis called me in a panic because somehow she saw your heart rate shoot up too high."

I stared at my watch. "I didn't know it sent that information."

"It reads your heart rate?"

"And other things - I haven't gotten a chance to go through the information it came with." I rubbed my eyes. Now I felt exhausted, but there was still so much to do.

"Does this mean we're courting now?" Silver gave me a lopsided grin.

I rolled my eyes. He was impossible.

My partner sat down next to me and started up the call.

"What in the Hells happened?" Lockonis demanded as soon as the call connected.

"We were asked to test the system," Silver said. I hoped he planned to do most of the talking.

Lockonis folded her arms and frowned. "Please tell me you took precautions and didn't just jump in."

"We've gone over the system and the reports from previous tests. I went first," Silver said.

"Not completely," I said quietly.

Lockonis turned her attention to me. "Explain before you give me a reason to fly down there."

Silver and I looked at each other for a moment. "I... I accidentally activated the system for a brief moment yesterday when my hand brushed one of the grips on the offense station. I didn't know it was active."

"As in fully activated it?" Lockonis asked.

"Yes," Silver said quickly. He could have control of the conversation. "I snapped her out of it after a few seconds."

"Now you really have to explain. Because I got no notice of anything out of the ordinary yesterday and today her heart rate was through the roof."

Silver sighed. "When I tested it, I hit resistance and couldn't get it fully activated. Same as every other caster. Ketayl immediately syncs with the system just by touching the grips."

I hugged my knees tighter to hide my shaking at the memory of being stuck.

"Ket, what happened in there?"

I shook thinking about it. "I couldn't get out. I could see outside. Hear the ocean. But I couldn't find a way back out."

Silver took over, "She could hear me, but not enough to make out what I was saying."

"Hm." Lockonis sat back in her chair. "On the off-chance you decide to toy with the system again, you might want to consider using a keyword. Something Ket knows to listen for and can follow. Granted, I'll be interested to read your report about how you got her out this time."

"It's not necessarily an option we should rely on." Silver rubbed his cheek again.

I felt awful about blindly slapping him. I wished he had found a different way other than kissing me. I had been better off not knowing what that was like.

"Alright, keep me posted. And Ket," Lockonis said, waiting until I looked up at the tablet's screen, "Don't go diving into unknown systems for a bit." Then she cut the connection.

Silver put his tablet aside and turned back to me. "What is it?"

"Why'd you have to do that?"

"Do what?"

I hid my face again. "How you pulled me from the system."

Silver let out a long sigh. "I could sense you holding on to the anchor I created, but I was struggling to pull you back. Too much more and I would have lost you again. Creating a stronger connection through a more intimate act was a gamble I had to take."

I made a noise of acknowledgment which was muffled because I still had my face hidden.

"Ketayl, we're both Elves. This isn't something uncommon between friends, okay?"

I nodded, refusing to lift my head.

"How about I take you back to the hotel? I think you've had enough today."

My head shot up. "No!" As embarrassed as I was, being separated was worse.

"Alright, let me go talk to the two outside and see if we can't work in peace for a bit. I expect you to be sitting in this exact spot when I get back."

I glared at him and then stuck my tongue out at his back. Childish? Perhaps, but I could deal with overprotective big brother mode over what just happened.

1 0

SILVER WANTED to keep working and I refused to go back to the hotel. In compromise, I sat to the side and read through the plans, directing him. We managed to get through the defense station's wiring in the room, but the source of the problem remained outside of the control room.

Now we were following the camera network back from the burned out screen, but Silver had lost track of it. Suddenly my partner jumped, putting his hands and feet on the sides of the ladder and slid down.

"I can't find where it came from," he said, tugging on his braid.

"We should dust for prints before coming back at it. I'll get the pictures you took uploaded to the case file."

"We can do it after supper."

"I'm not hungry." My appetite would likely be gone for a while still. I could not shake the last of the fear from having been stuck.

Silver stood over me with his arms folded. "You need to eat. And more importantly, we need to talk about what happened."

"I'd rather not." I fought down the heat rising to my face.

"You know Jake is going to pester you endlessly until you submit a report and it'll help to talk it over."

Maybe I assumed too much. He had a point about Jake looking

for a report, but I did not want to talk about my loss of emotional control. "I can draft up something tonight."

"No, you're sleeping tonight. All night."

I sighed. "Must you get this way?"

"If it means making sure you take care of yourself, then yes."

I rolled my eyes and returned to reading over the plans. The issues with the defense station continued outside of the room. It appeared to be a section the offense station also went to. Possibly whatever it was they were using as an amplifier?

Was there a way to reach it from another room? I would need to get the layout for the ship and hope someone else held the plans for the wiring. Why were these so incomplete?

The plans disappeared from in front of me. I glared up at Silver.

"You're done for right now. I know you have something, but it can wait." He knelt down in front of me. I backed away from his reaching hand. "I'm worried about how what happened might be affecting you. Just take this breather to regroup and we'll come back at it for a little longer."

I could fight him, but he could easily pick me up. "Fine."

Leaving the ship, our escorts drove us back to our vehicle. They would not leave the base with us.

Jonim caught up with us before we left. "Glad I caught you. You two done for the night?"

"No," Silver answered. "Just taking a break for supper."

The Dwarf folded his arms and looked up at each of us. "Given what happened today, I'd recommend taking the rest of the night off. Enjoy some of Sandpoint's food and entertainment. I can recommend you a place. Good food, live music, and sometimes a few interesting stories depending on who you talk to."

I shrugged to Silver. It seemed like Jonim wanted to tell us something.

"We're open to suggestions," my partner said.

"It's a place called 'Watered Down' though trust me, their drinks are anything but. The name helps keep it to mostly the locals. You folks have a navigation system or you need me to get you directions?"

"We can find it," I said. "Thank you."

Jonim gave us a salute and left.

I waited until we got off the base before I said, "Did it seem like he wanted to tell us something?"

"Might be why he gave us a recommendation to this place. Hope it's not a set up."

I shrugged. Only time would tell. "He'd be risking his career if it was."

"Sounded like telling us to go to this place is already risking his career."

"He's been the one to reign in Jake," I pointed out.

"True." Silver flicked the tail of his braid back and forth with his free hand. "I can't decide if Jake's behavior is a lack of experience as a weapons developer or something else entirely."

Now I was the one who was falling behind. "What do you mean?"

"He seems to forget things a lot. Very important things like his promise the system would work for any caster."

"Thanks for not telling them what I am." It had been the one relief within the mess.

"I figured you'd share it if you were comfortable. It's nothing to be ashamed of though."

I stared at my hands on my lap. "I don't know what you're talking about."

"Ketayl..." Silver sighed. "Every time the subject comes up, you're always hesitant to admit you're an Arcanist. You still do it with me on occasion."

I let out a shuddering breath, turning my gaze out the window, hoping this awkward conversation would end. He still seemed to not understand the problems I dealt with.

Rough fingers reached under my hair to rub the back of my neck. We were off-base with no one else to witness it so I relaxed in the seat and let him.

What bothered me still was we were no closer to the answer we were sent here for. Soon enough they would be demanding an answer.

"We should figure out a keyword," Silver suggested.

I blinked and sat up, confused by the topic of conversation. "A what?"

"A keyword, like Lockonis said. In case you accidentally touch the controls. I really don't want to get slapped again."

My face heated up at the reminder. I turned to look out my window. "I don't know. I barely could make out my name - I'm not sure what would come through stronger."

"Something unique to you."

"My name is."

Silver sighed. "A lot of people also use it or a variation of it. You didn't hear the other two when they used it."

"What do you suggest then?"

"Something unique to both of us?" He sounded hesitant to voice his suggestion.

His answer was not the one I was looking for. "What would be unique to both of us?"

"Could be something new. We could come up with something to use beyond this."

"For what?" Silver had my curiosity piqued - he must have some plan in mind.

Silver tugged on his braid as if he was nervous. The movement confused me. "I don't know. How about your name?"

"We just went over that - you said too many people use it." Could he make up his mind?

He let out a long sigh. "I meant what your name should have been."

"No," I said firmly.

"At least think about it," Silver said quickly. "It's unique to you and it could be to us."

"I don't know..." There was too much pain tied to that name.

A mischievous grin graced my partner's face. "I mean, I could just make up a nickname for you."

"No, I know your naming schemes. Let me think about it, okay?" He could be almost as strange as Ted with what he called things. I remembered catching him having referred to a pair of daggers we collected for evidence once as "Stabby" and "Stabber".

Silver grinned, but never took his eyes off of the road. I should not have said I would entertain the idea. Now he would be relentless.

We remained silent as he turned into the parking lot for the restaurant. Watered Down seemed like a respectable place at least from the outside.

"Ketayl." Silver stopped me before I got out. He pointed at my leg.

The holster. I forgot I still wore it.

"Just take it off and put it in your bag."

I nodded and tucked the whole holster in my bag.

It was rowdy inside. And crowded, though most were around the small stage cheering on whoever was singing.

Silver grabbed my hand after a minute and tugged me along as he followed someone to a booth along the windows and to the opposite side of the restaurant from the stage.

At least it might be quieter. I hoped I could convince Silver to talk more about how isolated the issue with the camera network was. I really did not want to climb up there again.

No, I needed to let Sparky take over by analyzing the images Silver took. Likely we would hear from him tomorrow. I should find the shielding. I thought it would have been installed throughout the whole system, but perhaps not with the prototype.

Not as if Jake's plans included it.

"Ketayl, give it a rest already," Silver said and dangled a menu in front of my face.

I glared at him and took it.

"Given it much thought yet?"

"Huh?" I had just opened the menu in my hands. He had not given me a chance to read it let alone think about what I wanted.

"About using your name."

Was he back on that already? "No. I've had other things to think about."

He reached over and rubbed my wrist. "And I want you to stop for now. We'll talk about what happened during the test when we get back to the hotel, but I want to get a plan in place in case you get stuck in the system again."

A small part of me whispered he created something unique to both of us. I shoved it back. It was not a viable solution.

"You okay?" Silver put the back of his exposed fingers against my forehead.

I swatted him away. "Yes, let me figure out what I want."

He let the conversation fall there until after the server took our order. "You sure you're okay? You got a bit flushed there for a minute."

"I am. Drop it."

A mischievous grin crossed his face. "Oh, I know what you were thinking about now. Don't tell me that was your first kiss."

"Back off," I ground out at him to hide my embarrassment.

"Well, let me just say that it was a honor and privilege to be your first."

"I'll slap you again if you keep this up."

He stroked the small patch of hair on his chin. "Would it be worth it?"

I glared at him for a moment, wondering what on Terra had gotten into him. Folding my arms across my chest, I decided to stare out the window. He was so childish sometimes.

He laughed and I refused to look at him. "Alright. Alright. I get it. You've been through Hells of a day again. Though I'm sure you would've preferred it be under better circumstances."

"Or not at all," I muttered. Something occurred to me. "How much of the effect of the system did you get by doing that?"

Silver stopped and stared at me. "Nothing because I kept myself anchored, why?"

"Are you sure because it might explain your current behavior."

"Nope, this is just me." Silver grinned broadly.

I rolled my eyes and returned to looking out the window. I still thought my theory held.

"Is the system actually operational?"

His question brought me back to the present. "I didn't try to use it. It might be, but I don't think it'll amplify the way they planned."

He sat back and toyed with the end of his braid. "If I don't like how this is being handled, I can only imagine how you feel."

I pursed my lips together while I organized my thoughts.

"Ah, heard we had some new guests this evening." I turned to find a male Dwarf standing at the end of our table. "Don't often get people outside of the locals."

"This establishment came recommended," Silver answered.

"Who sent you my way? Oh, where are my manners? I'm Caradoc Moltenborn, owner of Watered Down. I make it a habit to get to know who wanders my way. Especially if there's a good story to be told. My rule is 'give a story, get a story'."

"Commander Jonim Stormrider suggested we come here," Silver said.

"Joni? He doesn't often share, but it's always for a reason. You folks thinking of taking part in sing-a-long night?"

I stretched to look around him at the stage and saw someone else setting up, getting ready for a song.

"Maybe," Silver answered.

I turned back to see my partner staring at me intently. "No."

Caradoc laughed. "I think you've been volunteered, lass. Ain't had a pretty Elf like yourself take the stage in a while."

"I can't sing."

"Don't lie - I've heard you plenty of times," Silver said, grinning madly at me.

I looked at my partner like he was crazy. "That was once."

"No, you'll sing along with whatever you're listening to while you're working."

Heat rose to my face and I looked down at my lap. I had no idea I did that. He should have told me sooner so I could have made sure I stayed quiet.

Caradoc stepped aside as the server delivered our food. "Consider it. Especially if you can pull off something by Lindale - that'll be Hells of a treat for this crowd."

Why did he have to mention Mother's name? I sat silently staring at the plate in front of me.

"Ketayl?" Silver asked once the others left.

Too many things came to mind at once. I picked the least confrontational. "You should have told me so I didn't bother you."

"It was never a bother and I try not to interrupt you too often. I like listening to you."

I would have to be more alert to make sure I stopped the habit. I picked up my fork and poked at my food.

Silver sighed loudly. "I think you should go sing something after we eat."

"No."

"Listen to me first," he snapped. "He said his rule was 'give a story, get a story,' right?"

I eyed him cautiously. "Yeah."

"I think Jonim sent us here to get a story."

"And what does that have to do with me singing?"

He gave me an exasperated look. "Got to give to get, right? You've got the voice and the training. I don't."

"I don't even like playing my violin in front of people and you want me to sing?"

"You played in the Winter Solstice show the werewolves put on."

"And do you know how much they badgered me and how much time I put in practicing?"

"No, because you hid it."

I scrunched up my face. I had nothing to use against him.

"Look, this is obviously just for fun and most of them are probably drunk enough to enjoy just about anything. It sounds that way at least."

I glanced back at the stage where people were laughing loudly and singing along with the person on stage. "Even if I agreed, I wouldn't know what song."

"Give me your phone."

I sat up straighter. "What?"

"You heard me. I need you to unlock it also."

I rolled my eyes and handed him my phone. I had nothing on there I would not want him to see.

While Silver fiddled with it, I ate. I wanted to get out of here before I did give in to him. We could go back to the hotel and talk about whatever he wanted as long as I did not have to get up on that stage.

"This one." Silver slid my phone back to me. One of Mother's songs was pulled up.

I picked up my phone and read the title a few times before looking at him. "Why?" It was a simpler, but still an upbeat, pretty song.

"You seem to like that one."

"This is a bad idea." And worse that I actually gave it thought.

"Please? I have a feeling this is something important."

I bit my lower lip and looked over at the stage again. More people had shown up. Getting up on stage with the werewolves where I could not see the people watching had been one thing. I doubted the dim lighting here would hide the crowd as well. Maybe they would ignore me like they were currently ignoring the person up on stage now?

"Why don't you do it if it's just for fun?" I shot at him.

"Caradoc seemed more interested in having a female voice. It's been all men performing since we got here."

I closed my eyes and pinched the bridge of my nose. I could fight him all night, but he was right, I had to do this for the case. This may be the most ridiculous thing I ever had to do. "Fine."

Silver pulled my hand from my face and kissed the back of it. "You'll be great."

I COLLAPSED on my bed the moment it was in reach. It took me three songs before the person running the show convinced the crowd to let me take a break and still others approached me asking if I would go again.

Silver had made his rounds talking to people while I sat at the bar sipping a glass of water and fending off offers to buy me drinks. He remained silent on the ride back to the hotel and I only hoped I bought us something useful. At some point soon I needed to swear him to secrecy.

I listened to Silver taking off his boots. Why was I so tired?

My watch vibrated signaling a message. I managed to move enough to read it. Just Kitteren checking in.

Maybe she could help make sense of the conflict in my head about what Silver did. I rolled over onto my stomach, pulling my phone out in the process. Once settled, I replied to her message and asked her if she was free to talk.

"I'm going to go clean up," Silver said.

I nodded in acknowledgment and awaited Kitteren's reply. There was a good chance she was busy since she temporarily headed the Ghost Forest branch.

No sooner had the bathroom door closed than my phone announced my sister requesting a video call.

As soon as the call connected, she said, "*Ket, you look exhausted.*" There was concern on her face and that she immediately went to our dialect of common emphasized it.

"*Long day.*" For as short of a time as we had been here, it seemed far longer.

"*And the fact you're asking for a call worries me.*"

I sighed, not realizing exactly how out of the ordinary the request was. "*If you were busy you didn't have to. It's not anything pressing.*"

Kitteren sat forward, leaning on her elbows. "*Okay, what happened?*"

"*It's complicated. I... uh...*" I bit my lower lip, finding myself torn between being confused and embarrassed.

"*Take it from the beginning. You've got my attention with no one else around to bother us. Speaking of, where's your other half?*"

"*Cleaning up.*"

Kitteren raised an eyebrow at me, waiting quietly. The uncharacteristic behavior made me uneasy.

"I..." I paused, unsure if I wanted to continue. "*I just wanted to know what the physical boundaries in a friendship are.*" The words came out in a single stream.

Kitteren raised an eyebrow at me. "*Elven custom I take it.*"

I nodded. I regretted knowing little about my race's customs.

"*Anything. I have a friend in Great Tree I visit sometimes and we'll join, but there's nothing romantic about it. We're simply friends and enjoy the activity together. Sometimes we'll invite our current romantic interests to take part.*"

"*Oh...*" Her example made this even more complicated.

"*Ket, you need to tell me what happened.*"

Where should I start? "*The case we're working on has a prototype ship system and they asked if I would test it for them.*"

"*Okay, I'm lost, but keep going.*"

I bit my lower lip, figuring out how to summarize it. "*I got stuck in the system. Not physically - I mentally got stuck. I'm not sure if that makes sense.*"

Kitteren sat back in her chair.

"*I couldn't find my way back out. My partner tried, but he said he was losing his grip on pulling me back.*" I still kept to not using Silver's name out of habit.

"*And let me guess, he kissed you to create a stronger connection to do it.*"

My face heated up again and I looked down at the bottom of my phone. Either Kitteren was good at guessing or I took the action too personally.

"*It's not an uncommon practice for people having an out-of-body experience. What happened when you got out?*"

"*I hit him.*"

My sister snorted and then laughed so hard tears streamed down her face.

"*Kitayl! I didn't know who it was.*" I hoped using her other name would get her to stop.

"*Okay. Okay.*" She struggled to regain her composure. "*Have the two of you talked about what happened?*"

"*A little. He said it was common between friends and to not worry.*"

"*Well, for once he's right. Did you enjoy it?*"

"*I...*" It had been too brief and I had been scared at the time. "*I'm not sure.*"

"*You need to try it again without it being some weird extenuating circumstance. I know he won't say no.*"

I tried to glare at her through the video call, but I doubted it would work. What if I became even more attached? Look at what happened the last time I thought I would lose him. Then there was the fact he was interested in someone else and honestly, it was far too dangerous for me to get any closer.

"*Ket, just do it. You should know what it's like to have that kind of connection with someone.*"

"*Too close already.*" I heard the water shut off in the bathroom.

"*I'm thinking not close enough. I should probably let you go before he gets out.*"

"*Okay. Thanks.*"

"*Of course. Love ya, sis.*" Then she cut the connection.

I dropped the phone and my head to the mattress. This was a disaster.

How long I stayed like that, I was uncertain, but a gentle hand on my back got me to pick my head up. Silver sat on the edge of the bed, still dripping, wearing only the pants he wore to bed, and I put my head back down. "Tell me you at least got something out of that."

My partner laughed lightly. "Yes, I got more than an amazing show. I'm just not sure how we're going to use the information."

I struggled to sit up, managing enough to wrap my arms around my knees to keep from falling over. "What was it?"

"Jake's erratic behavior extends beyond the base. He's been overheard talking with people about the system who are neither military or part of Spelltech."

"Who?"

"Unknown. Drifters - people who come in and out of Sandpoint a lot. People suspected of criminal activity."

"Think maybe he's too wrapped up in the project and can't help but talk about it?" Despite my words, I remembered his request for me to sign documents about not disclosing information.

Silver shook his head. "It sounded like these were deliberate meetings, not just someone he met at the bar."

What could we do with the information? Tailing Jake would not be so simple - we were expected to be investigating the accident. And even then do we act on information gathered from an external source like this?

Jonim sent us so we would hear this information. I disliked the idea of being around Jake more, but if we were going to do anything about it, we needed to catch him in the act.

Rough fingers brushed my bangs back. "It helps if you talk to me."

"I'm not sure what to do with it either. We can't obviously abandon what we're doing to follow this lead."

"Let's just see what comes. At least we're aware he may be a traitor."

"A little strong, isn't it?"

"Is it? He and his company are currently doing business with the military and he's potentially selling military secrets to an unknown party."

I frowned. It was an easy assumption given what we had heard.

"There's other things we need to talk about."

I turned away from him. He always wanted to talk about things. Especially things I did not want to discuss.

Silver kissed my cheek. "And thank you for doing that. We may not know what to do with the information now, but we'll use it eventually. We also have a little credit there with them in case we find ourselves needing more information."

I should push him away and regain my space. Withdraw so the upcoming conversation would not occur.

"Can you walk me through what you did for testing the system?"

It was not the conversation I expected. "I pulled my power as tight into myself as I could. I was going to ease into the system."

"I'm thinking with your connection to the arcane being genetic you might not have had a chance. Did you feel anything when you touched the grip with the gloves on?"

"I could feel a thrum of power, but that was it."

"Good to know they work enough to stop the sync."

I nodded. This I could handle.

"What about when you got in?"

"I didn't have a chance to ease in. What happened in the room?"

"Immediately, the screens came on, the lights dimmed, and the blue ambient lights came up. The console was fully activated. I didn't realize the whole unit would turn until it moved. You had Hells of a grip on the controls because you kept me from falling when I grabbed the back of the chair."

"When did you realize something was wrong?" I needed to know if he knew something was wrong or if I had simply been in too long for his liking.

"Well, I noticed you went into a bit of a panic when you first synced, but you calmed down pretty quick. The first thing we noticed was you weren't responding to anything we said. Jake kept trying to give you directions."

I bit my lower lip.

"He seemed fascinated by your eyes though. I'm fairly certain he figured out you didn't need the screens to see outside since you never looked up at them. Any theories on how you are able to do that?"

How? I shook my head. "If you go over the information available, there's no reason anyone should be able to. Might have to do with whatever they're using for amplification. I also shouldn't be getting dragged into the system so easily either. Genetic connection or not, I'm still just a caster. If this was a normal defense system currently in use by the Navy, I would interact with the system the same way as anyone else."

"You are anything but 'just a caster'." Silver put his hand on the side of my face, leaning closer. "We should also discuss options for getting you out of the system if something happens."

I backed away from him. In getting me out, he connected to the system the same way I had, but I worried it affected him differently.

What he was asking though... It was a secret I kept for so long. The promise I made was to only to tell someone I trusted completely.

Glancing at Silver, I thought it over. There was no question I trusted him more than others. Even over Kitteren and my adopted parents. I still did not know why. I shook my head. I was not ready to release the information.

"Ketayl, I'm not going to lie, if you go in again, I'm not sure I'll be able to get you out without something else in place."

"We'll come up with something else."

"What? What is more unique than that? How many people currently call you by that name?"

"None."

"How many have ever called you by it?"

It hurt to remember the lives gone. "Three."

"Who?"

"Enough!" I snapped. My vision became blurry as tears formed. I could not afford to think about the past. I watched one die before me. Another run to his death. And the third I had no idea what happened after he told me to take Kitteren and run. When he never came for us, I knew he was gone as well.

Next thing I knew, Silver had wrapped around me. His head was alongside mine with his arms holding on tight. I shook even in his hold.

A sense of calm came and I pushed back which made him physically shudder. I was done being manipulated today.

"Please, let me help you," he begged.

"No. No more help. No more tests. No more letting people push me around. No more digging into things better left in the past."

"Now you decide to do this," Silver muttered. "We have work to do and we won't get anything done until you calm down."

I paused, debating his words. "I hate your logic sometimes."

He took my words as permission and I held myself back from fighting him. The calm came more slowly this time.

"Relax. You're still fighting me."

"Am not."

Silver pulled back and made a face. "Not actively, no, but your resistance is more impossible to get through than that forsaken system."

"Wait." I pushed him away. "What you just said."

"That you're still resisting?"

"No, my resistance is harder to get through than the system."

"What about it?"

"It may be the reason I can get through."

"You are the most stubborn person I know."

I rolled my eyes.

"But it doesn't discount your genetics playing part."

"I know, I know, but there's got to be something else because there's no reason for how I sync to the system." I got up and paced, biting the tip of my thumb.

I had been so lost in thought I had not noticed Silver standing in front of me and ran into him. I opened my mouth to apologize, but instead ended up grabbing his forearms as my earlier exhaustion suddenly returned. What had I been thinking about again? And where was his shirt?

"Go clean up and get ready for bed," he said softly.

Was that what I had been doing? Could have sworn I had been working on something. Silently I gathered my things and retreated to the bathroom.

I stared at myself in the mirror for a few minutes. What was it? Something about the system.

Anger rose quickly when I realized what Silver had done. I had been unprepared for the color change of my eyes. The iridescent colors swirled wildly around where the gray normally was.

So that's what it looked like. No wonder it unsettled people. I should calm down. After I dealt with him.

Twisting the doorknob sharply, I strode up to my partner who sat on the edge of his bed brushing his hair. "Never do that again." Then I stormed back, shutting the door behind me firmly.

"Ketayl, don't you think that's enough?" Silver stood next to the ladder I was on.

I refused to talk to him after what he did last night.

"I'm sorry, but you needed to stop and calm down."

The same thing he had been saying. I continued searching for fingerprints in the upper panel. Some of the debris seemed suspicious, but it was not my focus right now.

"Please talk to me. The least you can do is yell at me for what I did instead of this."

I sighed. I knew I could not keep up my silence forever and if he was still begging me to talk to him, then it meant he was not working. We had a lot to search through and it was going to take me time to scan all of these prints and get them to Sparky. Come to think of it, he had not contacted us yet.

Backing out of the panel, I said flatly, "Call Sparks and get an update." There, I talked to him.

"Not until you come down here and we talk."

There went my hope. I climbed back down and folded my arms, glaring up at him.

"I guess this is as good as it's going to get for the moment. Like I said, I'm sorry I had to do that, but you were pushing yourself too far.

Especially after what happened with the system test. I should have insisted we end yesterday after that."

I clenched my teeth at his overprotective behavior. "No."

"Would you just listen to me for once?!"

I jumped at his tone. I guess I had it coming. It had been hours.

"I saw the toll it took on you and I didn't act. I pushed you into the event at the restaurant so we could gain some insight. I should have taken you back and made you rest."

"I'm fine," I ground out at him.

"You're not. I let that stupid test go on for too damn long. I shouldn't have let it happen in the first place."

I glared up at him.

"You asked when I knew something was wrong. I knew something was wrong before you even sat down. I knew something was wrong the moment you synced. I knew something was wrong when you didn't respond to any of us. The longer you were in there the more panicked you became and I finally ignored them to pull you out."

I opened my mouth to retort, but he covered it with his hand. I shoved him away.

"I'm not done," he said sharply, "I got too used to letting you be in Ghost Forest and failed to do what needed to be done."

"Are you going to eventually argue that I did something wrong?" I asked flatly.

"What? I..." Now he seemed confused. He let out a long breath and tugged on his braid. "I'm not even sure where I was going with that anymore."

I shook my head. He could get so hot-headed at times he distracted himself. I started back up the ladder.

"Stop, please."

I had gotten up high enough I looked down at him. I raised an eyebrow, waiting for him to continue.

"Let me take over, okay? We need to get this stuff to Sparky and I don't know how to use the portable fingerprint reader."

"Alright." I got back down and shifted over to my new task. I had not been fond of being up in the ceiling anyway.

"Hey," Silver said gently, putting his hand on my shoulder. "Sorry about that."

"You probably want to take some time later at the physical training facility."

He grinned mischievously. "Are you joining me?"

"No." I went to go to my gear bag, but he stopped me again.

"How about we go back to Watered Down tonight for supper?"

I glared up at him.

"I'm not asking you to sing. It's a nice place and you seemed to like the food."

I shrugged. "I guess."

"Non-working meal," he stipulated.

"Only if you get back to work now."

"Yes, ma'am."

I rolled my eyes. Often times I wondered about him.

We worked for a while. I glanced at my watch and it was already well after noon and I had gotten hungry. Granted, I ate little for breakfast since my appetite was gone while I was still mad at him.

"Do you want to take a break?" I asked. I knew he needed to eat also.

Silver slid out from where he had been trying to get under the floor to see if he could find the source for the console issue. "Why, what time is it?"

"Almost 1300."

"Yeah. I'm not making any headway here anyway."

I sighed, crossing my arms. "After lunch I'm going to see if I can't get to the amplifier from another room. I need to know what we're dealing with."

"Any word from Sparky yet?"

I shook my head. "I should probably call him."

"After lunch."

I had been grateful for the quiet morning - no Jake, no Jonim. Just us and attempting to get to the bottom of this.

"I need to talk to her," Jake said loudly as we reached the ramp to get off of the ship. "For the last time, let me through."

I stopped and looked up at Silver. The scene before us explained the peace and quiet we had.

"I'm sorry, sir, but we have orders that under no circumstances are you allowed on-board while the investigation is ongoing," one of the guards said.

"This is ludicrous. This is my ship!"

"Actually," Silver said as he led the way down the ramp, "It's the Navy's ship you're borrowing."

Jake folded his arms and watched us as we came down the ramp. "Well, I guess that works too. Your reports are still missing."

"And you'll have them. Eventually. Right now our priority is figuring out what happened." Once Silver reached the bottom, he stood over Jake, towering above the Human man who shrunk back.

"Do you not understand how much I need that information?"

"We also need information and you haven't been forthcoming with it," I said.

Jake huffed. "I've given you access to everything. I know it's disorganized, but it's all there."

"Not what your amplifier is," I countered.

"That is proprietary information."

I shook my head. "Let's go," I said to Silver and walked away.

"What about you? You won't explain what makes you different from the others."

I turned on my heel. "That is personal. And with the reply you gave earlier apparently a trade of information is out of the question." Then I set off at a faster pace. I could not afford to lose my temper here - my power could start pushing at me at any point.

Our escorts hurried to catch up, leaving the soldiers guarding the ship to deal with Jake.

"Hey, wait!" Jake called.

Or not. I turned to see Jake running up to us.

"A trade isn't out of the question. You must understand I have to protect my business."

"Protecting your business would be cooperating with us," Silver shot at him.

"Yes, yes, of course. But I will only reveal the information to her." Jake pointed at me. "She is able to see the beauty of the system. Bring it to a level I had never thought possible."

"Fine, but we're headed to lunch. When we get back, we can talk." I quickly got in the car with our escorts.

I sat staring out the window while they drove, taking long, slow breaths to calm myself. Everyone remained silent.

Suddenly the car swerved and I slammed my head into the window hard enough to blur my vision for a moment. I held my head where I hit. *What just happened?*

We pulled over to the side and the escort not driving called in something at a rapid pace. I curled down, holding my head. What was it with hitting my head lately?

Silver got out to come around to my side, opening the door. He moved my hands gently before lightly touching my head near where I hit the glass. "You might want to consider wearing a helmet at this rate," he joked.

"Damn, I am so sorry, ma'am. I didn't think I swerved that hard."

I looked up at the soldier standing on the other side of my door. What was he talking about? Then I noticed the large crack in the glass. It was small, but it was still there. Had I really hit it that hard?

"She's got a pretty hard head. Do you have a first aid kit?" Silver said.

People were moving about again, talking, but I closed my eyes in hopes to stave off the building headache. What on Terra was happening here?

THE INFIRMARY WAS NOT GETTING lunch, but I sat still while Silver and the doctor poked and prodded at me again. Then there would likely be another call to Lockonis explaining what happened.

"Talk to me?" Silver asked softly.

"Hungry."

"Well, I'm fairly certain I was the reason for your lack of appetite this morning. Do you want me to see what I can find until we can make it to lunch?"

I started shaking my head, but the doctor held me still. "No."

"You should eat something," the doctor said. He stepped back. "It's not bad. Just some bruising. No reason you should have cracked the glass."

My head still hurt though. I refused to tell anyone because there would be medications being pushed my way. I did not feel like finding out which side effects I would have from those.

Jonim stuck his head in. "About done here? I've got some upset people demanding a conference call with these two."

"Yeah," the doctor said, "If there are any other problems, just stop by."

I slid off the bed and followed Jonim with Silver silently. We left the building with the infirmary when Silver asked, "Are you sure you're feeling okay?"

"Hungry."

He folded his arms and looked down at me as we walked. "Are you lying to me?"

I bit my lower lip. I hoped he would not see through my attempt to hide it. "Partially."

"What else then?"

I sighed, I needed to be more honest with him. "My head hurts, but I don't want medication."

Silver put his hand on my head as we walked and the pain lessened. "I can heal the bruising later, okay?"

"It's fine. Thank you though."

Jonim glanced back over his shoulder at us. "I'd offer more people for escort, but I ain't sure it would help. Starting to think someone doesn't want you folks here."

My head agreed.

Once we reached Jonim's office, he began the video conference call.

"What in the Hells is going on down there?" Lockonis demanded. She stood next to where Vince sat behind his desk.

I cringed at her volume. It made my head hurt again.

"Like I was telling them on the way, I'm starting to think someone doesn't want them here," Jonim answered. "The best proof we have right now is the crack in the window of the escort vehicle. Something hit it from the outside."

"And the inside," I muttered, rubbing my head.

Silver put his hand on my back. "The doctor said you didn't hit it hard enough to crack it."

Jonim eyed us for a moment before continuing. "It almost got lost in the confusion of the near accident. Thought the last time was just a reckless driver, but this is showing to be a pattern."

"You're not going, Lockonis," Vince said firmly.

"Someone's trying to kill them," she argued.

Vince sighed. "They would have made more direct attempts if that was the case. Right now I'm thinking whoever it is simply wants to scare them off the case. Any ideas?"

I shook my head and regretted the motion.

"No," Silver said as his spell washed over me again. "We've had a hard time getting information from Jake, but he wouldn't want to push us away. Especially not Ketayl."

Jake's personality was enough for me to not want to be around him.

"Though if he has business associates outside of the military who have interest in the project, they might not want us here," Silver continued.

"They shouldn't even be able to get on base," Jonim countered.

"How many civilians does the military employ here? How many does Spelltech?" I asked.

"It'd be impressive if they got through the background checks. We've also run them on Spelltech's employees before they're allowed access to the base."

Vince looked up at Lockonis. "I think I heard your next challenge."

Lockonis rolled her eyes. "Yeah, yeah. You just want me to stay home."

"Mostly. Do you want us to pull you?" Vince eyed us.

"No," I said quickly. I refused to back down.

Vince raised an eyebrow at me. "Do you want more help?"

"No," Silver said this time. "It'll only put others in danger."

"Keep us updated." Vince reached forward and ended the call.

Jonim crossed his arms and looked up at us. "Something tells me you got some interesting stories last night."

"Nothing we can act on at the moment," Silver acknowledged.

"It's been the same problem I've had. I'm supposed to trust Jake and his company, but too many things haven't been adding up and now this. And if people are getting onto the base who shouldn't be here, I've got bigger problems on my hands."

All I knew was I wanted at whoever was doing this. They had given me enough headaches thus far.

"Something tells me if she gets her hands on them, they're going to live to regret it," Jonim said quietly to Silver.

"You have no idea," my partner replied.

12

AFTER A QUICK LUNCH, we were back at it again since Jake was suspiciously missing. I walked through the corridors with a handlight and the copy of the ship's plans on my tablet.

Stopping to search for the lights would take too much time, though the dark corridors made me uneasy. I should be getting close to where I could access the amplifier.

Silver remained up in the control room attempting to track from that end again. Still no word from Sparky, but we also sent him a lot of information to process.

My footsteps echoed as I walked along the metal floor. I paused, unsure if I heard another walking or if I imagined it. No one else was allowed on-board. The exception likely the ones who made the rules, but they would have headed for the control room, not followed me down into the ship. Or if they had, I hoped they would have made their presence known.

No, no one else. I looked down at the plans and then back up at the doors near me. This one should put me close enough unless the room was shaped differently than shown.

It took shoving my shoulder into the door, but I managed to get it open. Panels sat aside, revealing the wiring behind the wall. Odd, but this whole thing had been odd so far.

Something glowing behind the wiring caught my attention. I set my gear bag and tablet down along the wall next to me and turned my handlight to the wiring. These looked to be shielded so I used my power to reach out and get a feel for how saturated they were with arcane energy.

As I suspected, the silicon composite had absorbed arcane energy, but without Silver here to give me an idea of how much divine energy had also been absorbed, I remained uncertain how close to capacity the shielding might be. Also if it would even absorb divine energy. This area was undamaged though. Somewhere between here and the floor above?

I glanced at the plans again. This wiring might not be for the defense station. I put gloves on before I moved the wires aside to see what glowed. The blueish light became brighter as I got farther in. The sheer number of wires through here seemed excessive, but some were probably for the rest of the ship's systems.

I examined the glowing blue orb with wires running to it. It must be bigger than my head. Was this the amplifier? The longer I studied it, the more I felt drawn to it. I had never seen anything like it. It seemed alien...

Or Atlantian. I took a step back, needing to get away from the pull. Had Jake actually found a piece of Atlantian technology? It would explain the results so far - no one would be compatible with it.

No, my theory was too far-fetched. He would never be able to recreate it for multiple systems. It might be based off of whatever he discovered as an archaeologist, but it was Terran made. Why keep this so secret? What purpose would it serve? Not with the way he hoped to have it implemented.

While this was all fascinating, I needed to find the source of what happened to the defense station. Stepping forward slowly, I turned my handlight inward to see the wires behind the glowing blue orb. Some came from the side, others from above - it was a disaster.

Everything appeared to be in order though - nothing appeared broken or burnt. Still, leaving this without documenting would be wrong. As I dug for my camera, the door slammed closed and I jumped, turning and falling back, my exposed shoulder brushing the orb.

Immediately I connected to the system and panicked. Silver was still upstairs. It would take him a long time to find me once he figured out something was wrong.

This time though, I could feel through the system with incredible clarity including both the connections going to the consoles as well as to the outside of the ship. My connection to the defense station shorted out quickly.

My vision remained in the room where I was, but I could shift between places. In the control room, Silver looked around at the screens. He rushed over to the offense station, flicking a few switches. He pulled his phone out and my watch vibrated with the incoming call.

I figured out how to pull back and tried to physically tear myself away from it. The pull to remain was so strong and my body refused to respond correctly. I was unsure I could do it.

Something else caught my attention - I could access other systems I should not be able to. I returned to checking on Silver. He ran out of the room when his call went unanswered, but stopped, not knowing which way I had gone.

The lights. I could turn on the lights. Sequentially, I turned the lights on, creating a path for him. I also turned the lights on in the room I was in. This room appeared unused.

While he ran, I pulled again. Finally I landed face down on the floor with a loud thud. It took everything I had to stay flattened to the floor. The promise of balance and calm was so strong. Part of me needed to return to it.

I heard someone in the hallway and hoped it was Silver. I could not find my voice.

The sound of doors opening continued until finally Silver shoved his way into this one. I managed to pick up my head enough to see his boots before returning to staying attached to the floor.

"What in the Hells is that?" Silver asked as he knelt down and pulled me to him.

I shook with the strain of resisting the orb's influence. My hand refused to listen and reached for the orb.

"No," Silver said firmly, pulling my arm down.

The door slammed shut again and I made a noise somewhere between a scream and a whimper. Thankfully Silver held on tightly because I would have run for the safety of the orb.

We sat in silence for several seconds before he asked, "Did you connect to the system?"

I nodded.

"Through that?"

I nodded again. "Hit me," I whispered. I needed to break the connection fully. I would be willing to suffer another concussion.

"What? No! Ketayl, knock it off. There's got to be another way. I mean, you were able to pull away from it."

I could not stop shaking and it only got worse.

Silver shifted me so I was tucked up underneath his chin and held my head to his chest. He wrapped a leg over my hips, pinning them to the floor.

My worry about getting free and reconnecting diminished, but had not fully been put at ease. I knew how to get away from him, but it required teleporting and right now I could not concentrate enough to do it.

After a couple of minutes of whimpering, shaking, and attempting to physically break out of his hold, a sense of calm began to push through the draw of the system. I eagerly let it through, knowing it was Silver doing it.

"That's it. You're going to be okay," he whispered.

Peace followed the calm and the shaking diminished. I was able to focus some again.

I needed to stay where I was despite the awkward position we were in. I could not say for certain I would not give into the small pull still coming from the orb.

"Can you talk?"

I took a deep breath. "Yes."

"What is going on?"

"I'm not sure."

Silver stroked my cheek with his thumb. "Okay, how about we start with why you touched that... thing."

"I... I hadn't meant to. I was getting my camera out to take pictures when the door suddenly closed. It startled me and I lost my balance."

He kissed the top of my head and held me tighter.

I struggled against the slowly strengthening pull of the system. "You're going to have to knock me out."

"No, Ketayl. I'm not entertaining that option. It still has a hold on you?"

I nodded. "It's getting stronger. Please?"

Silver shifted and I held onto him. "Let go for a moment. I want to try something, but you need to be in a different position. I won't let you go, okay?"

Slowly I released my grip on his jacket. He set me so I knelt on the cold, hard floor in front of him. I fought the pull of the system. The shaking started again and the chill of the room went right into me.

Large hands held my head and I closed my eyes when Silver rested his forehead against mine. The magic this time was similar to when he healed my concussion.

The world righted itself and my mind cleared further until I felt the final break from the system. Then the lights went out.

My handlight still shown on the floor where I dropped it. And of course, the blue glow from the orb.

"Can't say I expected that," Silver said. He held me at arm's length. "Are you free of it?"

"Yes, thank you."

Silver kissed my forehead. "See, we found another way."

"We should get out of here." I moved away to pick up my handlight and repack my bag.

Large hands stilled mine. "As much as I want to agree, I think we need to finish in here. Give me your camera."

Hesitantly I handed it to him.

"Can you find the lights?"

I moved toward the door, hoping the switch was as far from the orb as possible. Finding a switch panel, I tried a couple before the lights flickered on.

Silver was already looking through the wires. "I don't see any damage."

"I was thinking it might be back, but I'm starting to wonder about the system. I was able to access systems I shouldn't be able to like the lights and the cameras."

"So that was you. Thanks for leading me here." Silver went deeper into the wall. "Why were you planning to take pictures?"

"Just to document. I think the orb is the amplifier and it's based off of whatever Atlantian knowledge he acquired. The shielding has also absorbed quite a bit of arcane energy."

There was a pause before he said, "Divine as well."

I frowned. "It'll be hard to get an idea if it's hitting capacity."

"We should save the analysis for another time. I don't think it was the cause otherwise we'd be seeing damage here."

"Maybe we should head back up and call Sparks and see if he has anything."

"Good idea."

We only had the one handlight. Thankfully the door opened, though Silver needed to pull roughly on it. I led the way back up, the darkness being more frightening than before.

"I wonder if the lights turned off because you disconnected fully from the system," he idly mused.

"Maybe. I know I felt torn between wanting to break from it and wanting to return to it. Might be why the door closed also."

"Are you suggesting the orb is sentient?"

"No, but that's also a possibility. It could be riding off of the arcane and divine energies from all of the tests." It was a theory I could not ignore. "But I was more aiming at the system attempted to preserve itself by acting on my thoughts."

"That's not far from what I said."

"No, but mine is dealing with programming and me being the cause of it versus it acting completely on its own." A fine line, yes, but enough of one to make a difference.

When we reached the control room for the system, I sat on the floor as much away from both stations as I could and dug for my tablet.

Silver came and sat down next to me. "Wait."

"Why?"

"Do you want to be fielding questions right off?"

"Questions about... oh."

Silver had turned on the front facing camera on his phone. I was a mess. Sweat soaked with probably tear stains mixed in and my hair frazzled where it was not stuck to my face.

"I know you want an update, but let's break for a bit. I still have questions."

I sighed and withdrew my hand from my bag. I hoped it would have ended there.

"The door closed before you touched it?"

I nodded, pulling my phone out to use it as a pseudo mirror. Using my power, I cleaned up the mess as much as possible, spending some time getting my hair back in order. Then I realized he had not asked another question for a bit.

Silver sat, staring at the floor, flicking the tail of his braid back and forth rapidly.

"What's wrong?"

That snapped him out of his trance. "Your theory is sound except for that one piece."

"There are other explanations I'm sure. With as much residual arcane and divine energy as there is in the shielding that close to the amplifier, I can only imagine what it's doing to it."

Silver sighed and sat back, crossing his arms. "I just wish I was better versed in divine theory. Not that there is anything even remotely organized like it is with the arcane."

I tilted my head, awaiting an explanation.

My partner tugged on his braid. "Arcane theory is very scientific in its approach, right?"

"Yeah, you could say that."

He sat forward, rubbing the bridge of his nose - a movement he rarely performed. "Divine isn't - it's based off of the scriptures and beliefs surrounding each of the Gods. Anyone who takes a more pragmatic view of it is often shunned because they are not considered a true believer. There's a lot that could be learned from taking such an approach. Who knows what we could actually do if it was better studied."

I sat forward so I could look at him. "There's no one stopping you. Or at least I won't."

"I wouldn't know where to start. I fear much of my training was in how to fight. I've picked up a fair amount over the years, but nothing at the level of the scholars," Silver said.

"I think you've picked up more than a fair amount. Your curiosity led you to studying things outside of normal practices, right?"

"Yeah, but that's different from..."

I held up a finger. "It's really not if you think about it, but it's up to you if you want to pursue it. Like you said, who knows where it could lead."

Silver gave a short laugh. "Many would say you've been a horrible influence because you've had me questioning things I previously never would from the moment we met."

I shrugged. "Not trying to."

"I think I prefer it this way. You made Mason question his views."

I shook my head. "That one is because of how we work together."

My watch vibrating with a message ended the conversation. I turned my wrist over and read the short message from Sparky requesting a call.

"He knew we were coming for him," Silver mused, reading the message on my watch from over my shoulder.

My phone was still out and figured it would suffice. I started up the call and Silver put his chin on my shoulder.

"Must you?" I asked.

"Yes."

I rolled my eyes right before the video call connected. "What have you got, Sparks?"

"What don't I have is a better question. How all of this escaped the military, I have no idea." Sparky held up his tablet to read. "Jacob Martin has been getting money from outside sources. It's been going to various accounts around the world. It's not a small sum and it's growing."

"From who?"

"It's a lot of shadow companies upon shadow companies and the cyber team is still backtracking all of it, but so far, pirates. Or rather companies suspected of criminal activities who also happen to own ships. Primarily cargo, but you'll get the occasional yacht. Often seen armed."

"Pirates," Silver said flatly.

"And those fingerprints you sent, and you sent a ton by the way, most of them belong to Spelltech employees or military personnel. The rest aren't even in the system. So unless Spelltech has been slacking in making sure all of their people are properly documented, you've got people who shouldn't be anywhere near the system."

"Something Jonim was concerned about," Silver noted.

"Oh, wait, there's more. You'll love this one." Sparky sent a picture in place of his video feed. "I can see how you guys would have missed it because of the sheer amount of damage and collecting all of those prints. But right here," he said and a yellow circle appeared around a piece, "looks like it belongs to a transmitter of some sort. Don't suppose it's still there and you can send it to me?"

"Yeah, I can get it down," Silver said.

"Did you ever find the source for the defense station?"

"No," I admitted, "I found the amplifier though. Or at least I think it's the amplifier. It's somewhere in between."

"Those plans you uploaded are incomplete," Sparky said.

"Those are the most current plans," Silver said.

Sparky rolled his eyes. "How did this project ever get off the ground?"

It was another question we all wanted an answer to. "I'll upload the images we've got, but I'm not even sure what it is," I said.

"Don't they normally use a gem of some type to amplify?"

"This isn't a gem," Silver said.

"Anything else?" I asked.

Sparky shook his head. "Lockonis will probably have more soon regarding the personnel on the base, but last time I was in there, she was pissed, and frankly, I like not being charcoal."

"Thanks, Sparks." I ended the call.

"Now what?" Silver asked.

"Let's gather the piece and anything else that might belong to it."

No sooner had Silver left to go get the ladder from down the hall, I shuddered. I turned to stare at the offense station. The difference between accessing the system through the station versus a direct connection to the amplifier had been dramatic.

A body blocked my view. Silver said, "Ketayl, look at me."

I blinked, wondering how long I stood there staring.

"Is it still affecting you?" he asked.

"No. At least not in the way it was." My fear of the system at this point was a far cry from the pull it previously held over me.

"Okay, let me get this for Sparky and then we'll take a break - get off the ship for a bit. Maybe see if we can't find Jake and get some answers."

"That won't be possible," Jonim said.

Both of us turned at the same time.

Jonim crossed his arms. "We found him alright. But he not be drawing breath to speak anymore."

"He's dead?" Silver asked. "We just saw him a few hours ago. What happened?"

"Hung himself. Could use your folks' expertise 'cause it has all the trimmings of a suicide, but something doesn't feel right."

I looked up at Silver. "Not when we found evidence to support the sabotage theory. At least with the screens." I pointed at the ceiling where the shattered screen hung from. "We still need to find the source for the defense station itself."

"We should go see what happened. Where was he found?" Silver said.

"In the Spelltech warehouse." Jonim signaled for us to follow.

This case continued getting more bizarre.

WHAT JAKE'S previous tour did not show was another office hidden above the one we worked out of. This one was kept incredibly neat.

A suicide note printed and signed by him laid in full view on the desk.

I may not have liked the man, but I never wished him dead. I folded my arms and looked up at Silver. "This is getting more complicated."

My partner frowned. "The man had his secrets."

"That he did. Found him myself 'cause he didn't show up to the weekly progress meeting. He ain't used this office much. Most likely to come up here for a nap," Jonim said, "I take it he hadn't shown you this place."

Shaking my head, I bit my lower lip and looked around the sparse room. "He promised to show me information about the amplifier. Would you happen to know about it?"

Jonim shook his head. "That was his pride and joy. The higher-ups let him keep it to himself until we started seeing results."

I took a deep breath, considering the work ahead of us. "You want to message Sparks and let him know the case got bigger? I'll get started processing this."

"Want me to run interviews?" Silver asked.

"If you don't mind."

"You're better with this." Silver signaled for Jonim to move aside with him.

Even once he left to go talk to other people, I would not be alone - our escorts stood outside of the office door. Looking up at Jake's dangling body, I did not want to be alone in here. Even dead the man unsettled me.

Once I finished documenting, I would need help getting the body down. I wanted to get him out of here. Then I could search for the information he was willing to trade for.

Silver left with Jonim while I worked. I ended up needing to climb up on the desk to get pictures. Something sounded off under my shoes.

I tapped the top of the wooden desk with my heel, getting a hollow metal sound in return. I glanced at the escort who stayed, but his attention remained outside the door.

Debating what I should do, I noted the oddity and resumed my work, hurrying to get back to it.

Once I hit the point of needing Jake's body to be lowered, I figured it was as good of a time to get back to the desk. I knocked on the top of the desk, again getting the same sound.

I pulled out drawers and felt around, searching for whatever caused the metal sound. The top of the desk seemed rather thick and I looked for a possible secret compartment. Finding a seam in the ornate carving, I managed to pry the drawer open.

The inside was disappointing - prescription bottles filled the small drawer. They might explain Jake's erratic behavior. I documented what I found and moved on, needing to find something to keep me occupied until Silver returned.

Jake kept a collection of books on a shelf across from his desk. There weren't many, but perhaps some insight into the man. I browsed the titles. He had a few different collections of his essays. More collections of essays by others on Atlantis. I stopped when I found a book on beginner arcane theory.

Why is this here?

Gently I pulled the book from its place with my glove-covered hands. It felt frail despite the newer cover. The cover creaked in protest at being opened and inside was not what I expected. Foreign text and drawings scrawled across the pages, but still it seemed familiar. It was as if being able to read it was just out of my reach - a skill I merely forgotten though I could not recall having seen anything like it before.

Notes were stuffed in between the pages - attempts to translate the content. I recognized Jake's handwriting. Going back and forth between the original and the translation, I knew some of it was wrong, but no idea why let alone what the correct translation would be.

I stood in the corner of the room to read.

Was this what he planned on showing me? Eventually I made it to a section describing the orb. I knew much of the translation was wrong. Particularly about the orb itself.

Where had I seen this writing before and why could I not remember how to translate it?

Silver reappeared after some time. "You have some strange habits."

I rolled my eyes. "Take a look at this. I think this is where Jake got the idea for the orb."

He twisted to read. "I don't understand a word of it. Even the translation seems foreign."

I flipped through a few pages. "It's completely different from anything either of us probably knows and I doubt the accuracy of the translation."

"Wasn't he an expert?"

"Supposedly, but..." I glanced at the people within earshot. "Perhaps we should save this for later. We should get him down."

I got a larger bag out and put the book in as evidence, marking the bag. This one would stay with us. The rest I planned to somehow get to Sparky. We would need to coordinate with someone here to get it sent.

I wondered if we could send Jake as well.

"Jonim asked if we would wait for their coroner. I might have overstepped my boundaries, but I spoke with him about coordinating our efforts and sharing information."

I pursed my lips. I would rather have kept it in house, but we were at a disadvantage here. "It's a good idea."

"Were there any fingerprints?"

I shook my head. "Not unless there's something on the rope I can't get at until we get it off of him. Should probably check the rest of the room. Not sure why I didn't think of that sooner."

"You also had a pretty traumatic experience recently," Silver noted.

"Not sure I should ask," Jonim said as he came in with a trail of other Naval personnel.

I glanced up at Silver for a moment. "I think we need to sit down and make sure we're all on the same page. For right now, can we make sure no one goes on-board the ship?"

"Already in place, lass. Why don't we work together for now?

Especially if you folks don't mind doing the heavy lifting for processing evidence and making sense out of this mess."

I nodded. That was acceptable. "We'll need to high priority send evidence back to our lab. We can scan fingerprints here."

Jonim smiled. "I think perhaps we've been going about it all wrong this whole time. I'll be interested to hear what you have once we're finished here. And we can get whatever you need out."

"We'll need to get back on-board to finish collecting evidence," Silver noted.

"That piece definitely needs to get to Sparks. We should tape off the room with access to the amplifier - I don't want anyone else coming in contact with it until we know more about it."

"Sounds like you're formulating a plan," my partner commented.

I tilted my chin at the Navy personnel currently getting Jake down. "More manpower means we should be able to narrow down the source of the problem with the defense system faster provided things don't get more complicated."

"Let's finish up here and then go collect what we need from the ship and get it out."

The new information could wait. It was time to get to work.

It was just Silver, Jonim, and I on-board the ship. While Silver finished collecting what we needed from the ceiling, I stayed near the door, away from the stations.

"I see you have an aversion to the system," Jonim commented.

"Getting stuck was not my idea of fun," I said.

Jonim stroked his beard. "Now you've got to explain what your boy meant when he said you had a traumatic experience earlier. I'm thinking it's not in reference to yesterday's test."

I sighed and folded my arms, thinking about how to explain what happened.

Silver spoke first. "She went searching for the source of the defense station's malfunction, found the amplifier, and accidentally came in contact with it."

Jonim stopped and stared at me. "Wait, are you saying you can access the system without using either of the stations?"

"More than that," I said, resigned to the conversation. "I was able to access ship systems which shouldn't be connected. Lights, cameras, doors..."

"Doors? Nothing should affect the doors - there's no system to operate them."

I tilted my head, wondering why the doors closed.

"Did you actively operate the doors?" Silver asked.

I shook my head. "I thought it was the system acting on a self-preservation program or something like that."

"Then there was someone else on-board?" Silver asked.

"Maybe or maybe not." Jonim stroked his beard. "If the door is facing port or starboard, the rocking of the ship could close it unexpectedly. They didn't build this to normal specs. Tough to get open, quick to close on their own."

"I wouldn't rule out the possibility," Silver said.

"Normally I would tell you not to worry about it, but someone just showed up dead who I wouldn't expect to commit suicide. Not when his project finally started taking off. I'll have the footage pulled when I get back to my office."

Silver handed me the bag with the tag still blank. He shrugged. "Your handwriting is nicer."

I rolled my eyes and dug out a pen to fill it out. "When we get back to the hotel, I'll finish scanning the fingerprints into the file for Sparks. I hope we don't bury him."

My partner shrugged. "Eh, he's been wanting more of a challenge lately."

I tossed the evidence bag back at Silver. "He's about to get it. We should get this stuff sent. There's a lot and I'm certain the cyber team is going to enjoy picking apart his computer."

"You thinking there's something on that one? Can't say I've ever seen it on," Jonim said.

I crossed my arms. "If his financials are any indication, there could be."

Jonim stroked his beard. "I see I'm not the only one who's been questioning Spelltech."

"How did this project ever get approved to this point?" I asked.

Jonim sighed. "Heard something about Jake had a friend in the Navy who pulled some strings. It was a good enough proposal they didn't make him go through the normal channels. Being able to make better use of the casters in the military - they jumped on it. Frankly most of them just take up space and resources. No offense."

I shrugged. "If there's no specific purpose for them, I can see your problem. Sometimes it's hard to compete with technology."

The Commander grinned at us. "Yet neither one of you seems to have a problem."

Silver pointed at me. "She dragged me into this."

"I did not. You took the job offer from the Director," I shot back.

"Close enough."

I rolled my eyes. He could be such a child sometimes.

Jonim crossed his arms and looked back and forth between us. "I've got to admit, I am curious as to what made both of you different from every other caster we've had for this project. Especially you, lass."

"How many paladins have you had?" Silver asked.

"None. Not going to lie, lad, you don't look like one."

Silver's shield appeared on his left arm. "I try not to stand out too much. Besides, my old armor chaffed after a while."

I smirked at his answer. He rarely spoke about his time prior to the TIO.

"And you, lass? Don't tell me you're the arcane equivalent."

I shook my head, hesitating for a moment before I admitted, "Arcanist."

"Not familiar with the term."

Biting my lower lip, I looked to Silver who simply nodded. "My connection to the arcane is genetic."

Jonim frowned. "And here I thought the lad was being flowery with his words when he said you had a 'natural predisposition' for the arcane. Couldn't blame you for withholding the information from Jake. He would have started looking for every Arcanist he could get his hands on, which would have done the project no good."

"Why haven't you done anything about him before this?" Silver asked.

"Others have tried and gotten transferred. I've been collecting information and biding my time. The man had some powerful friends and I happen to like this place," Jonim said.

"And our presence provided a means to begin doing something about it," I concluded.

"You've got it, lass."

I sighed. There was little we could do about being used in this fashion. "We should seal the amplifier room."

Silver looked down at me. "I really don't think anyone else will have a problem with it."

I turned away from the others, but only enough to keep them in my peripheral vision. "I'd rather make sure I can't get into it. At least not easily."

Both men looked at me as if I had gone mad. I certainly began to think I had.

"I thought you said you had broken from it," my partner accused.

I took a deep breath. I could see his confusion. "I am, but I can feel the pull of the system just being near the amplifier."

"That explains why you wanted out of there," Silver muttered, packing his bag.

"Wait, are you telling me there's more to the amplifier than simply amplifying the magical energy sent to it?"

I nodded.

"But it doesn't affect you." Jonim pointed at Silver.

"I don't have the genetic connection to the divine. I also didn't touch the amplifier directly," my partner grumbled.

"Damn." Jonim appeared to be lost in his thoughts.

"What?" I asked after a few seconds.

He shook himself out of it. "I'm not sure it has anything to do with it or not, but Jake's erratic behavior started roughly around the time he completed the amplifier."

Silver looked directly at me. "We're sealing that room."

13

<hr>

ONCE SILVER and I finished collecting the piece we needed from the ship, we headed back to the Spelltech warehouse with Jonim. The casters and other employees stood outside arguing with each other. Jonim hurried over to break it up.

When Silver and I got close enough, Mason made his way over.

"What's going on?" Silver asked.

Mason paused, wringing his hands. "Depends, have you guys heard what happened to Jake?"

"Yeah," I said flatly. "We processed the scene."

Mason frowned. "Now everyone is up in arms about what to do next and who should be in charge."

Hearing a creak from the large shipping containers we stood near, I looked up, eying them suspiciously. Probably settling. "I would think that's for Spelltech and Naval Command to decide."

"I'm staying out of this," Mason said.

Silver crossed his arms. "Should we help him break it up?"

"Probably," I said, stepping toward the group.

"And you bring these people in and suddenly he's dead," the Dwarven arcane caster from the DAC said.

Jonim appeared to be at the end of his patience. "They ain't got nothing to do with Jake's death."

"Maybe not, but he was obsessing over her." The Dwarven woman who spoke before pointed at me. "What makes her special?"

The creak turned into something much louder and the top container tilted, threatening to crash down on us.

"Everyone run, now!" Silver ordered.

I did, but ran into the middle of the group, bringing my arms up overhead with my forearms crossed, my shield spell in place in time to catch the falling container. I grunted under the pressure of holding it up. Many of the people screamed and ran.

Pushing more of my power into the spell, I could only maintain the shield, not move the container. I took a step back, to keep my stance. I needed to keep it up long enough for everyone to get clear of it. The constant pressure drained my arcane energy reserves quickly. A couple of people cowed on the ground.

Silver came up next to me.

"Run. I can't hold this much longer," I said through clenched teeth. My legs might give out first. Either would get me crushed under the large metal container.

He brought his sword up behind his shield and created his protective bubble. "Let go - I've got it. See if you can push it back up."

I switched so my hands were out in front of me, wary when the container settled lower against Silver's shield spell. Conjuring the strongest wind I could manage, I slowly pushed the container back to where it belonged.

Another shield spell went up with Silver's. I glanced over to see Mason casting it. The arcane casters from the EAC and DAC stepped up and supported my wind spell with their own, moving the container faster. A third shield spell went up while we got it back to where it should be.

As soon as we got the container in place, the others moved away and I waited for Silver.

"Go!" He yelled and pushed me to run. The container creaked loudly as it settled in place.

The container crashed to the ground again half of a minute later. Once the dust settled, I noticed it had damaged the integrity of the container under it so it would not support another on top.

I folded my arms and turned my attention up to Silver. "Looks like we have another scene to process."

He crossed his arms and frowned. "We still haven't finished with the first one."

"Yer an Arcanist, ain't you?" the Dwarven woman from the DAC asked. "Ain't seen another mage cast that fast."

Turning, I found we had everyone's attention. I nodded.

"Jake kept sayin' you were special. Heard you got the system operational. Assumed he wanted to get a rise out of us again."

"I think most of us assumed that," Mason said.

"We should get to work," Silver said quietly.

"Yeah, and about you," one of the divine casters said. "I thought Mason was lying when he said there was a cooperative mixed magic team then you show up to be a paladin - the absolute last type of divine caster I thought would ever be able to work with what sounds like the extreme end of the arcane spectrum." He looked over at the mages standing together.

The EAC mage nodded at the assessment. "I'm feeling shown up here. Guess I got to step up my game if these two extremes can work together."

I bowed. "Please excuse us. We have quite a bit of work ahead of us." It never occurred to me before that Silver and I were on opposite ends of the spectrum.

"We might have to push back our dinner plans," Silver said.

I rolled my eyes. We just nearly got crushed and he was thinking about food. "You sound like Sparks."

Once we were out of earshot, Silver asked, "You okay?"

I took a deep breath before answering. "Using my shield spell like that drained a lot, but I'll be fine."

"That was certainly an interesting twist."

"Hm?"

"Getting them to start thinking about cooperating with each other."

I turned the corner and looked at the burn mark on the upper corner of the container. "Sometimes a practical application is a better example than theory."

"Could you have made it sound more boringly scientific?"

It would not be the first time Silver asked me that. We went around the fallen container. The metal box rested on its side, exposing the bottom. I dug in my bag for a pair of gloves. At this rate we would need to buy more.

Silver dug his camera out and we got to work. There were three dents in the bottom equal distance from each other along what would have been the backside of the container.

We would have to get up onto the container that had been below it to see if there were corresponding marks. We also needed check to see how the integrity of the container below was compromised.

While we worked, Jonim moved everyone in front of Spelltech's warehouse. They watched us while talking to the Navy personnel who showed up. At least we would not need to do interviews later.

Silver grinned down at me mischievously. "Can I kiss you?"

"What?! No!" My face heated up. What had gotten into him?

"They're watching us so intently I thought we might as well give them a reason."

I rolled my eyes and turned my attention to the containers still stacked. How could I get up there without using magic? We would likely need someone to get it down to check inside of it.

"Okay, how about a different show then?"

I turned and Silver had his shield out.

"You want up there, right? I can climb up with our gear bags."

It would not hurt to indulge him in this. Certainly would get our answers faster.

Backing up, I waited for him to squat down with his shield before running and jumping on it. It felt like he pushed me up harder than any other time we had done this.

I cleared the top of the container easily and flipped over to get myself more centered. Sure enough there were matching dents on the top of this one with corresponding burn marks. I peered over the backside of the containers to see if something had fallen off we should collect as evidence. Only the water lapping at the dock was below. Not likely to get anything there.

Silver made it up while I scanned the area below.

"Whoa. Be careful near the other side - it's really weak. And warm," my partner warned.

"Think someone heated the inside to weaken it?"

"That's a definite."

"Looks like they also gave it a push." I pointed at the indentations.

"Yeah, someone doesn't want us here. By the way, nice flip at the end there."

I shrugged. "Just wanted to get more centered on the container."

We went about our business documenting. There may not be much here, but it was still pieces to the puzzle.

It was late by the time we left the base for the day and I had hours of work ahead of me still. I needed to get everything uploaded and scanned. We managed to get a shipment out with high priority tags on it. I messaged Sparky as Silver drove to warn him of what was coming.

I grimaced at the reports I still needed to file. Resting tonight would be out of the question. I would still be able to function missing a day. It was the only way I would get caught up if I was lucky.

"We still need to get something in place." Silver's voice broke me out of my thoughts.

"What?"

"A keyword or something that'll work in case you come in contact with the system again. I don't like the fact the amplifier has that kind of affect over you."

"Oh. Um..." Why was this so difficult to come up with?

My mind reminded me he previously gave me a couple of options which would likely work. One I refused, but what would be the harm in telling him?

No, I refused to be teased endlessly and too often he found ways to do it. I really did not need to hand him another.

As well as I had no idea how I would feel hearing that name again. In my head that name was attached to people who died despite the fact so few used it.

I glanced over at my partner. As much as he loved to tease me, he also treated things I talked about with respect. He always wanted to listen to me. I never understood it.

"Don't think too hard on it. We've got other stuff to work on still," Silver said.

I rolled my eyes - as if I needed the reminder. "We should probably pick up something and head back to the hotel. There's a lot to go into the case file."

"You have a point. Why don't I drop you off and then go get something?"

"Okay." It would give me a chance to get started in peace.

Silver brought his bag up to the room before heading back out. I hugged myself for a moment looking around the hotel room. I used to love being by myself. Probably just a temporary thing because of the system.

Shaking my head, I sat down and pulled everything out. I set up both tablets to upload images from the cameras. Then I set to work on scanning in the few fingerprints we found.

Almost an hour later, my phone rang. Kitteren's name came up requesting a video call.

I sighed and answered.

"*Have you done it yet?*" A broad grin graced her face.

"*Done what?*" I had done a lot of things today. Some of which I would rather forget.

Kitteren rolled her eyes dramatically and gave a loud exasperated sigh. "*Kissed him.*"

"*What? No!*" My face warmed at her reminder of what happened.

She laughed. "*You've thought about it though.*"

"*No. I've been busy working.*"

"*Come on, Ket. You're in a beautiful vacation destination. You should take advantage of it.*"

"*What does being in Sandpoint have to do with that?*" Things like this I never understood.

"*It's a great place to try new things.*"

"*I'm good. It was a one time thing.*"

My sister smirked. "*I doubt that. And it happening because you needed to be pulled back to your body doesn't count. I know you're going to enjoy it.*"

It was my turn to roll my eyes. "*Why is this so important? I've got a case to solve that keeps growing.*"

"*What if he wants to kiss you again?*"

"*I'll probably end up slapping him again.*"

Kitteren gave a short laugh. "*Not the reaction I was expecting, but it'd be hilarious to watch.*"

"*How are things going in Ghost Forest?*" I asked, changing the subject.

"*Great. I really don't do much outside of the mounds of paperwork to be honest. You taught them too well. Let's get back to you. Where is he anyway?*"

"Getting food." I glanced at my watch. He had been gone a while. *"Not sure what's taking so long. I hope he hasn't run into trouble."*

"We are talking about Silver, right?"

"Yes, but there have been enough incidents we're certain someone is trying to drive us off the case."

Kitteren's face quickly became serious. *"Okay, what happened?"*

"Hit my head a few too many times," I joked, but my eyes slid to the door. If I could get Kitteren off of the phone, I could message him.

"Hasn't knocked any sense into you though otherwise you'd have tried it already."

Was she coming back around to that already? *"Too many near misses and this last one was more direct."*

"Hey," Kitteren said. *"You'll figure it out. But when this is over, you need to do something for yourself. I may not have details, but if you're this worked up over it, it's got to be Hells of a case."*

How was I worked up? I was concerned, yes, but I thought I kept it to myself.

I turned toward the door when I heard it unlock. *"He's back."*

"Not yet, Ket," she said as I reached for the button to end the call. *"Always get full confirmation first."*

I shifted nervously as the door opened slowly. Silver hefted a couple of bags while putting his wallet away and getting through the door.

He put the bags on the table next to me and then looked at my phone with the video call still connected. "Sorry I interrupted."

Kitteren shrugged. "We were just wrapping up anyway. Can you do something about her being so high-strung? Pretty soon you'll have to peel her off of the ceiling."

Silver crossed his arms and tilted his head at the screen. Even I did not know what to make of her words.

"I'll see what I can do," Silver said.

Kitteren turned her attention back to me. *"You need to do it."*

"Shut up," I shot at her.

My sister laughed and ended the call. I put my phone face down. Why did she constantly tease me about things like this?

Silver knelt down next to me. "Should I ask what that was about?"

"No."

"Well, considering you're blushing, I'm going to take an educated guess." Then he stood up and got the food containers out of the bags.

I glared up at him. He smiled down at me and held out a container.

Opening the small box, I found breaded cheese sticks. I picked up one and pointed it at him. "Don't start."

"Getting you one of your favorites won't get me a free pass?"

"No. And how come you were gone for so long? I started to worry something happened."

He sat down on another chair with his own food. "I went to Watered Down. I wanted to try something else."

"Don't suppose you happened to have picked up more than food."

He shook his head. "They already knew what happened to Jake though. Right now it's all speculation."

I dipped the piece I held in the sauce and twirled it around for a moment, frowning. "If it wasn't suicide, then whoever did it has likely gone into hiding. It's not like they're going to go boasting about it - not with the amount of work they went to make us question if it was suicide or not."

"You're also assuming Jake didn't decide to take his life."

"Guess even I'm finding it hard to believe. I don't want to write it off either in case there's a critical piece of evidence we might miss."

Silver sighed, pointing at my food. "Take a break and eat. We can work on this more after. Looks like you have a lot in progress."

I looked at the tablets uploading images still and the portable fingerprint scanner waiting for more input from me. "Between organizing all of this and the reports that still need to be written, I think it's going to be an all-nighter."

He raised an eyebrow at me. "Does this mean you're willing to go in later tomorrow?"

I tilted my head at him. "No, there's too much to do."

"Ketayl," Silver said and sighed. "Both of us will need rest if we want to be operating at full. I will make sure you rest."

I knew it was not an idle threat. He knew exactly how to get me to rest whether I wanted to or not. "At least can we knock out getting this stuff uploaded and organized? I've also got more from my watch to transfer."

"You do that, I'll draft reports. I'll probably complain about it the whole time, but they'll get done."

"Fine."

Silence fell between us and I moved onto my main meal by the time Silver spoke again. "I do want to talk about what has happened between us."

Not him too. "I don't think now is a good time."

"You told Kitteren."

I stopped and stared at him. Did he actually know?

"She's a little easier to understand than you when you speak in your dialect. And she's loud."

I glared at him. "You were eavesdropping?"

"I just told you she's loud. I could hear her in the bathroom with the water running."

I turned away from him. There went any future private conversations between me and Kitteren. "How long?"

"Rathal told me how he learned to understand Kitteren shortly after they arrived to relieve us in Ghost Forest. I don't have enough practice to translate when you speak it yet."

Which meant maybe two or three weeks at best he had been translating.

"To be honest, I can only pick up words here and there from Kitteren. Rathal was right - your accent is much thicker."

I set my jaw and stared at my box of food. Suddenly my appetite disappeared.

"Ketayl, eat. I need to learn it anyway. Sometimes you'll drop into it without realizing it and it'll be easier than asking you to repeat yourself."

His words did not help any.

"Besides, it could be useful as a means of private communication between us. Especially on cases like this. We'd be able to talk more freely."

"You don't seem to have trouble figuring it out," I spat at him.

"Words, Ketayl. I have to put what little I can make out into context and hope I'm right. I'm also more actively attempting to parse it out."

I bit my lower lip. I knew I would not stay mad at him for this. His points were valid. "How?"

"At least with Kitteren, if you slow it down, you can make most of it out. I still have a hard time keeping up with how fast the two of you talk."

Mouthing a few words, I slowed it down and realized it more or less did work, but there were still a lot of specific words to the dialect. Someone broke the code.

"Why did you tell Kitteren?" Silver asked.

His question made me sit up and look at him. "I'm not sure. I guess I was still confused about what happened and I've been trying to be better about communicating with her."

"It was certainly a confusing set of circumstances," Silver agreed.

I dug at my food a little more forcefully than I normally would. "We need to finish and get back to work if you want to get rest tonight."

Today I wondered if the weather would be against us. I eyed the strange clouds as we arrived on base. Hopefully we would spend most of our time indoors.

"Where do you want to start?" I asked Silver.

"Let's get back to the ship and track down the problem with the defense station. I know it's been bothering you that we haven't found the source yet."

"I'm leaning toward sabotage given what we've found so far." I pulled out my tablet and checked the tracking on what we sent yesterday. It should be arriving at the main office soon if it had not already.

A few more hours and it would be in Sparky's hands. I found out he had a knack for finding explosive devices I might overlook during the months we worked together. I never asked where he got the experience for it as I was unsure I would want to know the answer.

Once we picked up our escorts for the day, we headed for the ship. People rushed around the base as if preparing for something.

"Is something wrong?" I asked.

"Just getting ready for the wizard to arrive, ma'am."

I raised an eyebrow and looked at Silver who shrugged. "Wizard?"

The other escort explained. "It's called a wizard storm. Be Hells of a light show. You won't be able to stay on-board the ship once it rolls in. We'll give you as much time as we can."

"If a ship gets caught at sea during one, it's fine, but it's a precaution we have in place on base."

"Oh, thank you," I said.

A few silent minutes later, I was hugging myself against the wind as we ran up to the ship. Even the guards normally stationed here retreated inside. Our escorts remained with the guards and Silver and I headed down into the ship.

"How far do you think?" Silver asked.

"To be honest, I'm not even sure the plans are accurate for where the system goes. There were so many wires around the amplifier."

"So, keep following it one room at a time?"

I nodded. It would be slow going, but not as slow as chasing all over for the source.

While Silver pulled a panel off, he asked, "What was so special about the book you found in Jake's office?"

He reminded me it was still in my bag. "I think it's where his inspiration for the system came from, but I'm fairly certain his translation is inaccurate."

"You can read it?" My partner finally pulled the panel free.

I stepped forward and shined my handlight in, seeing only burnt out wiring still. "No. I know this is going to sound strange, but I feel like I should be able to and I know some of the translations are inaccurate, but I don't know why or how to correct it." I took pictures of the inside of the panel. Sparky might get something off of this - we were likely getting too frustrated.

"I'm thinking you've hit your head a few too many times in recent days."

I rolled my eyes. "Could also have something to do with coming in contact with the amplifier."

"Really don't want to consider that one. You're implying the orb can impart information."

"As a tactical system, it would be greatly valued if it could provide real time analysis of a battle, but I didn't see anything about it in Jake's notes."

"He also said you managed to make it do things he never even imagined."

I frowned. "I'm only seeing burnt out wiring here. It looks like it leads that way." I pointed in the direction they went. "I don't see how this type of damage could have traveled so far."

"I've given up on assuming this thing made sense."

"Probably a better idea." I followed Silver out the door. We planned to clean up later. With the time restraint, we wanted to move quickly.

We managed a couple more rooms before we were told it was time to leave. I had heard thunder a few minutes earlier even as far into the ship as we were and it continued to get louder.

When we got outside, the wind and the rain picked up to the point Silver held onto me. Even I was unsure if I would be able to keep from being blown off of the dock.

We hurried into Spelltech's warehouse with our escorts. All of us were soaked by the time we got there. Even the guards abandoned their post, taking up shelter in a small building just off of the dock.

I looked back out the rain-soaked windows at the strange cloud pattern passing over us. It appeared as if a tidal wave of storm clouds reached for the ground. Large ball-like clouds rolled over the landscape behind them.

"It's just a big thunderstorm, ma'am. Nothing to be concerned about. Doesn't happen too often, but it's better to be inside and make sure everything is secured," one of our escorts said.

Others in the warehouse gathered by the windows to watch the storm.

"Thank you. Just wish we could've gotten done what we wanted to," I said.

I turned my attention away from the windows and toward the back of the warehouse where the offices were located. Going through the computer would keep me occupied while we waited. I wished we kept the computer from his hidden office, but the one with access to the plans would have to suffice.

Besides, I wanted to dry off. I could use my power to do it, but the casters were already eying me cautiously.

"Since we're stuck here for a bit, I'm going to head to the office and see if I can't find something useful," I said quietly to Silver.

He nodded and signaled for me to lead the way. I was unsure if it was Jake's death or because of the storm, but all the other projects sat untouched.

I pushed my way into the over-packed office and dried both of us off. The room was as private as we were going to get. Then I sat down in front of the sole computer in the room.

"Did he give you access to it?" Silver asked.

I tapped my finger on the desk while it booted up. "No, but I can get in."

"What? How?" Silver leaned over my shoulder. Why did he have to be so close?

"I... uh..." I needed to be better about thinking through things like this. "I could never remember the passcode for my phone so I created an arcane solution to get in. It's the same concept."

"Have you done this before on anything other than your phone?" Silver turned so he leaned against to the desk next to the screen.

I mentally cringed at the question. "Yes..."

My partner raised an eyebrow at me. "Was it something you shouldn't have gotten into?"

I hesitated before answering. "Yes..."

"Okay, what?" Silver crossed his arms. "Your tales of mischief are always entertaining."

"Your phone and Kitteren's." I kept my eyes forward on the screen.

"When was this? I don't recall you ever getting a hold of my phone."

I sighed. It was bound to come out eventually. "In Mystic Port. I'm sorry I stole it from you, but I needed to figure out what was going on. It felt like everyone was covering something up." Which most of them were, but Silver had been as much in the dark as I had.

A hand touched my hair. "I think I understand. I might have done the same thing in your place."

I reached forward and touched the computer, working my way through the login screen to gain full access to what was on it. Part of me wondered if Jake continued to hold back information despite our assurances. He seemed extremely protective of his project. Maybe it was something else.

"Do you really think you're going to find anything useful in there?" Silver asked once I was in.

I shrugged. "I don't know. Figured it would give me something to do while we waited out the storm. You don't have to stay if you'd rather take a break."

Silver's large, calloused hand touched the side of my face and I turned to find out what he wanted my attention so badly for. "We should take this time to talk. If there's anything, it's probably on the one we sent to Sparky."

"We are talking." I went with the oblivious route, hoping he would drop the subject I assumed he wanted to bring up.

He gave me an exasperated look. "You know what I mean."

I sighed and turned away. "Right here and right now is a horrible place and time if you ask me."

"Then when and where?"

Silver would want a direct answer instead of letting me push it off indefinitely. "After we're done with this case and not here. Maybe when we get back."

"That's too long."

"Why?" I thought it too short.

"What do you mean 'why'? It's already been a couple of days," Silver snapped.

"Why do we have to talk about this? Strange things happened under stressful circumstances and I'm sorry I hit you." My words came out so fast I hoped he was able to keep up. And then dropped the topic.

"I'd like..." Silver trailed off and looked out the window of the office. "I guess this will have to wait. Get down and hide."

Immediately I used my invisibility spell and stood up to see what was going on. People with guns were rounding every one up and they weren't with the Navy.

What happened to our escorts? They were armed.

"I said get down," Silver hissed. He stood against my side to figure out where I was exactly. "You know what to do."

I went and hid under the table in the room, making sure to pull my long hair in with me. Silver put too much faith in assuming I understood what he meant.

He stood next to the table and waited for them. Less than a minute later one barged in with a rifle pointed at my partner. "You, out with everyone else."

I peered out enough to watch Silver put his hands up and walk out the door. No fight? My partner remained armed and he wore his armored jacket just as he had this whole trip.

Sneaking out the door behind them, I traveled along the wall away from the group our captors assembled. How did they get on base?

I covered my mouth to muffle the soft whimper as they shoved my partner to the floor. He sat with the others who worked in the warehouse - both Spelltech and Navy alike.

There were four men here - two Humans, a Dwarf, and an Elf. All armed. I made my way slowly around the warehouse, being careful to remain quiet.

Two Humans rounded up everyone while the Elf stood centered in the room. The Dwarf remained by the front door. As I got closer to the door, I spotted our escorts on the ground. There was blood, but not enough to have killed either one of them assuming the internal trauma was not worse. Their weapons were gone.

Giving the one near the door as much space as I could, I went around to the windows to see what kept our new door guard's attention. It was hard to make out through the heavy rain, but there were others - a lot of others - on the dock near the ship. Were they after the prototype system?

I could not get out. Not without teleporting and even then I had no idea where to go. How much of the base had they taken over? I would possibly be expending my arcane energy only to end up a hostage like everyone else.

What could I do? I was literally as trapped here as everyone else. Taking out the Dwarf would only alert the Elf and then they would all be in jeopardy. Trying to take down both of the Humans would result in the same. Going after the Elf...

I eyed the group huddled on the floor. They were not bound. Silver at least would act as soon as I did, but I would still need to take down the Elf and one of the Humans quickly which would leave me exposed to the Dwarf. I was not the one wearing armor.

As I stepped toward the Elf, he moved to get closer to the group held hostage on the floor. An argument had broken out between the Human men and Silver.

"Where is she?!" One of the men grabbed him by the front of his jacket.

"Haven't seen her since before you pulled me out here. Have you checked the bathroom?" The smirk on my partner's face told me he enjoyed antagonizing his captors.

And for as much as Silver walked the line with his statement, because I knew he could track me to some extent while invisible, he had not lied to them.

"Hey, you want the TIO up our asses also? Bad enough we'll have the Navy chasing us until we can unload the goods." One of the men near Silver stopped the other from hitting him.

The one who prepared to hit my partner looked down at the badge clipped to his belt. "Damn. Fine." He dropped Silver. "We still need to find the one that's loose."

"Tell us where she is and we'll let her live."

"You won't hit me because I'm with the TIO, but you'll kill her? You do realize we both work for them, right?" Silver asked.

I managed to get fairly close behind the Elf who seemed content to simply watch the events unfolding.

"Dammit, just tell us where she is."

Dropping my invisibility spell, I slammed a ball of conjured electricity into the side of the Elf's head. He fell to the ground instantly.

"Behind you." Silver smirked, his shield appearing on his arm and his sword sheathed on his belt.

I ran and slid on the floor between the two men as they turned, pulling out my staff and extending it to hit both of them at the same time. While they both fell from the hit to the groin, Silver's shield flew over me. I heard it bounce off of a couple of things before a loud grunt came from near the door on the other side of the warehouse.

"I think that's the longest throw I've seen you do," I said getting to my feet.

"You could have just said 'nice shot'."

I shrugged. "Now what?"

"Now what? Are you mad?! You put all of us in danger with that stunt," the Magister yelled, his face turning red. "We should have sat still and let them do what they want. Now we're going to die."

"Not my style," Silver shot at him. "And certainly not hers either. Let's get these guys tied up."

While they worked, I went back over to the windows to see what was going on. The torrential downpour made it difficult, but people still ran about the ship. Lightning struck the water not far away.

"What's going on?" Silver asked, coming up behind me.

"I'm not sure. There's people around the ship. I'm assuming not Navy since even the guards sought shelter."

He crossed his arms and stared out the window. "They obviously don't care about anything here. We're just the closest to the dock."

I raised an eyebrow at my partner. "You planning on letting them do what they want?"

"I didn't say that, but we need to know what they're planning. I need to go ask some questions."

Better them than me. He could get extremely intimidating when he interrogated someone. I learned not to interfere. The best thing I could do was keep watch.

A few minutes passed before Mason came over. "Want a temporary partner?"

"Huh?"

The priest wrung his hands. "Well, your buddy is busy making those guys crap themselves so I thought you might like company."

"Oh, yeah, sure. I'm afraid I'm not very talkative though."

"That's fine. I'm not much for conversation either. Well, at least not small talk."

"Could you teach Silver?"

Mason laughed. "You two are certainly an interesting pair. By the way, nice work back there in freeing us. I have no idea how the two of you came up with a plan before he got stuck with the rest of us."

"There was no plan. I couldn't leave to get help because I don't know how much of the base they've taken over. I might have ended up in the same situation."

"Telepathic communication?"

I shook my head. "I guess we've just trained enough together." So much for not being talkative.

Chancing a glance back into the warehouse, I hoped Silver hurried - even with the storm slowing them down, we would not have much time to stop whatever their plans were.

"IT'S THE SHIP," Silver said as he approached. "They plan on stealing the whole damn ship."

"The prototype system?"

"It has to be. There are no other projects built into it right now," someone in a Navy uniform said.

I sighed and looked out the window at the ship again. "Should we let it go and leave it to the Navy to catch them?"

Silver folded his arms and turned his attention out the window. "You, of all people, are suggesting we do nothing?"

"We'll be fighting not only an unknown number of enemies, but also the weather. There's only two of us and too many of them between us and the ship never mind who is on-board." I gestured in the direction of the chaos happening outside.

"Not just the two of you, lass," the Dwarf from the DAC said. "I think between the lot of us we can provide a distraction. As long as you two don't mind takin' point." Then she pointed up at the Elf from the EAC. "Want to make a game of it?"

"You know I'll win."

"Bah!" The Dwarven woman smiled broadly. "Grab a partner and let's get it done. We ain't dealt with Jake this long to let someone walk away with this project. You too Magister Prissy Pants."

The Magister turned his nose up in the air. "I refuse to partner with any mage not from the Arcane College."

"Ain't the point," she argued. "We pair with a divine caster for the best chance at pullin' it off. Not a one of us can cast as fast as the lass. And don't you want a chance to show all of us how high and mighty Arcane College mages are? You certainly boast about it enough. Especially a few drinks in."

"Not to mention after watching these two, it looks like we can have some fun," Mason pointed out. "I'm in."

As they organized themselves, I turned my attention to the remaining civilian and military personnel. Would they be okay when we left? I bit my lower lip. "What about everyone else?"

One of the Navy officers picked up a rifle we relieved from our captors. "I wouldn't want to provide cover fire in this storm, but we can protect the people here."

Silver put a hand on my shoulder. "How low did you run yourself with freeing us?"

I closed my eyes for a moment to make sure I gave an accurate answer. "Negligible. As long as you don't want me to teleport a group, I should be good for a while."

"Then let's do this." Silver flipped his sword around and the remainder of his armor appeared. Plates similar to the black, heavy textured material of his jacket covered his legs and his boots had a black metallic guard over them.

I raised an eyebrow at my partner. "At least you'll be better anchored out there."

"Really? This is the first time I've gotten to use the whole set and that's all you've got to say?"

I shrugged. He never mentioned Coburn had completed the set. I thought he still only had the jacket.

Silver shook his head and opened the door, the wind and rain threatening to push me back into the building. Once we got set up outside, Silver and I would make a run for the ship, attacking anyone in our way with the others creating a distraction and taking out the stragglers.

That was the plan anyway.

We gathered outside and the others immediately began casting for the initial distraction. The moment the spells went off Silver shouted, "Go!"

I ran behind my partner, hoping he would cut down the wind, but it shifted and I fought to keep moving forward. A familiar golden sphere appeared around us, making it easier to run. It also made us a target.

My partner brought his left arm back and threw his shield, hitting three of the four people running toward us with guns drawn. He stopped to catch it and I slid under his arm, throwing shards of ice at the one remaining.

Silver got ahead of me before I got to my feet and hustled to catch up. Fireballs and more ice hit others ahead of us. The bulk of the enemy diverted and went after the casters behind us.

The ship began pulling out of the dock. We were too far away with too many people between us and them.

Repeating our earlier pattern, my partner threw his shield again, getting three of the five heading for us. I slid under his arm, throwing a fireball between the remaining two, the detonation sent them flying.

We came up with this leap idea in training, but never attempted it in an actual fight. And certainly not something this extended. Our tactic would likely not work much longer if at all.

The ship continued to pull away, gaining speed. How would we catch up with it? Teleporting both of us would take too much of my arcane energy if I could even target it while it moved.

And there were still people barring our approach.

I pulled my shrunken staff from its holster and extended it. We needed to switch up tactics a little.

Silver again threw his shield and I used a quick flight spell to launch myself at the remaining enemies, plowing into them staff first. Flipping over it, I shrank it so as to not get caught and landed in a crouch. My partner caught up to me.

"We're not going to make it!" I shouted to be heard over the wind, rain, and rolling thunder.

"Just keep going! We'll figure something out!"

Many of the enemies on the dock ran to catch the ship before it left. Had the people on-board panicked and decided to leave their comrades behind?

They damaged the dock and the ship as it pulled away. How many were on-board?

We repeated our leaping pattern three more times before reaching the end of the dock. Teleporting, I could end up dropping us into the water and with the lightning strikes hitting out there, I could not risk it.

I shrunk my staff and shoved it back in its holster. "Hold on," I ordered, wrapping my arms around Silver.

Just as he locked his arms around me, I cast a flight spell hoping I was strong enough to carry both of us with it. Especially with the shifting high winds.

Landing roughly, I slid on the deck and hit a metal wall hard, dropping Silver en route. I put too much power into my spell to compensate, but we were on-board.

Silver pulled me behind another wall. I labored to catch my breath between the run and the flight. "Are you okay to keep going?" he asked.

I nodded. "Just need a minute."

"You low?"

"Not as low as if I had teleported us."

Silver touched the top of my head gently before peeking around the corner. "Looks like they don't know we're on-board yet."

"How many?"

"Dozen, maybe more."

"Close together?"

Silver nodded. "They're trying to shelter themselves from the storm."

I forced myself to my feet. "I've got this group if you don't mind getting any stragglers."

My partner grinned broadly and spun his sword at his side.

I peeked around the corner, solidifying the plan in my head. Why were they outside in the storm? It mattered little as I prepared myself.

Casting another flight spell, I dropped down in the middle of the group, slamming a ball of conjured electricity onto the deck, catching the people around me. I remained crouched down as Silver's shield flew overhead, taking out the couple I missed.

He ran by me and slammed another into the wall. He backed off a step to swing his sword at the enemy.

Without thinking through my actions, I grabbed Silver's sword arm. "Stop! We can't kill them."

"They'll just keep coming!"

"Can't interrogate the dead!" I pulled with all of my weight, but his arm would not budge.

He growled at me and dropped his arm. "Fine."

Taking a breath of relief, I took stock of our current situation. "Let's get to the ship's control room and see if we can shut down the engines. The Navy should have been alerted by now."

Silver led the way, but not before he kicked the man he slammed into the wall. We came across a couple more, both who my partner knocked overboard. What had gotten into him?

"Hey, knock it off! They could die out there," I argued.

Silver simply growled and kept a hard pace on his path to the control room. I slipped on the deck a number of times trying to keep up.

There were no others in our path, but I could not blame them for not wanting to be out here in this storm.

He peeked in the window to the control room. Crouching back down he held up three fingers to me.

I tapped my chest. The room would be too small for him to fight.

My partner nodded and put his hand on the door handle, checking to make sure I was ready before opening it. Springing inside, I unleashed a strong wind, throwing all three across the tiny room.

Silver jumped over me, prepared to fight whoever stood back up, but none did. He moved one off of the control panel, dropping him to the floor. "It's been too long since I last dealt with a ship." His gaze trailed over the controls.

Ship? I started to think I did not know the Elven man with me. "Should we call back for help?"

Silver shook his head and pulled back on a lever. The rumble of the engines ceased under my feet. "We've got bigger problems now." He pointed out the window.

I could barely make out a larger vessel in the distance through the rain. Reinforcements. "Did Sparks have to say pirates?"

"Got to admit he was right on the money for this one." Silver hauled the unconscious people out of the room, locking it behind us. "Any ideas of how just the two of us can protect the ship with enemies already on-board?"

I took a deep breath. "There's one way, but neither of us likes the idea." I pushed my way through the door heading into the ship and took off running. The dual-magic system would be our only chance at this point.

Silver grabbed me around the waist to stop my progress. "Ketayl, no! I can't risk losing you to the system."

An enemy showing up halted the conversation. While Silver dealt with him, I continued my run for the control room.

As soon as I got inside, I engaged one of two enemies in the room. The other appeared desperately attempting to operate the system.

Slamming a ball of electricity into my opponent's chest, I dropped the first one and turned on the second, but a shield hitting him beat me to it.

Silver dragged the one I took down out the door. "Would you stop for a minute? You can't do this! I don't know if I can get you out!"

I pushed the one slumped over in the chair for the offense station out of the way and switched it to operate both defense and offense. "If you've got a better plan, I'd love to hear it."

"Ketayl..."

"Kela," I said, sliding into the chair. I hoped giving Silver this information was right choice.

"What?"

"Use it or get slapped - your choice." Without waiting for further confirmation, I grabbed the grips, slamming my power into the system.

Immediately I was everywhere on the ship again, but more than the systems I should be in. I focused on getting the shield up and the "guns" ready to fire.

Coming in prepared this time, the system was incredibly easy to operate though I would have to push a lot of power into it to get out something useful. Once the shield went up, I shut the lights off in sections of the ship the enemy still occupied, also killing the emergency backup lighting.

It seemed once the system had been tied into the triggers, it could access any other system on the ship.

The other vessel rapidly closed in on us. They opened fire and I grunted as the barrage hit the shield surrounding our ship. I sent a few shots back, but unless I could actually hit something, I would be in for a lengthy fight. My reserves would likely not last long.

Looking for a larger target, I aimed for the waterline and noticed I caused more damage to the enemy vessel. My main problem was I was running low fast keeping up both the shield and the barrage.

After a few more seconds, I shifted to defense only. I could not keep up with both. It was an odd sensation: being outside the ship in the storm and feeling drenched in sweat at the same time.

The enemy vessel stopped its attack and retreated. Other Naval vessels appeared in my vision. I turned to see what was going on.

Helicopters headed for us and I shifted my power away from the shield emitters on that side so they could approach. It meant less I needed to throw my power into.

"Kela, it's over." Silver's voice was faint, but I heard it.

I backed out of the systems one-by-one as military personnel landed and took over the ship. I trusted Silver. I held onto the anchor he created, but was too weak to pull myself back. If I had more energy, I might be able to get myself out.

He pulled me, but it was slow and my grip kept slipping. The lure of the calm and balance the system offered made it harder to want to hold on. I could simply exist here. A short rest would make sense.

I barely loosened my hold and suddenly slammed back to where I should be. Feeling lips on mine again, I knew it was Silver and forced my hands off of the grips, wrapping my arms around his neck and held on to my anchor. I almost lost myself to the system and could not chance falling back.

Silver pulled me from the chair and between the kiss and how tightly he held on, I could not breathe. I managed to back away from him enough to get air.

He picked me up over the console and we sat on the floor. It took far too long for me to stop shaking.

"Just relax, Kela, you're safe."

"Can forget that name now," I said weakly.

"No, I like it. Nice shooting by the way. And thanks for not slapping me this time."

"Still can."

Silver laughed and gently rubbed the side of my neck with the back of his fingers.

I rested against him. I was too exhausted to talk anymore.

15

WE REMAINED on-board while they brought the ship into dock. I drifted in and out during that time.

"She's just exhausted." Silver's voice cut through the haze.

"So you managed to operate the defense side of the system?" Jonim asked.

"No, she switched it to operate both."

"We hadn't even discussed a broader test and you folks take it out into practical application. I'm thinking we're scrapping the project though. Ain't going to be able to use it with the current caster force and it wiped her out after a short battle."

"We also fought our way from Spelltech's warehouse and she got us on-board. Ketayl's resources aren't unlimited - she'd run herself down quite a bit by then." Silver stroked the hair near my temple with his fingers.

I wanted to argue with him, but could not find the energy to move. I listened as the thunder rolled in the distance. Silence fell in the room.

"Is the storm still bad?" Silver asked.

"Nah," Jonim said. "The wizard never likes to hang around long. Apparently just long enough for a bunch of pirates to think they can get away with Navy property. Looking forward to the stories to come out of this."

Silver stroked my cheek with his thumb. "I think we need to call it a day."

"If you weren't, I was going to kick you off base. Though, I'm sure your bosses will be wanting to hear what happened first."

"I've been expecting that call. Surprised they haven't already with the information her watch transmits."

"Probably haven't gotten it yet - you were pretty far out and the wizard likes to shut down communications. Normally we can patch into the camera network on-board, but it was a complete blackout. We'll download the security footage. Make sure copies get to who they need to."

My mind wandered while they spoke. I needed to make sense of everything that happened. The leaping tactic we came up with was more effective than I thought.

"I ain't trying to step on your toes, but I would feel a lot better if she got looked at. The lass ain't moved 'cept to breathe."

Silver sighed. "As much as she's not going to like it, I agree."

"Traitor," I muttered.

My partner laughed loudly. "Now I know you're okay, but you're still exhausted. At least consider it a more comfortable place to rest."

Jonim had laughed also. "If you can walk, we can get you to the infirmary. You and your buddy left quite the trail of pain and we only have a couple of ambulances."

"I can make it easier," Silver said right before he scooped me into his arms and stood up.

"Put me down." I pushed against him, but barely made an impression on his jacket.

"Just humor me, okay?"

I sighed and closed my eyes again. I could not fight him if I wanted to. Sleep would help. Then I could make sense of it all.

I knew we moved, but only could tell when we got outside because it still rained lightly. My eyes would not open again despite my curiosity.

"By the Gods, what happened?"

"Is she okay?"

"What do you need?"

"She's so low on arcane energy."

Voices I could not place got louder. Why could they not let me rest?

"She's exhausted from the fight and operating the whole system by herself," Silver said softly.

"She can do that?"

"The system is capable of it in theory. Never thought the damn thing would actually work."

"Or that anyone could manage to handle both."

"Excuse us," Silver said.

I expected to get put down in a seat, but it never happened. Silver stepped up onto something and then I felt the rumble of an engine before we moved. He slid down so I rested more on top of him.

"How low were you run?" I asked. My voice barely above a whisper.

He stiffened up underneath me. "I thought you were asleep."

"Too noisy."

He gave a short laugh. "I'm fine. It wasn't as long of a fight as I expected. You wore me out more pulling you back."

"Sorry."

"Don't be, but when you're feeling up to it, we really need to talk."

Of course he would and my actions likely confused him as much as they did me. Why did I hold on? Perhaps because I had been in there for longer and put so much energy into getting the power output the system should have had. Maybe it was the lure of the siren's call again.

I must have fallen asleep because I woke when Silver set me down on a bed. I reached out and grabbed his arm, not knowing where I was or what was going on.

"It's okay. You're in the infirmary. Just rest. I've got some calls to make," he said quietly.

I looked around and confirmed I was in the infirmary. Again. I sighed and rested my head back on the pillow, letting go of his arm.

Silver kissed my forehead. "Try not to give the doctor a hard time, okay?"

My brain did not want to process his words. I made a noise at him and went back to sleep.

WHEN I WOKE, Silver had not returned. I still felt worn and drained, but at least I could move.

I struggled to sit up and found myself attached to something. A couple of cables went under my tank top with another connected to my finger. What happened to the light sweatshirt I had been wearing?

The cool air got to me once the blanket slid down. What was going on? I followed the cables back to see what I was attached to and if I could disconnect from it.

"Oh, you're awake," a doctor said as he stuck his head through the curtain. "Let's get those off of you. We did it as a precaution."

I sat still as he removed the pads stuck to the upper part of my chest and the piece clipped on my finger.

"I'll let your buddy know you're up. Do you need anything?"

I opened my mouth to tell him no, but had to clear my throat to find my voice. "Water?"

"Absolutely. I'll be right back."

Part of me wanted to believe what happened was a dream, but I was fairly certain I had not hit my head again recently. I thought about what happened. How had we all missed the fact there were people who wanted the actual prototype? Was Jake killed for it or was it suicide? I needed to contact Sparky to see if he had anything yet.

How long had I been out? Maybe there had not been enough time for him to process much.

Where was my phone? And my stuff? I ended up leaving my gear bag in Spelltech's warehouse during the conflict.

The hostage situation. The fight to get to the ship. Taking over key sections of the ship until help could arrive. Syncing more completely to the system than before. Silver pulling me out.

I touched my lips. He had done it again and I could not fault him for it - I was ready to give up. The whole thing still confused me. Especially my reaction with holding onto him.

Kitteren would tell me this did not count also because of the circumstances. As it was I became concerned I had become too attached. Silver and I worked well together, but this could disrupt our easygoing friendship. It would be better to pretend it never happened.

I took a shuddering breath and pulled my knees up, hugging them. A cup appeared in my vision a few moments later.

"Oh, thank you." I took it and looked up when I recognized the hand holding it out to me. Why was Silver here?

"How are you feeling?" he asked softly.

I took a sip of water to give me time to think. "Confused. What's going on?" I refused to look at him again. I acted like such a desperate fool.

"Since you've been sleeping, I went back and got our gear. I also called Lockonis and reported in. Sparky had just gotten started on processing what we sent."

The plastic cup crinkled when I squeezed it. "What did she say?"

"I think she's mad she missed this fight. Jonim will be sending her the security footage as soon as he's gotten all of it. She's also not happy you dived into the system again, but agrees it was extenuating circumstances."

There would be a headache coming. I would likely get chewed out for my actions.

"The Navy is canceling any further tests to the system and dismantling it. We'll be taking the amplifier back. I've been promised it'll be in a box with very heavy shielding."

"Not silicon composite I hope."

Silver smirked and sat on the edge of the bed. "Lead I think."

Might be enough to keep the effects at bay.

"Also, we've been ordered to take a few days off after we finish tracking down the problem with the defense station. The main office will handle the rest. The Navy has the pirates in custody and I'm hungry so we should get out of here."

I debated if I should head to Great Tree during the downtime. I could consult with Father about my confusion and it would get me away from Silver for a few days.

Sliding forward, Silver took the now empty cup from me and held out a hand. I ignored it and stood on my own. I needed to back away completely. I became too lax about it over the past few months.

"Think you're up for a quick video call? Lockonis would like to see that you're okay."

I nodded. I was probably a mess, but I could deal. Food sounded good also. Might help with still feeling exhausted.

Silver pulled back the curtain and the doctor looked up from his clipboard - he had been heading toward us.

"Leaving?" the doctor asked.

"Yes," Silver answered.

The doctor tapped the back of his clipboard with a finger. "To be honest, I'm not comfortable with how exhausted you still are. It doesn't make much sense - the rest of the readings are fine."

"Arcane energy levels - takes longer to recover. I'm fine," I explained.

Silver folded his arms and looked down at me. "Normally I would argue against you, but even I know it's simply a matter of time for you to recover."

I rolled my eyes. "Thanks for the vote of confidence."

He patted me on the head. "I'll keep an eye on her. I think a quick stop at the hotel to clean up and food will help."

Both of those sounded fantastic right now.

"Let me get your sweatshirt first. It should be dry by now." The doctor disappeared for a minute before returning with the light-weight purple sweatshirt I had been wearing.

Taking it, I bowed. "Thank you." The movement left me slightly dizzy, but I forced myself to pretend nothing was wrong and strode out the door as steadily as I could manage.

Silver stopped me in the hall once the door closed. "You're not fine."

"Just a little dizzy. It's nothing." I moved away from him and set off at a quick pace.

Suddenly my feet left the floor and my back was against the wall. "Stop or I'm taking you back to the infirmary."

Silver held me at eye level for him and I glared back. I strongly debated kicking him. "Look, I'm tired, I'm hungry, and mostly I want to get out of here. Let's just make the call, get our stuff, and go."

"Wait, you're being reasonable?" Silver put me down.

"You go get stuck in that system sometime," I muttered.

He gave a short laugh. "Some good might have come out of it. Walk with me. It'll be easier to catch you if I need to." He wrapped an arm around my waist.

I sighed and put up with his coddling. "Thanks for doing all of that."

"I'm occasionally useful."

***

"KET, you need to knock it off," Lockonis said. "I understand it was the best solution, but can you not go to the extreme for once?"

I bowed my head. I had it coming. I never bothered trying to come up with a more sane solution.

"I'm just glad you're up and moving again. Silver already filled me in on what happened. Once you get done, I'm having the two of you take a few days off before coming back."

My attention went back to the screen. "We're staying here?"

"Why not? Sandpoint is a good vacation destination at this time of year. Unless you want to come back to the cold and snow."

I shook my head.

"Go play tourist for a few days and we'll talk when you get back." Lockonis ended the call.

Closing my eyes, I attempted to muster the strength to do something. Standing was taking everything I had.

"Lass, get out of here and get some rest. The two of you best be off the base within the hour."

"Thank you for letting us use your office. I'm guessing the mobile towers haven't gotten back up and running yet," Silver said.

"They ain't quick to fix things, that's for certain. Should be up again here soon though. They like backlash less."

Silver guided me to our loaner vehicle. I leaned on him most of the way. I had no memory of the drive back and little of getting up to the room. The moment I laid down on the bed, I fell asleep.

So much for getting cleaned and food.

When I awoke later, the sun was out, but it had gotten late. Then I noticed Silver's absence. I reached for my phone and only felt the cool top of the nightstand. I picked up my head enough to glare at the empty space. Then remembered my watch would get notifications provided I had not broken it during the fight.

It appeared to be in one piece. I twisted my wrist to get the screen to come on. Still worked enough to at least tell me the time. I cycled through and looked for new messages, but had none.

Dropping my head back down, I was still exhausted. And even more hungry than before. I supposed I could get cleaned up before Silver returned.

I dragged myself off the bed and got a change of clothes before making my way to the bathroom. The pound of the hot spray from the shower felt good against my sore muscles. I stood under it for a while before snapping back to reality and setting about cleaning the day's events off.

Staring at myself in the mirror wearing only a towel, I lifted my hand to dry myself off and then put it back down. I ached too much to do it. Something second nature to me and I thought twice about using it.

I jumped at the knock on the door, grabbing the towel where it was wrapped around my chest.

"Ketayl, you in there?" Silver asked.

I let out the breath I held. "Yes."

"Everything okay?"

"Yeah."

"Can I come in?"

"No. Just give me a few minutes." I hurried to get dressed, though it was slow going.

Several minutes later, I opened the door half-expecting Silver to be standing right outside. When I saw it was clear, I grabbed my brush and began working the tangles out of my wet hair. A couple of short brush strokes in and I gave up.

Then my brush disappeared from my hand. "Come on. I'll get it brushed," Silver said softly.

"It's fine. I can do it."

"No, you're still exhausted. You haven't even dried your hair like you normally do."

Right then I hated how observant he had become during the time I had known him.

I gave up the idea of fighting him as he prodded me out of the bathroom. I had not expected to see Jonim sitting in the chair in the corner.

He gave me a broad smile. "Lass, you look better than the last time I saw you."

That likely was not saying much. I could not find the energy to respond.

"Figured the least I could do was treat you folks to dinner. I'll get the others you recruited later. Impressive organization. Never thought I'd see the day they stopped fighting let alone actually work together."

Silver gently nudged me to sit in the chair at the desk.

"Thought you'd both also like an update. This little fiasco has the much higher-ups unhappy and they've opened a full investigation into how this happened. Pretty sure they've already contacted your bosses since you two were involved in helping us keep the ship."

"And the others at the main office have been delving into Spell-tech so they'll want whatever the TIO finds," Silver said as he sat on the edge of a bed to brush my hair. "What are they planning on putting the amplifier in?"

"We're treating the damn thing as if it's radioactive. I remembered you said anything silicon based is bad so we figured err on the side of caution. Especially since you'll be flying it back. It'll stay where it is until you've concluded your investigation."

I sighed. We still had more work to do. "Did Sparks call with an update? I can't find my phone and I'm not sure if I broke my watch."

"No, and I have your phone. I didn't want it waking you," Silver said.

"Hope I didn't," Jonim said. "Came by and knocked, but got no answer. Found your boy here down in the physical training room."

Of course Silver would be found there. I pinched the bridge of my nose to focus. They wanted to talk business and my mind kept drifting.

"You're lower than you should still be, aren't you?" Silver asked.

I sighed. "Yeah. The storm pushed the nearest ley line supplying this area away and the other mages were likely actively absorbing any remaining arcane energy after the fight. There isn't much around until it shifts back."

"How long?"

I shrugged. "Depends on how far out it got pushed. I'll be fine. It's just going to take longer."

"I'm betting food will help," Jonim said. He pulled out his phone the moment it rang. "Looks like I'm not off-duty just yet. If you'll excuse me, I'll meet you folks downstairs." Then he let himself out.

"Think you'll make it?" Silver asked softly.

"Huh?" His question startled me and I sat up straight. Had I drifted off?

Silver paused in brushing my hair and pulled the chair around and knelt down in front of me. "Would you rather I brought food back?"

I shook my head. "I think I need to move around for a bit."

I shifted uncomfortably when I realized Silver stared at me.

"Sorry, I was thinking about how to do your hair - I'm not sure how to get it the way you normally wear it."

"Doesn't matter. Could just leave it down. It's going to take forever to dry anyway."

Silver put his hand on the side of my head and rubbed my cheek with his thumb. I needed to pull away, but I ached too much to bother with the extraneous movement. He would want to talk soon enough and I could reset our boundaries then.

1 6

"YOU SHOULD HAVE SEEN these two go. It was like watching a well rehearsed dance," Mason said. Apparently the casters on the project decided to turn what I hoped would be a quiet dinner into a victory celebration.

I forced a smile and sat quietly sipping my water, hoping to eat soon. The others had begun drinking by the time we arrived at Watered Down. Silver joined in, laughing and chatting with everyone.

Playing with a strand of my loose hair, I tried to focus on anything other than what happened between myself and Silver. He did what he thought necessary. Why could I not just let it be? Why was I obsessing over how I reacted when I was free of the system?

"Ketayl," Silver said softly. He slid a basket of breaded cheese sticks in front of me. "Eat - you'll feel better."

I nodded and while my movements were slow, I managed. I asked him to order for me because I could not focus enough to read the menu. Perhaps I should have stayed back at the hotel.

He leaned down so he could whisper to me. "Is there something on your mind?"

"Just having trouble focusing. Sorry, you were right and I should have stayed behind."

Silver touched my hair gently. "We'll see how you feel after you've eaten and had time to get some energy from it."

My silent agreement was in picking up another piece to eat. Silver already explained my lack of energy, not that it needed much explaining after the display they saw even through the storm.

"Did you guys catch the rest of them?" I missed who asked the question.

Jonim smiled broadly. "Definitely. The lass hit them where it hurt and crippled the ship - they couldn't limp away fast enough. Now the fun part is figuring out how they got on base and if someone hired them."

"You folks certainly brought an epic tale tonight," the owner, whose name escaped me at the moment, said. "Thought it couldn't get much better than when Joni sent the lass my way. Though I don't think she's up for a reprisal this evening."

Heat rushed to my face and I hid it behind taking a drink of water. I hoped the topic of conversation ended there.

"Sounds like she's got more hidden talents than I bargained for," Jonim commented.

I prayed they would stop.

They laughed and thankfully the subject changed. I quietly ate while the larger conversation split off to smaller ones.

Eventually my basket sat empty before me and Silver moved it away before replacing it with more food. *How much does he expect me to eat?* My stomach reminded me I missed a meal earlier.

It did not look like something I would normally order. I looked at my partner.

"Just trust me on this one, okay? I know you usually go for something else, but your body needs fuel."

I raised an eyebrow at him. "Since when did you get into nutrition?"

"Well, you didn't give me much to do in Ghost Forest so I found new ways to keep myself occupied."

I rolled my eyes.

"Just eat."

"*You're such a pain sometimes,*" I said softly.

"Yeah, still can't translate."

I sighed and forced myself to eat. I felt a little better.

"When we're done, what do you want to do?" Silver asked. The others were engaged in another conversation.

With my mouth full, I gave Silver I sidelong glance. I swallowed quickly and asked, "What do you mean?"

"We've been ordered to take a few days off after we finish. Is there anything you want to do while we're here?"

I shrugged. It was not something that crossed my mind. I did not even know what Sandpoint had to offer.

"Anything in particular you're looking for? Adventure? Excitement?" the owner asked, reappearing at the end of the table near us with more food.

"Peace and quiet," I said flatly. "Think I've had my fill of excitement."

He winked at me. "I know just the place. It's a small resort, but I can put in a call and see if they wouldn't mind letting you in for the day."

"The beaches are easier to get to," someone else at the table said.

"Yeah, but they're always packed and loud," another argued.

So was this place, but it did not bother me as much as I thought it would right now. "I'll have to think about it. I've still got work before then."

"You need to stop working right now," Silver chided. "You've been analyzing what happened, haven't you?"

"A little," I admitted. I would not specify what though. It was not something I would classify as work.

Though Silver pointed out what I should be focusing on. I took to mentally cursing Kitteren for putting the idea in my head.

"Do you want to call it a night after you finish?" Silver asked quietly.

I opened my mouth to reply, but someone beat me to it. "Come on! The night is still young. You can't leave this early."

"You idiot, can't you see she's still exhausted? We all fought to get that damnable system operating. Actually using it has to be a few Hells."

"Wait, I don't remember any mention of it in the reports," I said.

"Did you have to get her started?" Silver muttered and took a drink. I wrinkled my nose at the smell. How could he drink that stuff?

"Not surprising," Mason said, "Jake would edit our reports before giving them to the Navy. He insisted it was because we didn't know how to write properly."

"More like he needed a few classes," I said flatly. "I had a hard time reading his papers."

"Papers?" Jonim asked.

I took a sip of water before explaining, "He's published multiple papers about Atlantis. He used to be an archaeologist. That's where he said he got his inspiration for the system."

"How do you go from digging up the past to creating cutting edge weapons technology?" Mason asked.

"More like trying to create and failing," someone out of my view remarked.

"Technically it worked, but I don't want to give him too much credit," Mason corrected.

I needed to read the book I took from his office. But how? There must be a cipher of some sort. I would have to go through more of his belongings.

"Stop working," Silver said sternly.

I looked down and realized I had been tapping the tip of my fork on my plate again. I had done the motion enough times for him to recognize the habit.

Frowning, I said, "I think we're going to need to go through Jake's personal belongings to make sense of it all."

"I'll arrange it," Jonim said, "but only on the condition you do as your partner says."

I sighed and tried to stay engaged in the current ongoings around me. But now I was concerned about the misinformation Jake kept feeding.

At least I had a little more energy and was able to focus more. This celebration still felt premature. There must be more going on.

I LAID in my bed staring at the ceiling. Why would Jake bring the project to the Navy if he planned to sell to the pirates? Why not sell the idea to them directly? Certainly they would be able to acquire the materials and manpower he needed.

Had he simply not known when to keep his mouth shut and tried to hide the problem he found himself in? Why was Sparky taking so long to process the evidence we sent? I needed answers.

Sitting up slowly, I made sure Silver remained resting. I knew I would get lectured if I disturbed him.

And I still felt exhausted, but my mind would not stop.

Sliding out of bed, I quietly padded over to the window, staring out at the city and the base beyond. Was the answer in his papers? In the book? Maybe one of the other books? On the computer we sent off?

I could send a message to Sparky requesting an update. What time was it there? He probably worked late and was asleep. Hopefully not under his desk in the office again. I used to do it and I wished he would not copy my habits.

Resting my forearms on the window, I hung my head. There had to be something else. Something we missed. Was I too close to see the bigger picture?

I shivered slightly at the coolness of the window, but refused to move as my mind ran in circles for a while.

Eventually strong hands pulled me back. Dammit, I hoped I would not wake Silver.

"How long have you been here?" he asked, his voice gentle. I doubted it would last long.

"I don't know."

My partner turned me to face him. "Is it the system?"

"No."

"Are you certain?"

I clenched my teeth. "Yes. You completely broke whatever connection I had to it."

"Then why are you up before me?"

I picked my head up. "What time is it?" It was still dark, though I noticed the sky had lightened to predawn.

"Shortly before dawn."

I had been up all night. I sighed and went to move away from him, but he held onto my shoulders. "Let go."

"No, not until you tell me why you're up."

"I couldn't rest, okay? I rested too much earlier in the day I guess."

"Kela..."

That name made me pause as brief flashes of the faces who used to call me by it crossed my mind. Why now and not previous times? I shook my head slowly. "Don't. Don't call me that."

"I only plan to use it when it's just us. Your secret is safe with me." Thinking on it, he had waited until it was only the two of us.

I clenched my teeth. "That's not what I said."

"And I like it so you're going to have to deal with it."

I sneered at him. What little power I managed to regain pushed at me as my anger rose - a sensation I had not had in a while, though it felt off. The power bled through into my voice. "*I do not...*" The world suddenly became disjointed and my legs gave out from underneath me. All my power was gone.

Silver caught me before I hit the floor. "Kela? Kela!"

"Told you not to call me that," I mumbled into his chest. Why was I so tired now? I closed my eyes.

"Dammit, how are you lower than before?" Silver muttered.

When had I made it back to bed? I squinted at the light in the room. Silver stood at the foot of the bed with a camera pointed at me.

I gave up and put my head back down.

"Are you going to be okay for a few minutes?"

I pulled the covers over my head. Why was he bothering me?

He gave a light laugh. "Okay, just rest. I'll check on you when I'm done."

Silence followed along with a sense of peace and tranquility. I let myself drift in the familiar sensation.

Where did I know it from?

After a while, as the sensation faded, a gentle hand with rough fingers brushed my hair out of my face. I remained still, drifting.

"Dammit, what am I supposed to do?" Silver said softly. "I don't even understand what happened."

"What happened?" I asked, my voice still sounding sleepy.

"You don't remember?"

"Just remember being tired all of a sudden." There was more - there had to be.

Silver slid off the bed and knelt next to it so he could be closer to eye-level with me. "I swear I didn't force you to calm down this time. I really don't know what happened. I don't know how to fix this."

"Fix what?" Why could I not follow what he said? What had I been worked up about? I forced myself to sit up. Silver was distressed about something and I needed to figure out why before I could decide what to do about it.

"How about we reset this conversation? Why were you up, I'm assuming, all night?"

Why? "Couldn't stop thinking about..." I knew that much. I struggled to get more. "The case. Think there's something more, but I don't have enough pieces of the puzzle."

"So nothing to do with the system."

"What? No! We've already been over this."

"Okay, how about what's been on your mind since you woke up in the infirmary?"

"What was...?" I forced down the heat rising to my cheeks. "That can wait." Forever if I had my way. "I'm concerned we're missing something important."

"Okay, just stop right there. No more work right now. You went from about ready to tear my throat out to passed out and I don't know what happened."

I tilted my head and tried to recall what happened. My power had pushed at me as my anger rose. No, that was not quite right.

Closing my eyes I dug past the obvious. My power had not reacted in that manner for months. Not even when Kitteren pushed my patience past the breaking point.

I had been gathering it. Maybe not consciously, but it moved more in that manner than pushing at my restraints. I may have been angry, but I really wanted to run. When I ran out...

Digging my hands into my hair, I groaned at my own stupidity. I had been so mad at him over something so simple and never paid attention to what instincts were running.

A weight landed on the bed and Silver tugged at my hands. "Look at me, please."

I released my hands from my hair, but refused to look up. "I did it to myself."

"How?"

"I wasn't thinking about it - it was more instinctive. I needed to leave and started gathering the energy for... something. To run? I just ran out."

Silver took a long, deep breath. "Where were you planning to go?"

"I don't know. Away is all. I originally thought I was reacting the way I used to, but it was something different."

"The way you used to?"

I rolled my eyes. "Can we stop for now? There's work to be done."

"Only if you promise we'll talk about it later today."

"Why is this so important?"

"So I know what to do if it happens again."

"I think you know by now."

"Okay how about so I know the signs and can avoid it?"

I rolled my eyes. I understood his concern, but there was no helping it once it started. Especially when I did not realize it was happening.

"Hey," Silver said and waited for me to look at him. "We will talk about this later. I really don't want you working until you've gotten more rest, but you're probably going to fight me on it."

"Not probably," I said flatly.

"Yeah, I should know better. Why do you think there's something else going on we need to be concerned about?"

"Why would Jake bother with the military?"

"It's a massive contract, right?"

"Yes, but not the most lucrative. Going into the private sector, he could sell to the highest bidder. And you said it sounded like the meetings he had outside of the base weren't by chance."

"That was the distinct impression I got."

"But how does all of this go unchecked by the military? Jonim seemed to keep quiet out of fear of his job. And why bother with the process? The private sector could supply him with the same opportunity without the oversight."

Silver stroked the small patch of hair on his chin. "Shouldn't we leave this to the others back at the main office and the military? It sounded like they planned on investigating how Spelltech got this far."

I glared at my partner. "I think there's something else going on. The whole set up has been bizarre."

"Okay, okay. We'll look, but we need to turn it over to the others to deal with."

I nodded. Unless there was something we needed to immediately deal with of course.

"I THINK WE FINALLY FOUND IT," Silver said after he pulled off yet another panel. "Surprised it was this far away. Also surprised there's this much wiring between the station and the amplifier."

"If you think about it, there would be far more wiring on something the size of a battleship. Plus it also makes sense to want to protect the amplifier," I replied.

Silver insisted I let him do most of the work finding the source while I wrote up the reports I was backlogged on.

I moved the portable keyboard for my tablet and got up, wanting to see what he found. Silver dug out the camera and took pictures.

Standing on the balls of my feet, I peered over his shoulder to the damage within. Halfway through the wiring burnt out.

"Is there anything in the bottom that looks like it could have triggered it?" It made no sense for it to be burnt out not connected directly to something.

My partner turned his handlight down. "There's some debris in here. Not sure if it's related."

"Can I see?"

Silver turned to look down at me. "Are you done with those reports?"

"Almost. Let me see. I'll know what we're looking for now that Sparks pointed it out."

"I can handle this," Silver argued.

"Please? I've done this enough times in the lab." I really wanted to see if it was sabotage or some random element connected which burned out.

Though there would be little reason for there to be an element here.

He sighed, fully turning to frown down at me. "Look, do not touch." Then he gave me his handlight.

"I can get gloves."

"No. I really don't want you near the system at all, but you're better at this than I am. I almost lost you the last time you were in there."

I had not the nerve to tell him I wanted to give up. I could put up with his overprotective behavior.

Shining the handlight down in the direction Silver said, I saw the debris. I knelt down to get closer and twisted to get a better look without touching the wires.

The wires moved and I glanced up to see my partner holding them out of my way. "Thanks."

I turned my attention back to the debris on the floor inside the wall. The pieces were certainly bigger than the ones in the ceiling. It appeared to have been clamped around the wires. It must have had a lot of power to send feedback all the way to the station.

Was it sabotage? Was it a repeater? I turned my handlight back above to look at the wires. The wires would have been spliced into a repeater.

I sighed and sat back on my heels. This would have to go back to the lab for full analysis.

"Done?" Silver asked. By his tone, I could tell his patience was thin.

"Yeah. I want to say it was sabotage, but I'm not certain if it was a repeater or not."

"Repeater? Haven't seen anything else of the sort so far."

"I'm fairly certain it shouldn't have been there, but I don't want to claim it until Sparks can process it."

"Alright, let me finish up here while you complete those reports."

I frowned and gave him back his handlight. We all had our tasks and Silver hated writing reports. Thinking on it, he would have submitted reports for what happened with the system. I bit my lower lip as I got settled. Should I read the ones he submitted? Would it put my mind at ease over what occurred?

Silver's back was to me and I could skim them quickly. I dove through the case file, looking for the reports Silver filed recently. I found the one in regards to nearly getting run over after the tire on our vehicle was slashed. There was one with what he learned at Watered Down.

Finally I found the one of our test of the system. Opening it, I was surprised at how short it was, but he always kept his words precise. He spoke about his interaction with the system and then the report stopped.

Raising an eyebrow at the half-report, I backed out and looked for the rest. Why would he divide it up?

I could not find it. Even his report about the attempted theft barely mentioned I used the system and nothing about me being stuck in the system. I leaned back against the wall and crossed my legs at the ankles. This was absolutely strange.

"You're supposed to be typing," Silver said, his voice muffled from inside the wall.

I mentally cursed the fact the keyboard clicks were loud. Should I ask about his missing reports? Granted, I omitted certain details also, but for Silver, it was downright strange. He may keep his words to a minimum, but normally he made sure to note everything.

He backed out of the wall and turned to look at me. He held a bag in his hands with what looked like the debris from the floor inside the wall. "Alright, what are you doing?"

"I, um..." The tablet in my hands was suddenly far more interesting. "Just reading."

"Reading what?" he asked as he filled out the form on the bag.

I hesitated. Would he be mad if I told him I read his reports? They were in the case file. "Just refreshing my memory on a couple of things."

"Like what?"

I shook my head and pulled my keyboard back onto my lap before precariously balancing my tablet so I could get back to writing. I needed to get back on task.

"Hey, what were you trying to remember?" Silver asked, squatting down next to me.

"I'm sorry, I read through your reports because some things still don't make sense to me. You omitted some events so I'll just have to figure it out."

"Lockonis ordered me to send her more detailed reports directly. I think she wanted to keep others from seeing it who don't need to. I still have them on my tablet. Let me finish up here and then we can get this stuff sent out and head for lunch."

Now I found myself torn between being relieved he was still thorough and embarrassed about what his reports might contain. It made it difficult to focus on the report I should be writing.

Not that explaining the sensation of being locked in the system was easy to begin with. The more I thought about it the more I sounded crazy to myself.

"Want to talk about it? You haven't said much about what it was like in there. Might help put the pieces together."

"No thanks," I said quickly.

"How about when you let go this last time?" It was impossible to miss the anger in Silver's voice.

I clenched my fists. "I had nothing left."

"There's more than that, isn't there?"

Clenching my teeth, I glared at my tablet even though it was innocent in all of this. He would never understand the draw.

"I understand you were exhausted, but why let go?"

I took a deep breath and rubbed my face, hiding from my partner for a brief moment. "I was so tired and I needed to rest. If I let go, I could recover for a little while. Once the fighting ended and I backed out of the systems it was so peaceful in there."

"And then you held on when you got out."

"I was afraid of falling back in. Look, I know it doesn't make sense and I've been trying to make sense of it since it happened."

Silver let out a soft huff. "No wonder you've been irrational."

I glared up at him.

"I'm not being a jerk. I'm fairly certain I would be also given the circumstances."

Shaking my head, I packed my things. I needed to get out of here. It was cold, the floor was hard, and I was hungry. Mostly I needed to get away from the system and any reminder of what happened.

"With this, we're technically done. I'm guessing you don't want to be."

Taking a moment to stand up, I hiked my gear bag up on my shoulder. "I really think there's something else going on. There are far too many inconsistencies."

"It could simply be Jake wasn't a good business owner or wanted to sell to multiple parties. Why not use the military's resources to develop the system?"

Sometimes I attempted to dig too much when it was a simple answer. But to develop such a complex system that tempted pirates enough into trying to steal from the military? And what about the lack of actual oversight?

Who sabotaged the system? At least the part we were certain about.

17

JONIM OPENED the door to Jake's apartment and my heart sank. It looked like someone ransacked the place. Either that or he was a slob. Given the original office we dealt with, I remained uncertain.

The mound of dishes led me to believe the latter more.

"I'd like to tell you this is just how he was, but I ain't never seen his place before today. Hard to believe he could afford a place like this. Treated it poorly."

Now that Jonim mentioned it, once one looked past the mess, it was an impressive place. The woodwork throughout and stonework on the counters and around the fireplace alone appeared expensive. I picked my way carefully through the apartment. Where to start?

Silver stood next to me. "Are you sure you want to go through this?"

"I can do it myself if you want to start your downtime early." I needed him to stop doubting me.

My partner folded his arms. "No, I'm not leaving you to work yourself to death. I'm just not sure if we're going to find anything here. I don't immediately see anything telling us he worked here."

I pursed my lips while I thought on it. Silver had a point, but we could only see the common, kitchen, and dining areas. This place seemed pretty large and there might be an office.

Then there was also the fact we needed to check-in at the front desk downstairs. I turned to Jonim. "Is it possible to get a list of the people who visited Jake?"

Jonim stroked his beard. "Don't see why not. I'll go ask. You two okay here?"

"Yes, thank you." I gave our escort a short bow.

Once the door closed, Silver asked, "What're you thinking?"

"The people he had been seen meeting. They could have come here to do business. I'd like to know who we're dealing with."

"Who Naval Command is dealing with," he corrected.

"You know what I meant. Having background information on these individuals will help put this thing into perspective." I moved forward into the apartment, wanting to get a better idea of the layout, taking pictures as I went.

Reaching with a gloved hand, I opened the first door in the hall-way. Bathroom. I continued down the hall, opening the next door across the hall from the first. This looked promising - a small office with another computer. I planned to come back to this one.

Further down the hall was Jake's bedroom. It had a large walk-in closet and the moment I opened the door to the attached bathroom, I was shoved back. My head hit something hard as I fell.

The world went out of focus and I could make out the colors of Silver fighting the person who I assumed pushed me. Voices were distorted. My partner yelled at the person as he pinned whoever it was to the floor.

Then the pounding began. I struggled against the disorientation and the pain to get up. What if there was another here?

"Dammit, stay down!" Silver barked. Who was he ordering?

Then it sounded like he spoke with someone else at a rapid pace. This case had been nothing but a chain of headaches.

I managed to get to my hands and knees when Silver yelled again, "I said stay down! I'll knock him out and sit on you instead."

Me? Why should I stay down?

Suddenly there were more people. Someone pulled me back to sit against the wall.

I jumped when two sets of unknown gloved hands reached for me. I backed away, but could only plaster myself against the wall and let out a distressed whine. Everything remained out of focus and voices distant despite the people talking directly in front of me.

"Can you give me a minute?" Silver's voice cut through the white noise. "I'll help you with her."

The hands backed away. They kept talking. Why did my partner's voice cut through?

People moved about. Eventually a figure who looked like Silver came over and knelt down in front of me. "Ketayl, what's going on? How badly are you hurt?"

"I don't know," I whispered, but it sounded like I might as well be screaming. "Hard to hear and everything is blurry."

"Can you let these people check you? I'll be nearby."

Sitting still was the best answer I could give. Maybe now he would believe me about there being something else going on.

It took a few more minutes before I could make out other voices. Longer for my vision to clear and by that point I held a cold pack to my head.

The Dwarven woman of the pair combed through my hair gently with her fingers searching for where the blood had come from. I kept shifting the cold pack out of her way. The Dwarven man who accompanied her was busy writing something down.

Silver argued with another Dwarven man on the other side of the room. Jonim stood over our intruder who was tied up on the floor. The side arm in the Commander's hand never wavered even as he joined my partner's conversation.

Great, another call to Lockonis was coming and now I needed to explain why I insisted on pushing for more. With my luck she would order us off the case.

The headaches just kept coming.

Silver came back over to us. "How is she?"

"Fading in and out. No loss of consciousness though so that's good news," the male Dwarven medic answered.

"Concussion?" Silver asked.

The Dwarven medic tilted his head, looking at me. "I'm fairly certain, but it's been hard to tell how bad. Her symptoms are all over the place."

Silver gave a short laugh. "Well, it's not the first one this week."

I glared up at Silver. This had gotten ridiculous.

"That good of a week, huh? We can take her to the hospital, but I'm not sure they'll figure out much else without doing a bunch of scans," the male Dwarven medic said.

"No," I said firmly.

Silver sighed, looking down at me. "You sure? I can handle things here and come pick you up later."

"I'm sure. No hospitals," I stated firmly.

"Okay, okay. Geez, you can be so stubborn," Silver conceded.

"It may still happen if I can ever find the cut," the Dwarven woman who combed through my hair said. "I'd rather have them handle closing it with as much hair as you have."

"No," I reaffirmed.

"That means you'll have to let me do it," Silver chimed in.

I rolled my eyes and sat still. My head cleared slowly. Maybe I just needed the cold pack.

What I really needed was to get back to work. Why did this have to get more complicated? Why could I not have listened and let it be?

"Any chance you know why he was in here?" I asked. I needed something to focus on.

"No, he shut right up," Silver said, folding his arms. "I'll try again when we have a better place to talk. Since he's a civilian and on private property, he's going to be held by the local law enforcement until we can send him somewhere else."

Silver really had things under control. I felt even worse for just sitting here while people poked and prodded at me.

"And if you keep this up, I'm not going to be able to heal you for a while," my partner added.

Because I absorbed divine energy for whatever reason. I could not use it, but I would become over-saturated and needed to wait between sessions when he healed my shoulder last summer.

Silver eventually joined in combing through my hair, but between the two of them, they had no luck finding the cut. The medics packed up and left as did everyone else, except Jonim.

My partner finger combed my hair, getting it back into some semblance of order. I still nursed the cold pack.

Jonim was on the phone and walked out of the room. I could hear him continuing down the hall. It sounded like he was having about as good of a day as I was.

Silver knelt down in front of me as soon as I felt him tie off the end of my hair. "Okay, how did you do it?"

"Do what?"

"Heal yourself. I found where the cut should have been, but I wanted to keep this between us."

I tilted my head in confusion. "I didn't heal myself."

"Then how in the Hells did it heal? And you're far more coherent than when they first began examining you."

I pulled the item in my hand away from my head. "Cold pack?"

Silver sighed right before he took my head in his hands and leaned his forehead against mine. I pulled back, but his grip, while not painful, was firm and I was unable to move.

It was a minute or so before he backed away. "The divine energy you absorbed is disappearing rapidly and if you had a concussion, it's gone now."

What he said made no sense. I absorbed it before and it never acted this way. "Can we save this for another time? I'd really like to get what we need to done and get out of here before I find any more surprises."

"Yeah. I'm going to need to do some research anyway."

I raised an eyebrow at him. "Never thought I'd hear you voluntarily doing research."

"I do it all the time in what interests me."

"Like?" Now he had my curiosity.

"I'll leave that for you to figure out." The broad grin on his face told me he thought this was a game.

Shaking my head, I made my way back down the hall to the office. Jonim sounded like he was in the front set of rooms.

I put my bag down just inside the door and dropped the cold pack next to it. This room was less of a disaster, but still enough of a mess it could take a while.

"Hey," Silver said quietly. His tone got me to stop and look up at him. "Don't overdo it, okay? If we need to, we'll come back another day."

"And find someone else hiding in his bathroom?"

"The military is assigning a detail and I've requested the security footage. To get more than just this guy though, we'll probably have to contact Lockonis to get the proper paperwork."

I sighed, my shoulder slumping. "Can we not tell her about this?"

"She already knows. You missed most of the conversations."

This was not my week. I leaned over the short chair and powered up the computer. Getting what we needed and out of here was my top priority.

Something cold rested against my head. "I don't need it," I told Silver.

"Humor me."

The computer immediately went to the main screen - I never saw a login request. Poor security?

The background caught my attention. It was a propaganda piece from the Free Terra Foundation. While not personally familiar with the group, I got the idea from the image they wanted the Terran Council dissolved and for the territories to be free to govern themselves.

Last I knew the territories were free to govern their own way for the most part, but the Terran Council handled issues on a global scale. The group was something I would need to research.

"Ketayl," Silver said softly, "We need to get this to the main office. This looks much larger than we can handle."

I clenched my jaw, knowing he was right, but wanting to do this myself. Sighing, I caved, hoping perhaps this would extend our duties further. "Yeah, I'll shut it down and dismantle it. Let's get this out right off. We can come back for the rest."

"You two are done."

I turned upon hearing Vince's voice. Why was the director of the TIO here? Two others who I had not met before stood outside the door to the small office.

"I've already gotten the reports you found the source. That was the extent of your duties. Pack up and get out of here - go finish updating the case file. Start your downtime tomorrow," Vince ordered. He signaled the two men with him to enter.

I looked nervously at the men who flanked us. "Sir, I think there's more to this."

Vince eyed me for a moment. "There is, but it isn't your job to continue the hunt."

"Why not?" I could not leave this partway done. We had come this far.

I shifted back as Vince moved to stand over me. It was not often I could sense the power rolling off of him, and right now he made it hard to breathe. My own pushed back enough so I could continue to stand my ground.

Vince stared me down. "You cannot take on a faceless organization such as the Free Terra Foundation. I'm not risking the two of you further. Get going."

Silver put his hand on my shoulder. "Come on. We have our orders."

I stood my ground. I came here for a job and I intended to complete it.

"I'll have you removed if I have to," Vince said.

I clenched my teeth, glaring up at the director. I finally looked away and stormed over to my bag, gathering my things. I told myself fighting over this was not worth potentially losing my job.

It did not help. I bit the inside of my mouth, to quiet my agitated power. Rarely did it respond to my emotional state since I broke whatever spell had been put on my reserves a few months ago.

Setting off at a quick pace from the apartment, I punched the elevator button and stalked back and forth, waiting. Silver remained silent all the way back to our vehicle.

"Kela, what in the Hells has gotten into you?" Silver snapped at me once we were in our vehicle.

I clenched my teeth at his continuing use of that name, but unless I could come up with a better reason than I disliked it, he was going to ignore me.

"Me?" I snarled at him. "We had this. Why didn't you back me up?!" I think that stung more than being pulled off of the case.

"Because I'm tired of watching you get hurt!"

I sat back, staring at Silver with wide-eyes. The previous thought of I did not know him returned.

"I can't protect you from an unknown enemy. This is one fight we need to walk away from."

"I don't need you to protect me," I grumbled at him.

"Yeah, because I sure as Hells don't know how to protect you from yourself." Silver threw the vehicle into gear and we left. He was still mad, but his driving was at least controlled.

"What's that supposed to mean?"

Silver merely growled at me and continued driving in silence. What was going on with him? I needed to focus. Get the remainder of the information filed and then I could take some time away from my partner.

———

"Kela…" Silver said softly. He finished whatever he was working on a while ago and sat across the room watching me.

I clenched my teeth at the name.

"Ketayl, you need a break. We should talk."

"Not interested," I snapped.

Silver took a deep breath before continuing. "No, you need to understand why I chose the path I did."

I continued getting images uploaded and tagged.

"I may not have backed you up with the Director, but we can't take on an organization like that. There's a pretty good chance they were or at least worked with the pirates. We can't be a visible part of this case."

I stopped and tilted my head at him, dropping my tablet to my lap.

"We're already after one faceless organization, do you really want to take on another?"

I shook my head and returned to my work. It was true we normally trailed one, but it felt wrong giving up this far in.

"Talk to me?"

I sighed, putting my tablet aside. "I don't like leaving this unfinished."

"I never said I did, but this isn't our fight. They know who we are - we have to leave and let someone else take over. They've come after us more than once already and I'm fairly certain they aren't happy they were unable to acquire the ship. We should probably go to Watered Down tonight."

I raised an eyebrow at him. How did he go to reasoning why we needed to leave the case to food?

"They deal in information, right? All we have to do is let it out that we're off the case and hopefully we'll be left alone the rest of the time we're in Sandpoint."

I bit my lower lip considering his words. Vince must have foreseen the same thing. I had gotten too focused on the task at hand. "Fine."

Leaving work unfinished still did not sit well with me. Given that thought, I picked up my tablet again to continue working.

"What do you want to do with our downtime?" Silver asked.

"I haven't thought about it. I'd like to spend it alone." I had a lot to think about and it would be better without Silver around.

"That's not a good idea."

"Silver, I…" I paused, trying to come up with a much more polite way to say what I wanted, but gave up. "I really need some time alone."

He came over and knelt down next to me, touching my cheek gently. "And you can have it when we get back. Right now it'll be safer if we stick together."

I sighed and shifted away from him before rubbing the bridge of my nose. Was there any possible way to get out of this? I understood the dangers we currently faced, but I knew he would want to take the opportunity to talk. I needed to think through everything and come to my own conclusions first.

"What're you thinking?" Silver asked softly. He reached for me again and I moved away.

"I need time to think without any outside influences," I said.

"Then let's see if there's any information floating about someone wanting us before we decide on a course of action." Silver stood, grabbing his wallet off of the nightstand. "Besides, it's getting late and I'm hungry."

"You're starting to sound like Sparks," I said, putting my tablet aside.

"I've been keeping an eye on him because someone's got to make sure he doesn't fall into your habits." Silver held a hand out to me.

I rolled my eyes and took the offered hand. He stayed still after I was on my feet.

Looking up, his attention was down at me. Was he lost in thought on something? "I thought you were hungry."

"Yeah. Yeah, I am." Finally Silver backed away so I could have some room.

"I'm not going to have to pay to get the information out, am I?"

Silver smirked at me. "I'd love it if you did, but I think we've got enough credit there to cover."

Then I would refuse to get up on stage again.

18

IT WAS busy again at Watered Down. As we were led to our table, I stiffened up, feeling eyes on me, but could not tell if they were friend or foe. Thankfully we got a table where I felt a little less exposed.

Silver leaned across the table, taking my hand in his. "What's wrong?" he asked just loud enough to be heard over the noise.

I bit my lower lip, debating if I should say anything, but the last time I had this sensation, he took me seriously. "Do you feel like you're being watched?"

He tilted his head, eying me carefully. "No, but I'm not as attuned to it as you are. Good or bad?"

"I don't know. Couldn't tell when we were in Mystic Port either."

Silver let out a soft huff. "You had both trailing you then."

I caught sight of the owner making his way over to our table and pulled my hand back. "Ah, my favorite Elven couple. Bring me anythin' else good?"

"No," Silver answered first. "We've been taken off of the assignment. I'm afraid we'll be leaving soon. Just hoping to get a few quiet days."

"A shame. Lass, any chance I can convince you to take the mic one more time before you leave?"

I shook my head. "Not tonight."

"Keep it in mind. Oh, I need to make that call for you. See if my friend has room for two more. I'll make sure I get you an answer before you leave. I'm afraid I can't settle my debt with you tonight, but..." The owner paused, stroking his beard. "I might be able to, but not in the traditional way. I'll get back to you." He waved and left.

I tilted my head, confused about what just occurred. This might be more problematic than I wanted.

"Have you figured out what you want to eat?" Silver asked, breaking me out of my thoughts.

I picked up my menu to refocus, but my mind continued wandering back to the short conversation. I chose something I had ordered previously before returning to the puzzle at hand. It felt like I witnessed a secret coded conversation between Silver and the owner.

"Talk to me?" Silver asked, rubbing the back of my hand with his thumb. When had he taken my hand again?

This was more like the Silver I knew, but his actions during this assignment still bothered me. I pulled my hand away again. "I think I missed what actually went on during that conversation."

"I'm not entirely certain either, but we'll have to wait and see what Caradoc says when he comes back."

Silence fell between us and was only temporarily broken when we placed our orders. A vaguely familiar face came up to the table. "Hey! Haven't seen you two since you came in for those files." I searched for a name in my memory. Was it Aris?

"Sorry I haven't had a chance to make good on getting drinks," Silver said.

Aris waved off the apology. "You two have been busy. Been the talk of the base."

I bit my lower lip and stared at my glass of water. With knowing there were people on base who should not have been, it was not good news to me.

"We finished what we came here to do so we'll be leaving soon," Silver said.

I looked up when I caught movement. Aris sat down next to Silver. "Too bad. You guys livened up the place. The only entertainment we got outside of the casters fighting was Mr. Martin losing his mind over something," our Navy friend said.

Perhaps there was more to us being removed than simply attempting to take our duties too far. If we caused as many problems on the base as Aris suggested, it was no wonder they wanted us gone. Had we really caused so many problems?

"Ketayl?"

I looked up at Silver. "Sorry, just thinking about how much trouble we caused for them."

"Nah, you guys gave us something to talk about. We don't have much to do without any major projects going on and Spelltech didn't actually want our help for anything."

"Really?" I asked. Aris had my attention.

"Yeah, anyone who got assigned was either kicked out within a couple of weeks or ended up relegated to guarding empty rooms. Not many people got a chance to actually look at the projects Spelltech had going on. Didn't sound like any of them were functioning though. Except for the ship system and we didn't think it worked until the fireworks started."

Silver turned his attention to our friend. "It was never mentioned the system had been operational before that?"

Aris downed the rest of his drink. "No. Well, there were rumors someone finally got it up and running, but without them taking the ship out for a full test, we assumed it was just Mr. Martin going off again."

I shook my head and took a sip of water. I hoped Silver dropped it there. If we were the talk of the base, adding information about me operating the system only made me a bigger target. I could not afford to have Silver getting caught up in the potential fallout.

The appetizer Silver ordered showed up. He slid the basket of breaded cheese sticks over to me. He looked down at Aris. "Can I get you a refill?"

He looked at my partner for a moment. "Yeah, I'd appreciate it."

They slid out of the booth and Silver patted my shoulder before he left. Wrinkling my nose at not understanding what was going on, I focused on the food in front of me. Why was Silver always wanting to feed me so much?

And what was going on with him?

The momentary feeling of loneliness was overridden by the sense of being watched. It disappeared temporarily when Aris came over. Or maybe I had been too distracted.

I scanned the area to see where Silver had gone. He stood over Aris at the bar, leaning down to talk with him. After both of them received their drinks and my partner paid, Silver leaned down to speak directly to Aris' ear.

I turned away at the intimate display. I pushed the basket of food away and closed my eyes. I really did not know the man who I considered my closest friend.

"Can't say I saw that comin'," Caradoc commented. "Guess I can't figure them all out, though you Elves are always tough."

Glancing up at the owner, I picked up my glass of water. "I apparently don't know him either."

"Cheer up, lass. I brought you some good news."

I raised an eyebrow at the Dwarven man.

He handed me a brochure. "Won't be able to schedule any of their services since they're overbooked, but my friend said you're welcome to enjoy the private beach. They're very discernin' about their clients so you won't have to worry about someone causin' a ruckus."

I looked at the brochure. "Thank you. I'm not sure what we're doing yet."

"I think you'll enjoy the quiet. Read through it when you get a chance. There are also a number of museums and the such in the area if you're into that sort of thing. Talk it over with your boy. I'm sure the two of you can make the most out of the time you have." Caradoc patted my shoulder and left.

I cringed at the sensation. I wished people would not touch me.

The brochure in my hands felt a little stiff in the center. I opened it to find a business card. Flipping it over, it read: "Relax, you two are covered."

I raised an eyebrow at the message. I missed something. I tucked the card away in my pocket and looked through the brochure. The Sandrock Resort claimed to be the best Sandpoint had to offer. It continued on to the amenities and I mostly skimmed it, looking at the pictures provided. I guess I could pretend to be a tourist and the private beach looked like it would be quiet.

Silver slid into the booth across from me. "You haven't eaten."

"Not hungry." I kept my eyes on the brochure. "Where's your friend?"

"He was waiting for his husband. They're seated over closer to the stage. Nice people."

What I witnessed and what Silver said refused to add up in my head. I shoved it into the growing pile of not understanding Silver. A pile which bothered me more the larger it grew.

The brochure disappeared from my hands and the basket reappeared. "I said I wasn't hungry," I shot at him.

Silver sighed. "No, you're being stubborn. You need to eat. Did Caradoc say anything?"

I glared at my partner for a moment before relenting and picking up one of the breaded cheese sticks. "We're welcome to use the private beach, but they're overbooked for any services. Also suggested checking out some of the museums."

By the movement, I could tell Silver flipped the end of his braid back and forth on his lap. What on Terra was he contemplating? I yanked the card out of my pocket in frustration and tossed it across the table at him. "Here, since you seem to know what's going on."

He slowly picked up the card, watching me. He read the information before he slid out his seat and came over to my side. Silver reached to wrap his arm around my shoulders as he sat down and I pushed myself away from him. I was done with all of this. I would take the cold and the snow if it meant being left alone.

"Hey, settle down. Let me explain," Silver said quietly.

"Do it from the other side of the table."

"Ketayl, just give me a moment, okay?"

I glared at him, but where was I going to go? I was stuck between him and the wall. I crossed my arms and sat still, forcing myself to not react to him putting his arm around my shoulders.

"Easy." I shuddered at his warm breath on my ear. "I'm sorry I haven't been better about keeping you updated. What this card means is that they're going to keep an eye out for us while we're still here to keep any potential trouble at bay. The resort will be an easy safe place." He rubbed the side of my neck with the back of his fingers.

I wanted to shove Silver away, but he was giving me information. I was unsure if I could hold out through the end of what he planned to tell me.

"When we get back, we should plan out our remaining time as well plan for if something does happen."

I bit my lower lip in contemplation. He was so far ahead of me in thought. I struggled to figure out how all of this happened without my notice.

"Think you could also stop looking so angry for a bit?" Silver nuzzled my ear with his nose.

I shifted away as much as I could. "You're done." I pointed at his side of the table. I did not give a damn about anything else he had to say at the moment.

My partner sighed and moved away. Once he sat down on his side again he said, "I'm sorry. I guess I got carried away."

I forced myself to eat what was in front of me so I kept my mouth shut on what I wanted to say. Eventually it would get said, but not here where information was so readily acquired and traded.

WHEN WE GOT BACK to the hotel, Silver excused himself to go clean up. I plugged my phone in and paced for a minute, deciding on a course of action. I stopped when I saw his tablet on his bed. I picked it up and sat down on the chair in the corner. He said I could read his reports.

Using my power to feel through the electronic locks, it opened to a book he had been reading. I knew he had a preference for under-cover law enforcement stories, but the few paragraphs in front of me felt a lot like how this evening went at Watered Down. Except I was unaware of the part I was supposed to play.

Snarling at the device, I got up and tossed it back on his bed, grabbed my room key and left. I hit the elevator button with more force than necessary, stalking back and forth while I waited for one to arrive.

It was not long before I was downstairs and out the main doors. I turned along the walking path with no route or destination in mind. The sun began to set and I cared none for how it looked. I knew I should calm down and think through what happened rationally. I just refused to at the moment.

By the time I calmed down enough, I found myself on a path surrounded by trees. The sun had dropped below the horizon and the last bits of daylight were fading quickly. Where was I?

I reached for my phone, patting my empty pocket. In my haste, I left it behind on the charger. I hung my head at how blind I had been in my anger.

"Alone and disarmed without a way to call for help. Not the wisest choice."

I jumped and turned at the voice. Arcane energy already gathered in my hands. I stood down when I realized it was Vince.

"Though technically I suppose you're never disarmed and I'm certain you could make enough noise to get help. Doesn't answer the question of why you're out here alone."

I glared up at him. "I need time to think, sir," I snapped.

"Still testy I see. I didn't pull you for a lack of competence or to punish. I wanted you to complete your task, but it's too dangerous to keep you on this assignment. I won't take away the downtime Lockonis promised, but despite the friends you've made here, I don't want the two of you separated. It takes time to get an enemy like this shifted to chasing someone else, especially with the wounds you gave them."

I clenched my teeth and paced, not yet calm enough to have this conversation.

"Do I have to order you to stay together?"

Taking a deep breath, I resigned myself to my fate. "No, sir."

"Good, now head back, finish up, and get some rest."

"I, um..." I looked back down the path I had been walking and bit my lower lip. Now it was completely dark. "I'm not sure where I am."

"I'll let him guide you back," Vince said, motioning with his chin at the tall figure running down the path.

I stepped forward and squinted. Then I caught sight of the long braid swinging behind him. Silver. I was not yet ready to deal with him. Turning back to tell Vince that, the director was gone. I scanned the area around me quickly, but there was no sign of the man.

Silver stopped next to me, his hands on his knees, trying to catch his breath. "Dammit, Kela. Don't run off on me like that."

I folded my arms and turned away from him.

"We talked about this: it's not safe to be separated."

"You could have stayed in the room," I shot at him.

"Kela..." Silver stood in front of me and went to brush my bangs back.

I pushed his hand away. "I'm not a character in one of your books!"

"What?" The word came out of his mouth so softly I nearly missed it. He stared at me with wide eyes. "I never said you were."

"Then what was that earlier at the restaurant?"

"I, um…" Silver looked down at the ground, rubbing the back of his head. "Like I said, I'm sorry I got carried away. I never meant to make you uncomfortable."

I growled at him and stalked back and forth, trying to calm back down. I ran my my hand over my hair and tugged the ends of my long bangs. This was getting us nowhere.

"I guess I owe you a name," Silver said.

"What?"

He tugged on his braid for a moment. "You told me your name so I guess I owe you the name of who I'm interested in."

"No! I don't even want to know," I snapped. "You can keep it to yourself."

After a minute of silence, Silver sighed. "Why don't we head back? Maybe take a detour along the way."

I paused and raised an eyebrow at him. "Fine." Being out here was not getting work done.

I let Silver lead. Part of me felt bad for responding the way I did, but I had not had enough time to think straight. Perhaps tonight while he rested I could work through the conflicts in my head.

One thing did nag at my mind. "How did you know where I was?"

Silver turned his eyes to the ground. "When you didn't answer, I called to have you tracked. I thought something might have happened to you."

Tilting my head, I tried to figure out how someone tracked me. "I accidentally left my phone in the room."

"I noticed, but your watch can still be tracked."

I looked down at the small device attached to my wrist. *Traitor*. It showed the time and a notification I missed his call. "I didn't even notice you called. Sorry."

He reached as if to touch my hair and then backed away. "It's okay. You're safe and that's all that matters."

Silence again fell between us. The path split and he headed down what seemed to be away from the hotel.

"Um, isn't it this way?" I asked, standing at the split.

"Yes, but I want to take a detour."

I bit my lower lip and stared down the path we should be taking. "We should finish our work first."

"It can wait. Come on." Silver came back and grabbed my hand, tugging me along the path of his choice.

"But the Director said…"

"We can take an hour or so." Silver turned back to me with a smirk on his face.

The path went around a small pond with shops on the other side. Silver insisted on getting a snack and we walked back the way we came as we ate.

He stopped me and pointed at a bench on the side by the pond. This was more like the Silver I knew, but something was still off. With our food long gone, he sat there staring at the water, flipping the end of his braid back and forth.

I stayed quiet, unsure what would happen if I broke his moment. After a couple of minutes, he stood up, walking closer to the edge of the water.

"There's an idea I've been wanting to propose to you for a while now," he said without turning around. "It seems to be both the perfect and the worst time for it."

I crossed my arms and sat back, waiting.

"Just, hear me out, okay?" Now he turned around to look at me. He tugged on his braid nervously.

I nodded.

Silver turned away from me again, taking a few steps. "I, um… Well, since… Dammit!" He pulled hard on his braid.

"Just say it."

My partner stopped and looked at me. "Sorry. It's just… Never mind. We both grew up around Humans and are used to Human customs, right?"

I raised an eyebrow at him. "I wouldn't necessarily consider the Arcane College the epitome of Human custom."

He gave a short laugh. "I guess you've got me there. My point is I've been wanting to explore what it means to be Elven and I hoped you might explore it with me."

His proposal made me sit up straighter. "Meaning?"

Silver knelt down in front of me. "Kela, there's no one else I would want to take this journey with. I'm not going to push you into anything you don't want to do, but maybe we could give it a try. At least for the remaining time we're here."

I sat back in my seat. It was not the answer I had been looking for.

"I need further clarification on your proposal." Then I realized I had gotten comfortable with him using that name. It should concern me, but my attention was split at the moment.

My partner sat back down next to me. He was certainly fidgety. "You were talking to Kitteren recently about Elven custom, right?"

Then it clicked what he proposed. "Oh, um..." Heat rose to my face. "I don't think that's a good idea. Not with me."

Silver brushed my bangs back. "It might help you stop being afraid of your power. We'll take it one step at a time. Think of it as a way to explore without the commitment of a romantic relationship."

I bit my lower lip and looked down at my hands folded in my lap. He had an interesting proposal, but it still sounded too dangerous. I found myself too confused given what occurred during this trip to give an answer. "Why did you say this was both the perfect and the worst time?"

"It's the worst time because I'm probably only complicating things for you."

"And perfect?"

Silver gave a short laugh. "Because our downtime here seems like a prime opportunity to start."

"I appreciate the offer, but..."

"Please try. Just for the time we're here," Silver blurted out. He quickly took my hand and threaded his fingers through mine. "This is all I ask to start. It doesn't have to become something much more than this unless you want to."

I stared at our intertwined hands. We had shared more than this before his proposal. I wanted to see no harm in it, but between my growing power and the potential hidden enemies...

"We need to stick together anyway, right? It can't hurt." Silver sounded desperate.

I closed my eyes, trying to end the internal conflict. It would be better if I was on my own, but if I did not stay with him, I would be ordered to. It mattered not what I wanted. Three days - I could survive three days of his proposal. "Alright."

Silver stood quickly and pulled me from the bench into a tight hug, kissing the top of my hair. I hoped I could get some understanding of his recent behavior through this.

19

I STARED at the ceiling from my bed. *What did I agree to?* The sky began to lighten meaning I spent the entire night making sense of it all.

I had been unable to figure out Silver's erratic behavior. Or how I felt about what had occurred.

I spent so much of my life being concerned about the well being of others that I put my own priority last. Putting myself front and center in this was both foreign and uncomfortable. Had I agreed because I simply wanted to make Silver happy?

But how he acted while retaking the ship... It was as if he never gave killing them a second thought. Was there something I missed? Was it something from his past? For as much as he attempted to pry into my life, he rarely ever said anything about himself.

I rolled over onto my stomach and pushed my pillow out of the way, resting my chin on my arms. Between all of the previous fights and training sessions we went through together, I had never seen him as aggressive as he had been during that fight.

A weight rested on the side of the bed before a large hand rested on my back. "Please tell me you haven't been up all night again," Silver said softly.

"Then I won't tell you," I muttered.

"Kela..." He stroked my hair. "What is going on? Why couldn't you rest?"

"Needed time to think," I muttered.

"And?"

"Didn't get anywhere."

Silver sighed. "I'd ask if you want to talk about it, but I think I know the answer."

I huffed lightly.

"Come sit with me? Maybe the dawn will illuminate an answer for you."

I held my tongue. I had sat with him during his morning rituals before and it was simply a time of peace and quiet for me. The sun would provide me with no answers. I waved him out of the way so I could get up.

Silver knelt on his bed and I moved the chair at the desk to face the window. He looked at me. "You can sit with me."

"I'm fine." I knew what I agreed to, but I still planned on keeping my distance as much as possible.

My partner frowned, but turned his attention back out the window. The clouds in the distance might bring rain. Perhaps I should check the weather for the day. We had yet to plan how to spend our downtime. I reached for my tablet.

Before I could pick it up, there was a hand over mine. How fast had he moved? "Whatever it is, it can wait," Silver said gently. He took my hand in his. "Come sit with me so you can focus."

"I was checking the weather."

He kissed the back of my hand. "And it can wait. Come on."

I sighed and let him lead me. I only had to put up with this for three days, though hiding from him on the flight back would be next to impossible.

Silver directed me sit down on his bed, facing the window, before he knelt behind me, wrapping his arms around my waist. I shifted, hoping he would get the hint, but he stayed firm. I gave up convincing him to release me. He needed to concentrate.

The sense of peace and tranquility which came with his morning rituals did little to settle my unease. Nor did the sun give me any answers.

I yawned as he continued to hold me during his prayers. I wondered what he prayed for or if there were certain words he offered up each day. I closed my eyes for a moment, enjoying the warmth. My power slumbered in the effect Silver created. It was similar to being in the system: calm, balanced. I could rest here.

I jumped when lips pressed against my cheek. What was going on? Where was I? Was I stuck in the system again? Then I realized I still sat in Silver's arms.

"I'm sorry, I didn't mean to scare you. I probably should have insisted you rest instead of sitting with me," Silver said softly.

I shook my head. "I didn't mean to fall asleep on you."

He tightened his hold for a moment. "You needed it. You still need more than you got though."

"I've survived on less."

"Kela..."

"You're never going to stop calling me that, are you?"

"No. I love it."

I sighed in resignation.

"At least you stopped looking like you've seen a ghost when I use it."

I moved away from him, hugging myself. "The others are all dead. You should probably stop calling me it because I'm pretty sure that name is cursed."

"Tell me about them."

I shook my head and hugged myself tighter. I could not afford to think about them.

"Surely you have some good memories with these people. I assume two of the people who called you 'Kela' were your biological parents?"

I nodded, my throat too tight to speak.

"You said there were three. Who else?" Silver stood behind me with his hands on my shoulders.

As Silver pressed, the walls around those memories cracked. "Please stop."

My partner came around and squatted down to get eye level with me. "This all happened over 50 years ago, right? Have you not mourned for them before now?"

I shook my head and looked down at my feet. There had been no time. Not with people pursuing us relentlessly while also keeping Kitteren alive and safe. I could not afford to then nor could I now.

"You remember more than you let on, don't you?"

I clenched my fists to stop my shaking. "Stop prying - I don't want to remember."

Silver pulled me down to sit on the floor with him. I had not the energy to push him away. "Shh. Let's make some new good memories with that name, okay?"

I remained silent. What if history repeated itself? As angry as I had been lately at my friend, I could not live without him.

"Hey, our short trip last night wasn't so bad, was it?"

I shook my head and yawned. Why was I so tired? I had gone days before without rest.

Silver stood up with me in his arms. I moved to get out of his hold, but it was firm. Quickly he set me down on my bed. "Get some more rest and let me plan today, okay? Besides, I doubt many places are open at this hour. Dwarves tend to not like early mornings."

My answer was pulling the blanket over my head.

***

OF ALL THE places Silver could have picked, he choose a geology museum. I glanced at the rain outside. At least we were indoors, but why this?

It was interesting enough, though I knew little about geology. I turned to the giant geode I stood next to. The purple crystals contained within were pretty. I had no idea what I should be examining about it. This one seemed more for decoration since there was no sign in front of it explaining the rock.

I sighed and looked at the large room I currently stood in with its bright, pristine displays. Perhaps I would find it more entertaining as we explored the museum.

"You don't have to look so bored already," Silver said with a teasing tone. He came up beside me, wrapping an arm around my waist.

I forced myself to stay still, reminding myself of the agreement. "You took a while."

"The bathrooms are made for Dwarves."

"We are in Dwarven Territory," I pointed out.

The gentle push from him prodded me along. I let him lead, completely at a loss of where to start in here. Slowly we made our way through the exhibits in this room. Silver never rushed me as I read and studied what was before me.

This trip had become more enlightening than I expected. At least from an arcane perspective given how spells and information could be stored. I needed to remember to delve further into crystal systems to see if there was a difference in how each worked.

The next room contained exhibits regarding mining. After that was information on erosion. Another on fossils. Some were interactive, allowing us to touch or in one case, dig. Silver seemed to enjoy that one and I sat, watching him. *Ever the child.*

If this was how our agreement was going to play out, I saw no harm in it, though we spent time like this before now. Just without him being quite as tactile.

I shifted in my seat as I watched him. How had we grown to needing each other? Would we be in this position if I had not gotten hurt?

Biting my lower lip, I considered this new perspective. Silver had always been protective. It was simply in his nature. His strange behavior remained unexplained.

Thinking back to the case we first met on, Rathal exhibited similar swings in behavior. Savanas mentioned he was always immature due to his age. He was younger than Silver, but they were both considered children by Elven standards.

But Rathal's extremes were due to being influenced by a necromancer's spell. I was fairly certain it was not currently the case with Silver.

This was getting me no where, but I was afraid to ask. His desperation last night still worried me.

"Come try this." Silver beckoned to me.

I shook my head. "I'm fine watching." I smiled softly. It actually was amusing to watch him play with the exhibit.

He moved the sand back over what he managed to uncover and stood up, coming to sit next to me. "Everything okay?" His arm was around my waist again.

"Yeah," I lied. I needed to figure this out on my own.

"You've got to be getting hungry. I know I am." Silver grinned broadly.

The moment we left the museum, I felt eyes on me. Forcing

myself not to look around desperately for the source, I slowly scanned the area as not to look obvious.

Silver leaned down speak in my ear. "You're sensing it, aren't you?"

"Yeah."

"Inside?"

"No."

Silver kissed my cheek and straightened back up. "At least the rain let up. In the mood for anything in particular to eat?"

I shook my head, struggling to keep up with the change of topic. There was little we could do here. With any luck, we could lose whoever it was in the vehicle. Or I was simply imagining things. I truly did not know.

As Silver drove, the rain came down again.

I stared in the side-view mirror, not really seeing, when I thought I noticed a pattern with a particular vehicle. I sat up straighter and paid more attention. "Silver, is there a car following us? The white one about two cars back."

"I'm not sure. We've been on major roads since I first saw it. We've made the same turns as others in front of us."

I bit my lower lip. Being inside a vehicle, I could not tell if I was being watched.

"Pull up Watered Down on the navigation system," Silver ordered.

"Why?" I swear I would never keep up with his changing topics.

"It's probably the safest place we can go right now and I don't know how to get there from here."

I quickly pulled it up for him and sat back to watch the car in the side-view mirror again. We had a while to get to the restaurant.

———

THE WHITE CAR followed us through most of the trip. It continued straight when we turned down the street to get to Watered Down. I wanted to breath a sigh of relief, but in truth, I had no idea if they were following us or not.

When we got into the restaurant, the hostess immediately showed us to a room past the main dining area. It looked to be a private party room. All of the window blinds were closed.

Vince sat at one of the tables, eying us as we were escorted in.

"Got to say your instincts are good. Give me your loaner keys and have a seat."

I hesitantly took a seat at a table over from Vince while Silver handed him the keys to our vehicle. He handed a different set to my partner. The Director unnerved me with his stare.

"I won't lie - there's been more than a passing interest in the two of you. Your gear bags have been moved back to the jet. You and I need to talk about the book you held." Vince kept his attention on me.

I bit my lower lip when he mentioned the book. I opened my mouth to give a reason and closed it again. There was no excuse for me to have taken it in the first place.

"Can you read it?"

I tilted my head at the Director. It was not the line of questioning I expected. "Only the notes, sir."

"Silver's face says otherwise."

I looked over at my partner. He turned away from me. I narrowed my eyes at his silent admission.

Returning my attention to the director, I took a deep breath before I explained, "I can't read it, sir. I feel like I should, but I can't. Likely an aftereffect from handling the system."

Vince folded his arms. "Sounds like a reasonable hypothesis." He stood up and went to a door at the back of the room. "Stay alert and stay armed when you can." Then he left.

I glared at Silver as soon as Vince was gone.

My partner raised his hands. "I'm sorry, I didn't mean to."

I sighed and sat back in my chair, folding my arms and crossing my legs at the ankles. I closed my eyes to focus on figuring out how to deal with the problem at hand.

We were obviously swapped vehicles. They relocated our gear bags which meant likely the enemy knew where we were staying. Why not cut our downtime short and send us back? "We're bait, aren't we?"

Silver stroked the small patch of hair on his chin. "Probably, but at least we get to have our downtime."

I shook my head at his optimism. This trip continued to get more complicated.

The sound of things being placed on the table caused me to open my eyes. Caradoc smiled at me. "No need to worry, lass. This be a safe place. Your boss told me you were on your way here so thought I'd get a little ahead and get some food made. He left some other gifts for you as well." The Dwarf nodded at the back door to the room.

A couple of bags sat next to the door. I raised an eyebrow at Silver who shrugged back at me. He got up to go investigate.

"Thank you. Sorry we've caused problems," I said.

"Bah! Been needin' somethin' to liven things up around here." Caradoc waved me off. "Eat, relax. A couple of my people be takin' your loaner for a long drive. See if we can't confuse the blokes. It be a bit rainy for the beach today. Hope the geology museum was interestin' enough."

I stopped and stared at Caradoc. "How did you know we were there?"

"One of my regulars works there. We keep an eye out for each other. Now eat and relax. I ain't be needin' the function room today so feel free to stay here as long as you'd like."

Sighing, I sat up to see what Caradoc brought. I immediately grabbed one of the breaded cheese sticks and started munching. We spent quite a while at the museum and it had been a lengthy drive to get here so I was hungry.

Silver came back over with the bags, setting them down on one of the chairs. "You'll probably want to go through yours."

"Why?"

"There's a note."

I gave a soft huff and stayed where I was. The note could wait.

"We'll probably need to change also."

I raised an eyebrow at Silver. Wiping my hands, I got up to look. He held up one of the bags to me. I took it and sat back down peeking in. An envelope sat on top of fabric. Taking the note out, I set it on the table before carefully picked up the garment underneath. "A dress?"

Shoving it back in the bag, I tore open the note. There were a few cards inside. The note contained information of where we would be staying and to use the enclosed card to get whatever we needed. I looked at the three cards in my hand. Two were key cards and the other was a generic funds card.

Grumbling, I grabbed another breaded cheese stick from the basket. "I hate dresses."

Silver laughed lightly.

2 0

I SHIFTED UNCOMFORTABLY, tugging the cream colored sun dress to see if I could get it to cover more of my legs. I wore the provided swimsuit to make it not quite so bad.

Silver took the change of attire to mean we needed to change our normal appearance. He had redone my hair, braiding my bangs back into the rest of my hair and wrapped the small braids around to tie the rest off at the base of my neck.

Glancing sideways at my partner as we walked toward the next museum he chose for the day, he looked about as comfortable as I did with the tank top, shorts, and sandals he received. He had pulled the top of his hair back, but otherwise left it down. At least his shorts were longer and he got a lightweight sweatshirt to hide the bracers and belt he wore for his weapons and part of his armor. He stretched and clenched his hands again probably from missing his fingerless leather gloves. It was strange seeing him like this.

Silver glanced at me while I fidgeted again and smirked. "You can leave it alone, you look great."

"At least you're better covered." I went through the suitcases loaded in the new loaner vehicle - both were packed with similar items.

"This is not what I prefer to wear, but we should be harder to spot."

I looked up at his hair. "We still kind of stand out with our hair color. I might blend in better if we were in the Northern Isles."

"Now that you mention it, there were a lot of redheads in Mystic Port. Well, unless you plan on dying your hair, there's not much we can do. My height could also attract attention."

While I was short for an Elf, I still stood taller than the Dwarven population around us, though I could blend in with the tourists far easier. I bit my lip, considering the hair color problem. Plus both of us kept it extremely long.

"Alright, what are you thinking?" Silver asked.

"An illusion to at least change hair color, but it would take a lot of concentration to keep it going and I can't create an illusion bracelet right now."

Silver looked down at me with a raised eyebrow. "Such a thing exists? Why wouldn't they have supplied us with them?"

"I make them. It takes a couple of weeks because I have to tailor it to the individual. Even with changing only hair color, it could take me a few days since I haven't made any for a while so I'm out of practice."

Silver pulled me to the side. "Only you can make them?"

"Lockonis can also, but it takes her longer. Because of the time it takes and the cost of materials, it isn't used very often."

My partner pursed his lips. "I guess that's out of the question then," he said staring off in the direction of the museum.

This situation started to feel like what happened in Mystic Port except this time I had some idea of what was going on.

I jumped when Silver stood directly in front of me and leaned down. I must have stopped paying attention for a minute.

"Can you focus your invisibility spell on certain items?" he whispered.

"I, um..." I tripped over my words as he wrapped an arm around my waist. "I've never tried it. On what?"

"My jacket. I dislike not having it when we're this vulnerable."

We left it in the back of the new loaner. "Maybe? I'd have to try it, but it would still show pressing on any clothes you're wearing underneath."

"Might be enough. We'll talk more later." He kissed my cheek.

Once Silver moved away I could breathe again. This man continued to throw me off.

The entire time we spent in the armor and weapons museum, Silver would make similar gestures, though most not quite so intimate, but it certainly made it hard to concentrate. At least most of his attention was on the displays.

As he studied an ornamental Elven suit of armor, I sighed and moved away, needing space. A much more flowing outfit caught my attention. It did not seem to provide much in the way of protection, though the craftsmanship was beautiful with curls accenting each piece. The high leather collar and small shoulder guards sat over a blue gown. A thick leather belt formed a large diamond at the front before coming down into the band. Intricate leather bracers finished the ensemble off.

A Dwarven woman came up alongside me. "Not too many take interest in our Sorcerer's Armor." Her shirt told me she worked for the museum.

"Sorcerer's Armor?" I had yet to read the information attached to the display.

She brightened up at my inquiry. "Aye. It's such a rare piece to find as mages found this to inhibit their castin' so this type of armor was only ever worn by sorcerers, though the later Elven warmages would wear heavier armor than this. We managed to get the robe recreated for appearance, but the leather is original."

I pursed my lips. "How was a sorcerer different from a mage?"

"Well, lass, the stories about sorcerers were they had an innate ability to wield the arcane. Since being labeled as a sorcerer ended up havin' a bad connotation, the current day term is Arcanist."

My eyes widened at the word Arcanist.

"Perhaps yer already familiar with the term then. Sorcerers were highly sought after when war broke out. Children who showed to be sorcerers were taken from their families and trained to fight. Didn't matter what race. They were the hugely destructive force in any military. Many went into hiding to avoid being conscripted."

Had my biological mother done just that? I tried to recall the rumors that circulated through the village. The information escaped me. It was too easy to focus on the insults they would throw about us when they thought my mother or I were not around.

"Even if we had the original robes, the enchantments they used for further protection and to enhance their destructive abilities would be lost to most people. I'm hopin' we can find some from the other races someday. Be a wonder to see how each developed armor for their casters, though as you can see, our full suits of armor tend to draw in the crowds better." She gestured to the growing number of people in this room.

I eyed the crowd warily before returning to the Sorcerer's Armor. Silver had moved on from what he had been looking at, but had not gone far. "Do you know who this belonged to?"

The curator shook her head and pointed at a display not far. "See that Warmage's Armor over there? We got it as a donation at the same time. Said it had been left in her care, but the owner never returned after the Racial War ended. It would have been nice to track the history of the armor since an intricate piece like this would have been passed down through the generations of a sorcerer family and the robes would have held the family crest as well as the individual's insignia. Though I doubt you would see somethin' like this in use today given the lightweight armors which offer better protection."

I raised an eyebrow at my companion. "You said the military took the children. How were there sorcerer families?"

"Aye, I did. And they did. There were exceptions though. They often left the sorcerer families alone in that regard, but they were required to train their children to fight 'cause when the time came, you better believe the military would be callin'. For ones not from sorcerer families, issues came up where genetics could skip a generation or give it to one child in a family and not another. And it was easy to take a child from a strugglin' family. Sorcerer families usually didn't suffer from the genetic issues and would often be required to mate with other sorcerers." She paused and scratched the back of her head. "Sorry, lass, guess I tend to get a bit excited about this. Most people just want to know about the armor, but there's so much more behind it. All of them, really. Sorcerer families disappeared after the Racial War for the most part. Can't right blame them after only being used as tools of war for generations."

"It's okay. I think it's interesting." While educational, it was also a nice distraction from the chaos Silver and I seemed to have found ourselves in. "Would sorcerers wield weapons at all?"

My companion's face brightened. "Some, though most often they were merely tools for amplification. Most favored staves, though a few would carry a lightweight sword or dagger. Wands were rare as those were more preferred by mages."

Nowadays few casters carried anything. I itched to have my staff on me, but the dress was too short to cover the holster.

"I'll be right up," the curator said, holding down the button attached to her headset. "Sorry, lass, duty calls."

I bowed and watched her leave, wishing we had time to talk more. Turning back to the Sorcerer's Armor, I gave consideration to delving into the topic further when I got back. Maybe some of the answers I was looking for were buried in history.

I sensed the familiar presence before an arm wrapped around my waist. "You seem interested in this," Silver said. "Sorcerer's Armor?"

"It's the old term for Arcanist," I said quietly.

Silver stood completely still for a few moments. "I can see why this would interest you."

I shrugged. "I need to do some research, but I may have a solution to one of our problems."

"Oh?"

"Later." If I could figure out the armor spell and how to enchant it on an article of clothing, it would make Silver less exposed. Though I did wonder why being without the armored jacket bothered him so much. When we first worked together he wore his original armor rarely.

I let Silver lead and set the pace through the rest of the museum while I pondered the idea of enchanting clothing. My partner had done it to the gloves he bought me while we were in Ghost Forest. I needed to consult him first, but here was not the place for it. Not when we had no idea who to trust.

I stood staring at the large, elaborate room we had been moved to at the resort which was supposedly overbooked. Silver moved about, investigating the place, while I tried to add it all up in my head.

My phone rang, ending the loop I found myself in. I glanced at the caller before rolling my eyes and walking to the opposite side of the room from Silver. At least it was not a request for a video call. *"Hey."*

"You still in Sandpoint?" Kitteren asked.

"Yeah. We leave in a couple of days."

"And?"

"*And what?*"

"*Have you kissed him yet?*"

I rolled my eyes, keeping my back to Silver. "*No. It's not a good idea. I'm already in over my head.*"

"*Why?*"

"*Kitteren, it's...*" I stopped, realizing I was running from her. While telling her about the fact we were being used as bait was out of the question, I could tell her about Silver's proposal. I turned in time to see my partner disappearing into the bathroom. Taking a deep breath, I continued, "*I made the mistake of agreeing to a proposal he gave.*"

"*Which was?*"

"*He wants to take our remaining time and use it to explore Elven custom like we talked about.*"

There was a pause before my sister asked, "*How far?*"

I shrugged, and then shook my head at the pointless movement. "*I don't know. Doesn't sound like very far. Kitteren, he can understand you to some degree and overheard our conversation. It won't be long before he can understand what I'm saying.*"

"*And this is a bad thing?*"

"*Ugh! Yes!*" I paced. "*This used to be just for us.*"

"*Ket, he should learn. He's closest to you and you drop into it sometimes. While I agree we're essentially losing this by inviting others in, it isn't going to change us. I know this is going to sound wrong coming from me, but trust him, okay?*"

"*I'm not sure I know who he is anymore,*" I muttered.

"*Wait, back up. What do you mean you're not sure who he is anymore?*"

I cringed, not thinking before I uttered the words. "*It's probably just the stress of the assignment getting to him.*"

"*No. No, there's something else. Come on, Ket, tell me.*"

I sighed and eyed the closed bathroom door, dropping my voice so he hopefully would not hear me. "*He's been acting strange. I've seen him almost out of control during a fight and then he begged me to accept this proposal of his.*"

"*You got hurt, didn't you?*"

"*What? Where did that come from?*" Had I missed part of the conversation?

"*I noticed he gets wild when you've gotten hurt. And let's not talk about when you've been hurt and there's nothing for him to take out his frustrations on. You're everything to him."*

"Well, I shouldn't be," I shot back. *"I'm too dangerous to get close to."*

"Get over yourself, Ket. You need him as much as he needs you and if he can get you to realize you're no threat to the people you care about, then I'm not about to argue."

I pulled my phone away from my head and stared at it for a moment. My thumb hovered over the end call button. Shaking my head, I returned to the call. *"You're a brat, you know that?"*

Kitteren laughed. *"That's a new one coming from you. And if you really have a problem with his behavior, then you should talk to him about it."*

I sighed. If only everything had not gotten so complicated. Right now I was forced to trust Silver despite my unease.

"Ket, I know most of the time you'll do something just to get me to stop bothering you about it, but you really need to do this for you."

"I'll think about it."

"Guess that's the best I can hope for right now. I better get going. Meetings and all that fun boring crap."

"Thanks, Kitteren." The inane conversation helped hold most of my worries about our current situation at bay for the brief time.

"Anytime, sis. Love ya." She ended the call.

I stared at the ceiling and let my arms hang. It had been a long day.

Hands touched my shoulders and I jumped away, dropping my phone. I turned ready to defend myself - arcane energy already in my hands.

"Calm down. It's just me," Silver said softly.

"Don't sneak up on me." I dropped my hands, releasing the gathered energy. I slowly knelt down to retrieve my phone, my body protesting the movement.

"I'm sorry, I thought you heard me." He stepped closer and brushed a stray lock of hair out of my face as soon as I stood back up. "You're really scared, aren't you?"

I scrunched up my nose and turned away, refusing to answer.

Silver stepped in front of me. "Kela, don't lock me out. We're in this together."

"It should only be me," I whispered.

"What? No. No, don't you even think about taking off on me."

I shook my head and walked away. "I'm not, but you shouldn't be involved."

"Well, I was right there fighting with you so I made it my problem also."

"I don't think that's why they're after us," I said softly. Before now I had pushed the thought back.

Silver squatted to be eye level with me. He searched my face for something. "What are you seeing that I'm not?"

I took a deep breath. "I'm the only one who managed to use the system and worse, we've both seen how the system was built."

He straightened up. "You're suggesting they don't want revenge."

"I wouldn't rule it out, but we hold information." Or in my case, I held a different key. I gave Silver a sidelong glance. *What if they used him to convince me to do something?* I closed my eyes and clenched my jaw. So many scenarios were before me. So many ways this could end horribly.

"Stop," Silver said firmly.

I looked up at him.

"I know you love to theorize, but right now we're safe. We have people looking out for us. I'm not going to worry about something which might not even happen."

"But..."

Silver covered my mouth. "No buts. Worrying and planning for the worst isn't going to help."

I shoved him away and glared at him.

"Figured you wouldn't like that, but you need to listen. Let's enjoy the remainder of our time here. Why don't you pick what we're doing tomorrow? I looked at the weather and it'll dry up, but I don't think it's going to be a good beach day."

I stared up at him. "How can you not be concerned about this?"

"I am concerned. Which is why I'm hoping you can find at least a temporary solution for my missing armor."

"I..." I told him earlier I might be able to do something. Pushing past him, I went for my tablet, sitting down on the edge of the bed. "I'm not sure I've ever seen how to enchant an article of clothing. Supposedly the Sorcerer's Armor, specifically the robes, would be enchanted to increase armor and destructive capabilities."

Silver sat down next to me, leaning over my shoulder. "It's not too difficult. Just time and energy consuming. Provided it works the same for the arcane as it does divine."

"First I need to find an armor spell. It may not be as strong as your actual armor, but it should offer some protection."

"I'll take what I can get."

His statement made me pause. "Why is it bothering you so much? You didn't wear your armor much when we first met."

"That armor was impractical. This one is easy to wear all the time and I guess I got used to it. Besides, if you're right and they're coming for what we know, I'd rather have one less thing to worry about when the fight comes."

Now I knew he was concerned, but he preferred to wait and see which scenario came to pass instead of planning ahead. I stood up and moved to one of the chairs in the room. "Why don't you get some rest? It's going to take me a while to research if this is even possible."

"Kela, it's still early. I don't need to rest yet. Not to mention you need rest too."

I waved him off. "It's probably safer if we don't rest at the same time anyway. Besides, there's only one bed."

"We've rested together in a bed before. This will be no different. Wait, are you suggesting we take watches?"

I hesitated before I answered, "Yes." Was it so strange of a suggestion?

"No, you'll use it as an excuse to stay up all night."

"This is going to take me at least all night."

Silver knelt in front of me and took one of my hands, kissing the back of it. "Then don't. I need you rested more than I need armor. We can take tomorrow morning to do some research and test ideas, but we can't hide all day."

I stared at my partner. "I don't understand you most of the time." Shaking my head, I went back to my research.

"What? You don't understand if it comes down to a fight, having you too exhausted to help is going to be worse than being without armor?" Silver snapped at me.

I snarled at him. "Not just this. Things you've been doing... It's like I don't know you." I covered my mouth. The words were out and I could not take them back.

Silver stared at me. He opened his mouth to say something, his face tight with anger. He took a deep breath and sat down on the edge of the bed, facing me. "What have I been doing?"

This calm was more unsettling than dealing with his temper. I bit my lower lip for a moment. "I didn't mean to say anything..."

"Well, you did. Now let's deal with it. What have I been doing to make you question me?"

I closed the cover on my tablet and stared at it. "Well, there's how you acted on the ship. It's like you never even gave a second thought about wanting to kill those people." I peeked up at my partner's face.

He closed his eyes and his jaw was set. "I hoped you never had to see me like that, but I couldn't hold back. Not in a kill or be killed situation with someone to protect. If you hadn't grabbed my arm, I wouldn't have stopped." Silver turned his gaze to the floor.

I tilted my head, unsure how to continue the conversation.

"I, um..." Silver pulled part of his loose hair over his shoulder to tug on. "I didn't always live in Ocean's Edge. No idea where I'm from other than somewhere in the Inner Sea region. Lived at the Central Seat for a while, which is where I learned to pilot a larger vessel similar in size to the prototype if you were wondering."

That bit of information had me curious, but at this point it was unimportant.

"Shortly after I took my oath to become a paladin my master's group was ordered to secure a new settlement on the southern side of the Inner Sea region on the edge of Troll territory."

Putting my tablet aside, I went and sat down next to him on the bed. Silver tugged harder on his hair and I put my hand over his to get him to stop. He clenched his jaw tighter.

He looked at our hands. It seemed to free his lips. "The nearby Troll tribes would raid us weekly if we were lucky. Usually every few days we were fighting them off. I got really good at killing. I stopped thinking about it. I had people to protect and the surest way to make sure an enemy didn't come back to try again was to make sure they were dead."

"How long were you there?" I asked softly.

Silver let go of his hair and took my hand. "Five years, maybe more. I lost track after a while. We were so busy fighting and rebuilding, we never actually got the settlement beyond the basics. Then we were pulled and sent to Ocean's Edge."

I had no idea what to do. "Why didn't you want me to know this?"

"You were so afraid of driving people away if they knew about your past and mine is literally coated in blood."

I leaned over so I could look him in the face. "I'm still here."

Strong arms wrapped around me tightly and Silver shook. I managed to get an arm free to hold onto him.

After a while, I said, "You lied when you told me you didn't have anything interesting."

"Huh?"

"When I asked you while we were in Mystic Port."

Silver sat up and blinked, rubbing at his face. "I guess it's a matter of perspective. I don't find it interesting. It's one of those times I'd just as soon forget."

I sat back on the bed, staring out at the ocean view. "What about this proposal of yours? This isn't what I expected from you either."

He put his hand behind his head, his cheeks reddening. "I guess I really have confused you. Like I said, it's something I've been meaning to put before you for a while now. It's... I should..." My partner took a deep breath and hung his head.

"Why did you wait?"

Silver sat back up and looked at me with wide eyes before turning to look out the windows. "The timing never seemed right and I was content with what we had. Thought maybe we would simply fall into it, but when we got back from Ghost Forest everything reset as if our time there never occurred. And ever since you connected with the system, I felt like I've been losing you. Almost lost you in there the last time."

Silence fell between us and we both stared out the window at the fading day.

"They're going to need both of us even once they get the information on the system, aren't they? You can operate the system and I can pull you out."

I closed my eyes. I hoped I was the only one who considered that scenario. "Maybe."

"Why do you think they moved us and are hiding us if they want to use us as bait?"

"I'm not sure. Make it look like we're not bait? I'd have to run it by Kitteren, but I'm not about to tell her the situation we're in."

"So that's not what you were getting worked up over when you were talking to her earlier."

"No."

"Tell me?"

"No."

"Can I guess?"

"No."

Silver sighed. "Well, you're no fun. Let's go for a walk and maybe we can figure out what we're doing tomorrow. It's a bit stuffy in here."

2 1

____

SILVER HELD my hand as we walked. There were others from the resort out and walking through the paths because the sky had begun to clear. I wanted to stop and focus. I needed to figure out if this sensation of being watched was real or if I was mistaking the quick glances from the people we passed.

Though likely Vince had people following us and I could not tell friend from foe. There were also the friends we made recently in Sandpoint. I squeezed Silver's hand tighter.

My partner looked down at me. He squeezed my hand briefly in return and turned his attention back to where we were walking.

After our conversation, I understood better what was going on, but still needed to fully process the information. He said something about when I stopped him. I let out a soft huff. It looked like we managed to keep each other in check, but I continued to worry about my growing power.

The path left the cover of the tall, flowering bushes and opened up along the water. The people walking around us thinned out to the point I had not seen another for a couple minutes.

Silver tugged me over to where the walkway jutted out over the water.

I stepped away from him and up to the railing, taking in the moon reflecting off of the water. I wanted to stay in this moment of calm.

Silver came up next to me, wrapping an arm around my waist. I took a deep breath, enjoying the peace. The world could wait a moment.

"Kela," Silver said softly.

He was already looking down at me when I turned my attention to him. His hand went to the side of my face and he leaned down. Then he grunted as if in pain.

"Silver?"

His hand went to his neck and he pulled me to the ground with him. He used his body to cover me and his shield appeared behind me. I stared at the dart he pulled out.

His movements became sluggish and I struggled under his weight. "Silver!"

"Get out of here," his voice started to slur.

"Not without my partner," I hissed at him. My wrist vibrated and I tore my watch off while I was out of the enemy's sight, stuffing it down the front of my shirt and inside the high neck swimsuit top I wore as a bra.

People closed in on us with rifles. I saw two, but I could not see behind me.

"One shot. Go low," Silver said. Without anything further, he stood up and threw his shield.

I conjured a strong wind and knocked back the two I could see.

Silver caught his shield a second before it disappeared and he fell. I tried to catch him, but his weight dragged me back down. I put up my shield spell before checking him.

My partner was unconscious and more attackers surrounded us. The ones I knocked back stood up. Where were the people keeping an eye on us?

I held onto Silver tightly, not sure what to do. I would have to drop my shield spell to teleport and it would take time to get both of us out of here. Too much time.

One of the attackers walked into my shield spell, bouncing off of it, falling down. The next closest person laughed at him. "Well, we're lucky it's gone this smooth. We knew we'd have some resistance."

"You sure we've got the right ones? I mean, look at her - this can't be the girl who took back the ship and that guy went down way too easy," another said.

I prayed they decided we were the wrong people. I kept my shield spell up anyway.

"Not my problem if they aren't as long as I get paid," one from behind me said. "Now be a good girl and drop this barrier. Make things nice and easy."

I looked down at the unconscious Elven man I held. I jumped when someone pressed against my shield spell. I clenched my teeth at the additional strain.

Gun fire went off in the distance. Was help on the way? I needed to hold out until they arrived.

Another pushed against the shield. I held onto Silver tighter as I struggled to keep it going. I absolutely had to get him out of here, but how?

A third pressed and my shield spell shattered like glass. Disappearing shards fell around us. Something stung me in the back of my shoulder and my vision immediately blurred. I immediately turned my focus to teleport Silver, but the fog kept me from completing it before blackness took over.

THE FIRST THING I noticed was my wrists hurt a lot. I hung between my outstretched arms. My feet were on the ground and I struggled to get them underneath me.

"Ketayl?"

That name in Silver's voice sounded strange. I managed to crack my eyes open. It took me a moment to find my partner chained to the floor on the side of the room. Bars were directly across from me and a metal wall with a door beyond that. Our cell was fairly large and unfurnished.

"Remind me to listen to you next time," he said.

I let out a soft huff. My head hurt too much to roll my eyes at him. "Where are we?" My mouth was dry and my voice cracked. I licked my lips.

"I'm not sure. On a ship I think. I haven't seen anyone."

Even with the pressure relieved from having my full weight hanging, my arms ached. I studied the restraints.

"Why didn't you run?" Silver asked.

I shook my right arm a little to see how loose the manacle was. "I told you I wasn't leaving you. I... I'm sorry, I couldn't hold out until help arrived. Couldn't get you to safety either." I hung my head.

"Hey," Silver said softly and shifted so he knelt as close to me as his restraints would allow. "You did what you could. Now we need to find a way out of here."

The screeching of metal on metal stopped our conversation and we both looked toward the door as the bolt slid open. Three Human men entered. Two of them carried a large black case between them. They entered our cell.

"Wasn't too hard getting both of you. Lost a few causing the distraction, but that's the price of business," the man not holding the case said. I assumed this was the leader.

The men behind him set the case down on the floor near the bars. A fourth came in carrying a covered tray and set it down on the floor on the other side of the room from Silver. He departed quickly.

The men who carried the case took up spots next to us. The one in front of me grinned broadly. "I think you and I will have some fun later." He trailed his fingers up my thigh.

Snarling at the man, I jumped, grabbed the chains, and kicked him square in the chest with both feet. He stumbled backwards, tripping over the case.

The one on Silver laughed at him. The leader looked down at the man I kicked as he got up off the floor hurling curses. I pulled hard at my restraints, snarling and ready to kick him again. My power wild and ready for a fight despite my low levels of arcane energy.

The leader turned his attention back to me. "Oh, so you do have some spunk. Worry not - I'll have him removed from this duty. I'll have no harm come to our guests."

An Elven man came in this time and pulled the one I kicked away. Once the Elven man shoved him out the door, he returned, standing out of my reach.

"Funny way to treat guests," Silver spat. He moved at the man standing next to him and got punched in the stomach for the effort.

The leader shrugged. "Until we come to an agreement, consider this me protecting my assets. Though in one way I should thank the two of you for stopping that tactless display some of my former colleagues thought appropriate to reclaim what was ours."

"The ship belongs to the Navy," Silver argued.

"But the system is ours. We loaned Jacob Martin a good sum of money and equipment to get his company started. Not to mention the connections and other miscellany to get him going quickly as a successful weapons developer." The leader signaled to the men to go to the case. "We already have the plans, but he withheld a vital piece."

The cover lifted barely an inch when I sensed the pull from what sat inside and backed away as much as possible. My wrists burned, but I needed to get away from that thing. They lifted the lid to show the glowing blue orb nestled deep inside.

"You're afraid of this and yet you're the only one to master the system. Curious." He signaled for the men to close the case. "If you're wondering, this is the one from the ship. It's good to have friends in the Navy."

They took the case back out the door and returned.

"What do you need us for?" Silver asked.

"I'm fairly certain I gave you your answer. Your female friend here can operate the system and you can get her out. You will be her care-taker. It also makes a nice little package, being able to keep the two of you in line should one of you attempt to break this deal. Though it would be interesting to see you try as we're over 200 miles out."

Too far for me to be able to teleport myself let alone both of us.

"I don't think you understand how hard it is to pull her out of the system," Silver said, his eyes toward the floor. "I might not be able to if she goes in again."

"After reviewing the information, we're modifying the system to compensate. We'll start with a conjured defense barrier and keep her time limited. I assure you, our standards are far higher than that of Spelltech."

The Human man guarding Silver pulled a knife out and held it to my partner's throat.

"Stop! Don't!" I begged.

"Easy, child. This is a show of goodwill," the leader said.

The Elven man who guarded me went over and undid Silver's restraints.

"Now, I can only afford to have one of you free in here at the moment until I'm certain we have an understanding. There's food for both of you on the tray." He left first followed by the two who quickly closed and locked the cell door.

My legs gave out from under me when the bolt of the door

beyond slammed home. My wrists hurt from the sudden weight of my body pulling against the restraints, but it mattered not to the situation we found ourselves in.

Silver struggled to his feet, coming over and picking me up. He held me with one arm and brushed the hair which had fallen out of the braids out of my face. "Ketayl. Ketayl, look at me."

I rested my head on his shoulder - everything felt heavy. Lifting my head to look at him was too much right now.

"Kela," he whispered in my ear. "I'm going to do everything I can to get you out of here." Silver rested his head against mine. His hand undoing my hair. Once my hair was down, he threaded his fingers through it, rubbing my head. He stayed holding me for a while, whispering assurances.

Despite his attempts, I could not see a way out of this. I shifted to get out of his hold as I was sure I was heavy.

"Can you stand?"

"Think so," I said as I put my weight on my feet.

"Okay, I want to see how bad your wrists are."

I stood with my head hung. My arms had only a slight bend in them at my full height.

"You surprised me," Silver said softly. He held one of my elbows to get the weight off of my wrist.

"Huh?" I turned to look up at him.

"When you attacked. I guess I got off lucky with only getting slapped." Silver's smirk sat wrong against the tension in his face. "By the grace of the Gods, I wish they at least made it so you weren't putting so much strain on your arms."

"It makes sense: even if I wasn't low, the pain makes it hard to concentrate." I read about it years ago at the Arcane College. As well for a traditional mage, it kept them from being able to use their hands for the cast. "Sorry I slapped you," I mumbled.

Silver lowered my arm and stood in front of me. He reached behind his neck with both hands and undid the clasp of his necklace. He held it for a moment, looking at the small sun pendant before clasping it around my neck.

"What are you doing?" I asked as he tucked it down the front of my swimsuit top. A small thrum of power emanated from the pendant.

"Praying the God of the Sun can light the path to free you from the system if it comes to that." Silver rested his hand over where it hung under my clothes and then raised an eyebrow at me as soon as the heel of his palm pushed against where I stowed my watch. He leaned down and whispered in my ear, "Something?"

I bit my lower lip thinking through how to word it without being obvious. "*Time,*" I whispered it in my native dialect of common and for the first time hoped he understood me. I also prayed someone had the sense to track the small device before we got out of range of the communication network.

He mouthed the word against my ear. Then he smiled before he kissed my cheek.

My partner moved back to examining my wrists. His power washed over my arm. "I'll have to be careful with this since you absorb divine energy. Don't let your full weight hang for too long. I'll hold you when I can to give you a break."

Closing my eyes, the small thrum of power coming from the pendant pulled my attention. It was warm and comfortingly familiar. When his power washed over my other arm, I realized why it felt so familiar. It resonated the same as Silver's power. "How long have you had this?"

"Hm? The necklace?"

"Yes."

"Depends on which part you're asking about. I don't remember a time I haven't had the sun, but I've needed to change the chain out a few times over the years."

I returned to the familiar sensation. Was it possible the pendant absorbed magical energy and attuned itself to my partner over the years?

I caught Silver rubbing the area the pendant usually hung around his neck. "Have you used it like this before?"

He shook his head. "I'm trying to come up with ways to make it easier to call you back no matter how far-fetched. I'm hoping it'll be a physical anchor for you. I've never taken it off except to change the chain."

"Then you should..."

Silver put a finger over my lips. "I'm not taking it back until we get out of here."

I sighed and shifted away from him. "Go eat. I'll be fine."

Once he moved toward the tray, I looked back up at my current predicament. Thick chains were bolted to the ceiling and there was no way I could pull out of the manacles around my wrists. If I had more arcane energy, I might be able to teleport out, but I lost too much maintaining my shield and we moved away from the ley line. By the time I regained my arcane energy levels, I might not be able to concentrate enough to pull it off. Where would I go though? I would only put Silver in danger if I did.

"Here," Silver said softly. He held up a bottle of water.

I shook my head.

"Please, you need to keep up your strength."

"I'll wait until I can get down." They would have to let me down at some point otherwise I would never be able to use their system. I refused to be degraded further.

"We don't know when that will be. We don't even know when they'll be back," Silver argued.

I bit my lower lip. "They have to hookup the orb at least. I'm not hungry anyway." Thirsty, yes, but I could manage.

Silver grabbed my chin and forced me to look at him. "You need to listen to me here."

I stared at him with wide eyes and nodded under Silver's intense gaze. He held me for a moment longer before shifting to give me water from the bottle he carried.

My partner was careful and deliberate with how much he gave me of anything. He ate with me at the same time.

I shook my head as he went to give me another piece of bread. "No more. I'm going to be sick." The nausea had grown steadily and I was uncertain the cause.

Silver put the food in his hands aside, and made a soft hushing sound, cradling my face in his hands. "It's okay."

"This is degrading," I voiced out loud.

"Well, it might be fun under different circumstances." He gave a half-hearted smirk. "Definitely could do without the chains though."

I sighed and admitted, "I swear I'll never understand you."

"Maybe someday, but right now I still need to come up with more ideas to make sure I can pull you out."

"Do you have any yet?" It was something I could focus on. Maybe not help with, but I would try.

Silver bent down and moved the tray to the corner. He kept his back to me. "I do, but you're not going to like it."

I looked up at how I was attached to the ceiling, moving my arms a little, causing the chains to make noise. "There's already a lot I don't like right now. I don't think one more thing is going to matter."

"It matters to me."

I stopped analyzing the chains and tilted my head at him.

"I, um..." Silver stood over me. He touched my face, running his thumb over my bottom lip. "I hoped for better circumstances to share this with you."

"Wait, share what?" I stepped back, but my current predicament kept me close to him.

Silver stood there for a moment staring at me. "You really are oblivious."

I was about to give my partner a hard time for his words when something caught my attention. I twisted to look behind me, as futile as the gesture was.

"What is it?"

My eyes went wide as I analyzed what caught my attention. "We're moving toward a ley line. An extremely dense one."

"What's a ley line? I've never heard you talk about them until this trip."

Shifting back to the most comfortable position I could manage, I explained, "Normally I don't pay attention to them. There's typically enough arcane energy in an area I don't concern myself with where one is. Ley lines are like wind currents of arcane energy, but they don't shift nearly as much or as often. On land they disperse and spread out making them more indistinct."

"But we're out in the ocean."

I nodded, hanging my head. "I've never been near something so concentrated before. I don't know what will happen."

"We've flown over the ocean a few times now."

"We've been too high in the atmosphere to be affected."

"Okay, I get it - you're likely going to have a power spike. Can we get back to how to make sure I don't lose you to the system?"

"How about how to get out of here?"

Silver clenched his jaw and looked down at me, his face tight with anger. "You should have run all of those scenarios already and realized there are too many unknowns to formulate a plan. And where can we go so far out to sea?"

"Yeah, well, you've been planning so much for me using the system, I assumed the idea escaped you," I shot back.

Silver grabbed my head and leaned down quickly, stopping only a couple of inches from my face. It took a few warm breaths on my face to realize his attention was lower.

The necklace warmed and a strong desire from it to complete the connection washed over me. I followed the impulse and stood on the balls of my feet, pressing my lips to his.

I bet Kitteren would insist this did not count either given the circumstances.

After a moment, Silver moved his lips and I followed his lead, unsure of what I was doing. All I knew was how absolutely wrong this was kissing my best friend while chained to the ceiling. I could not tell if any part of it was right.

I blamed his necklace, which I only received contentment from.

22

<hr>

"WE'VE MADE a number of improvements to the system," the leader said. "The original lacked imagination, and, as you yourself pointed out, a lack of zonal shielding. Something we consider of great value."

I trailed behind him, my hands bound in front of me with guards both in front and behind. Silver followed with his own guards. My power resonated with the ley line. The close proximity to it made me slightly nauseous and despite my arcane energy levels being back to full, I wanted to collapse to the floor.

My legs took action on the thought and I dropped to my knees. I would have hit the deck if the guard behind me had not grabbed my arm.

"Dammit, let me help her," Silver said.

"Oh, come now. You haven't even gotten to see the control room. I thought you would be excited to see the improvements," the leader said, kneeling down in front of me.

And to think, I had initially been excited about this assignment.

"You kept her chained up for how long? What did you expect? She's not going to be able to operate the system," Silver yelled at him. I heard movement behind me followed by my partner grunting in pain. He was getting hurt because of me. *How am I supposed to protect him like this?*

The leader stood back up. "It's a simple test today and depending on how things go, we may be able to make adjustments to your accommodations. Something to keep in mind as we work together."

I hissed at the pain from my arm when the guard pulled me back up. I swayed on my feet for a moment before being pushed forward. I stumbled to keep up with being mostly shoved along.

"At least let me help her," Silver begged. "You want me to be her caretaker, then let me care for her."

The leader stopped and signaled at the men behind me. I closed my eyes and hung - my legs too tired to support my weight.

Another pair of hands took me away from the guard holding me. The pendant warmed against my skin.

I lost track of time and where we were until a familiar sensation pulled at me. I cracked my eyes open as Silver maneuvered us through the door.

This control room bore a similar layout to the prototype, but contained only one seat in the center. Instead of the control panel I expected, the orb sat on a stand in front of the chair. My breath came quick as panic set in. I shook my head, my eyes glued to the orb. "I can't..." I whispered.

"No need to be afraid. With eliminating the console, you should be able to better sync with the system. Right now all we need to do is check to make sure it's operational. You don't need to conjure anything."

Two men stepped forward with their guns raised and another two pulled me away from Silver. I pushed back with my legs, desperate to get away from the orb. "No! Please! You don't understand what that thing is."

I was too weak to overpower the men who shoved me into the chair and forced my still bound hands against the orb. Immediately, the sense of calm and balance greeted me. It spun the sensations around, acting as if it was happy to see me. I pushed back against it, but had nothing left to fight with.

All I could see was ocean for miles. The system took my despair at the sight and sent it away. What was I supposed to do?

I spent some time looking around outside to get a sense of where the defense system emitters were. I searched for offensive weaponry, but there was none. I came back inside the ship, going through the ship via the camera network. I briefly wondered if they knew I could access other systems.

This ship was larger than the prototype. A cargo ship? I remained uncertain.

"Kela," I heard Silver whisper. "It's time to come back."

The system blocked the anchor. Something warmed against my chest, creating a clear path back. As soon as I stepped through the gate, I took a deep breath and threw myself against the back of the seat, tearing my hands away from the orb.

Silver was practically on top of me, his hands holding my head. He had a look of relief on his face. "Thank the Gods."

I turned to the orb and whimpered, the desire to touch it again strong.

"You haven't fully broken from it, have you?"

I shook my head.

"Curious. I was wondering what caused the earlier reaction from her. In any case, it looks like we can proceed as planned with future tests. You're dismissed." The leader waved us off.

The guards took no time in getting us to move. Silver held onto me tightly even after we left the control room. I drifted as we walked, still partially connected to the system. I could still access the cameras, but it was difficult to control and harder to hold onto the farther we walked from the control room.

With more exposure, I might be able to maintain the connection for longer and at a greater distance. I could get Silver to freedom once the circumstances were right. They would have to return to port sometime.

"Can't you take the restraints off of her?" Silver asked. I came back to the present.

We sat down, but my hands remained bound in front of me.

"No. We have our orders," one of the guards answered.

The bolt slid home on the door before Silver spoke again. "Are you still under the effects of the system?"

I nodded. "You're dampening it." It could be a problem for maintaining control. I sat in a tug of war between Silver and the system.

"Let's get you free of it and then you're eating and getting rest. We can talk about what happened after." Silver did not wait for a response before he put his forehead against mine and the last vestiges of the system disappeared. Once he was done, he kissed my forehead and sat me up against the wall.

"Guess I should be glad I'm not hanging again," I muttered.

"We even got a cot."

"Luxury hotel."

Silver laughed lightly. He went and got the tray from the corner. "Here." He held up a piece of bread.

I did not fight him this time. My hands might be free enough to get food to my mouth, but the previous strain on my arms and the weight of the manacles kept them immobilized.

How long would it be until I found the opening to get Silver to safety?

TESTS CAME at odd intervals and I had not seen daylight beyond what the system allowed for however many days we were held captive. They stopped letting Silver come to the tests once they found they could simply pull my hands away from the orb. They took him out to go see the sun rise every morning, but I lost track of how many times now.

More and more was being connected to the system. I managed to get the zonal shielding working and they added some offensive weaponry. I could not get the output they wanted no matter the configuration and I explained over and over that the orb was not an amplifier, but it had fallen on deaf ears.

I hung heavily between the guards as they brought me back to the cell. We were in the elevator when I noticed something on the wrist of one of them. I recognized one of the illusion bracelets I made at some point and stared at it.

The guard saw what I stared at and glanced at his friend. "Soon, kid, okay?"

"We need to figure out a big enough distraction," the other guard said.

I hung my head and flitted through the system for a moment, analyzing what was connected and what they were in the process of adding. "I can do it. Make sure you get Silver out of here."

"You're in no condition..."

"Wait, hear her out. What's your plan?"

I kept my head down, grinning. "If you can get the ship closer to the ley line, there will be fireworks." It would be harder for me to be closer, but I would need the constant stream of arcane energy to blow the system.

They dragged me the rest of the way and tossed me unceremoniously through the cell door. I collapsed onto the metal floor and stayed there, the tug of war between Silver's necklace and the system making it impossible to move.

Silver picked me up, stroking the side of my face gently. "Tell your boss to lay off the tests for a while. She's absorbed too much divine energy. I won't be able to break her from it soon."

I heard nothing but the sound of doors shutting.

"Dammit! I swear I'm going to kill every last one of them on this ship."

I leaned as much into my partner as I could before I said, "*Friends.*"

"I think you're delirious." It had not taken him long to learn my dialect as it was what I primarily spoke to him here, though he never spoke it back.

Taking his hand from the side of my face, I put it over where his necklace resided and pressed until I knew he felt the watch between us. "*Time.*"

Silver pulled my head to him and muttered against my lips, "Certainly took their's."

The effect had become too strong for Silver to break the last of the connection, even with me not touching the orb, without a more intimate connection between us. He previously voiced his concern he would eventually have to do more.

Until it came to that point, I refused to ask what more was.

I closed my eyes as he kissed me, letting the sensation of his power removing the last holds of the system bring me some measure of peace. His sun pendant warmed against my skin and resonated with his power.

"Maybe someday we can share a kiss without it being an extenuating circumstance," Silver said quietly.

I let out a soft huff.

"May the Gods help me. I'm not sure how much longer I can watch them torture you like this."

"*Free you soon,*" I said, my voice not making it above a whisper. I was content here.

Silver curled around me and cried just as he had the past few tests. I worried this place had broken him. The sooner I could get him out of here, the better.

23

I STAYED CURLED UP TIGHTLY on the cot. Being in so much concentrated arcane energy made me sick. Silver sat beside the cot, stroking my hair. He backed away and I cracked open my eyes to see my power manifesting itself across my skin again. The iridescent tendrils disappeared quickly.

My body kept doing it to burn some of the excess off. Soon it would not be enough to keep the overload in check. Especially as we continued moving into the ley line.

Silver returned to stroking my hair. I let myself drift.

"No! I can't break her out of it if you make her connect again," Silver pleaded. "Can't you see she's also sick?"

I opened my eyes to see the same two guards as before standing at the open door to the cell. Mustering the strength, I pushed myself up into a sitting position. "It'll be okay," I said.

Standing took more effort and I suddenly became lightheaded, making me want to sit back down. I managed to put one foot in front of the other and followed my escorts.

We were in the elevator when one spoke softly, "We're ready whenever you are."

I hung my head and rubbed the bridge of my nose. "On my signal after I get back." I could not risk Silver's safety.

"What's the signal?"

"Trust me, you won't be able to miss it." It would be hard, but I needed to overload one of the arcane guns.

The remainder of the walk was silent. I dragged myself through the door to the control room. The leader folded his arms.

As typical, I took a seat in the chair in front of the orb and waited for directions.

"You've been so cooperative, I'll have to consider giving you an upgrade to your accommodations, but I fear it won't happen today."

I sighed and stared at the orb. The thought of another test made me weary, but it would help with the excess arcane energy.

"Today will be short. I want you to bring the four new cannons online and run diagnostics on them. My people will review the information at the terminals."

I sighed and reached for the orb. It again greeted me with some level of enthusiasm. I pushed it aside, determined to get on with my task. I had grown too used to the calm and balance it offered to be affected by it anymore.

I first pulled up the camera for our cell. Being able to see Silver kept me focused. He paced and tugged on his braid.

Moving on, the cannons were simple to locate. I picked one and ran the startup sequence I found. It appeared as if these could be run by either myself or someone at a control station for the cannon. These would not require me to put energy into more than controlling it. Curious, I poked around a little more while it started up.

These cannons were still energy driven, but would draw from an internal power source. The system pushed its calm and balance at me. I noticed it did when it thought I was getting off-task. I ignored it.

Once the first cannon was up and running, I ran the diagnostic and moved onto the next one to repeat the procedure. With each cannon, I gathered more information, learning how they worked, and more importantly, how to wreak havoc with them.

As soon as I ran the last diagnostic, someone pulled me away from the orb. My vision would take a minute or so to readjust back to where I was.

"You've done good work today. I think you've earned a reprieve for a day or so from further tests," the leader said.

I was hauled from my seat and out the door, my bare feet tripping over the lip on the door frame. I cringed as I hit the bruises already there. We were in the elevator again before I could pull enough of myself back to be able to see.

"You okay, kid?"

"Will be."

"I don't think she's up for it."

I flitted through the system, watching to see what the others were doing with the cannons. They seemed only interested in the diagnostic reports. "Will be. Need Silver." It was as far as I wanted to share my plan. This all depended on how much I could hold onto the system from a distance, but the enemy certainly made it easier with adding those cannons.

A guard stood in the hallway outside of the room for my cell. He shoved a box at me when I got close enough. I took a step back to steady myself. "A gift from the boss." Then he opened the door.

They shoved me through the big metal door and again through our cell door. Only staying upright by running into Silver.

"You could be more gentle with her!" he shouted at them as they left.

I moved the black material on top and smirked at what had been hidden beneath.

Silver gave up growling at them and moved to kiss me. I shifted away. "Let me at least dampen the effects until I can break it," he snapped.

"*No.*"

"You can't stay connected to that thing. I don't know what it'll do to you. Your eyes are still completely arcane covered."

"*Time's up.*" I took my shrunken staff and shoved the box at Silver.

"What do you mean? Oh."

"*They don't know what they gave me.*" I mentally left the room and went to the first cannon, starting up the power core, locking down the firing sequence, and frying the control station for it. While I set up the second, an explosion rocked the ship. I was forced back to the cell after two.

Silver wore his armored jacket and had called the rest by the time I returned. Another explosion rocked the ship.

The guards entered, rushing to get the cell door open. "Well, lady, that was Hells of a signal. Going to have to tell me how you did it later."

"I need to get to the control room," I said.

"Gods help me. Ketayl, you can't risk it," Silver argued.

I extended my staff before looking up at my partner. "I'm not going to stop you. Don't try to stop me." I strode out of the cell before I got sick on the concentrated arcane energy again.

"Ma'am?" one of the guards asked. "We need to escort you out of here."

I clenched my jaw for a moment before I ordered, "Get Silver to safety. I'll tear this place apart myself."

Two more guards ran down the hall toward us with guns drawn. I put up my shield spell and pushed my way down the hall. Being this close to the ley line gave me a constant stream of arcane energy. They would run out of bullets first.

A different shield went flying past me. It took out the two guards and Silver stepped up alongside me to catch it.

My friend smirked. "You're not the only one who wants revenge. Not letting my partner go it alone."

I jogged to keep up with Silver's long strides, but slowed after only a few steps. I was too unstable with the excess arcane energy to do more than a fast walk. My feet were also bruised and cut from being dragged around barefoot.

The guards got up and took aim again. Silver rushed them, cutting them down with only a couple of swings. My partner turned to look back at me. "You know it's kill or be killed, right?"

"I know. I'm done caring." Then I noticed his sword remained sheathed. Silver wielded a shorter blade - the one he called out rarely.

"I think letting these two burn off some steam is going to be a better bet," one of our escorts said behind me.

"Boss might get mad, but I'm up for some fun."

I was about to ask who the boss was when the elevator doors opened and more enemy guards ran at us. Silver engaged with the fastest two and I teleported past them. I brought my staff down on the floor, sending a strong shockwave down the hallway. The people before me were violently thrown into the walls and some back into the elevator. When they hit the floor, they did not move.

Silver caught up with me as I kicked one out of the way of the door. "You really are done caring."

Our escorts quickly hauled out the two I knocked back into the elevator.

As the elevator moved up, my connection strengthened. "Think I can get one more," I said before mentally diving back into the system, beginning the overload process on a third cannon. I came back once I completed my task, my connection weakened too much to reach the last one.

The elevator doors opened as another explosion rocked the ship. Our escorts were off first, shooting down the few in the hall. Silver charged forward as more came out of different rooms. His movements immediately appeared wild, but he was efficient. While he sliced one, he would slam his shield into another until it was their turn to meet his blade.

Blood coated the walls as he went. I levitated through the carnage, needing to burn off some of the excess arcane energy anyway.

I turned when the elevator behind us buzzed, signaling an arrival. I conjured a fireball, throwing it into the elevator before the doors opened enough to let anyone out. There was an explosion and then nothing other than the sound of Silver fighting.

"Hope we didn't need that," I commented to our escorts.

"There are other ways up."

Silver waited for us when he ran out of enemies. "Did you kill the people in the elevator?"

"Probably. The elevator is out of order."

My partner snorted and opened the door to the control room. "Are you sure about this?"

I sent bolts of electricity at the workers in the room watching them collapse at their stations before responding, "I will destroy this system with or without your help."

Our escorts moved to haul people out of the room.

Silver grabbed my arm before I could reach the chair. He pulled me to turn around and face him. His lips were on mine before I could protest. There was no power except for his necklace resonating against my skin. "Give them Hells," he said with a strained smile.

I nodded and took my seat. With what I planned, I would cripple the ship in the process. I slammed the large amount of arcane energy in my control into the system, quickly finding and setting the final cannon to overload before connecting to the arcane guns. I watched the chaos on the main deck as the final cannon exploded, taking out a chunk of the above deck with it.

One-by-one I pushed my power into overloading the smaller

guns, chaining them to go off one after another. Once I finished, I turned my attention to the shield emitters, forcing them to overload as well.

Something on one of the cameras caught my attention. Among the chaos I caused, Vince lead a team, taking out those who crossed their path, but otherwise they seemed to be on a particular course.

Now I knew who the boss was.

The only thing left now was to burn the wiring and see if I could destroy the orb. The system forced its calm and balance at me, siphoning off some of my arcane energy. Self-preservation?

Burning out the miles and miles of wiring was tedious and time consuming. I lost my view through the ship as the span of the system became smaller. By the time it was just me and the orb, I labored to breathe and had nothing left to fight it with - it pulled the arcane energy away from me faster than I could gather it.

Another presence joined the system. Silver appeared before me.

Panic overrode anything the system threw at me. "What are you doing here? You need to go while you can!"

"Not without you." He closed his eyes to the calm and balance the orb pushed. "It's time to go home, Kela." He took my hands and floated backward, pulling me along with him.

The system pulled at me, keeping me where I was. Stuck in the tug-of-war between the two, Silver's necklace flared, creating a golden-white barrier around us, breaking the orb's hold.

When we got out, my vision shifted back immediately and Silver knelt on the other side of the orb, his hands over mine. I pushed our hands away from the orb. He grabbed me by the wrists and pulled me out of the chair, away from the source of so many of our problems this trip and held onto me tightly.

Vince stepped up to the orb, signaling the people with him to take care of it. "We need to get the two of you out of here." He held my staff out to me.

I pushed Silver away to take the weapon and tilted my head toward the door. I moved as quickly as I could manage, stopping short when the leader came through. Before he could bring his gun up, I closed the distance with a burst of a flight spell and struck him across the head as hard as I could with my staff.

He dropped. Part of me hoped for more, but he remained still on the deck.

Our earlier escorts led the way to the extraction point.

Silver broke ahead of them as soon as more enemies came at us.

"You know we're supposed to be the ones fighting to get you out of here, right?" one of our escorts asked.

I kept walking. "Do you plan on stopping him?"

"No, ma'am. Just feeling useless."

A group of enemies coming from a side hall behind us stopped any further conversation. Our escorts turned to engage. I stepped in front of them, first sending thousands of ice shards at the group to distract them before chaining a lightning spell, branching it out, watching it multiply from one enemy to the next. They dropped in a wave.

"Save your bullets. I have power to burn being this close to the ley line," I said.

"Really feeling useless."

"We're close to getting above deck. The extraction point won't be far from where we exit," the other escort said.

Silver stood down the hall waiting for us. Blood dripped from his blade and his shield with splatters over his face and armor. What disturbed me most was his braid hung down his back. Even in training, when he stopped like this, it would always be over his right shoulder. Would I lose him to the past in this escape?

I turned to attack the coming footsteps when our escorts stopped me. Vince and the people with him caught up to us. "Let's move," he ordered.

They pushed past us. Silver fell in behind them while our original escorts took up a position behind me.

We made it a few more yards down the hall when I heard lots of loud footsteps coming from behind. Clenching my teeth and drawing arcane energy to both of my hands, I dropped my staff and turned around, hurling two fireballs down the hallway. I was done with interruptions.

I threw my shield spell up to fill the entire hallway as the fireballs went off, protecting us from the blasts. The force of the explosions made me slide back.

Someone behind me let out a low whistle as I reclaimed my weapon.

Silver stepped in front of me as I went to pass him. "You still here?"

I took a second to realize he was concerned about the fairie making a reappearance. "Yeah. You?"

"Yeah. Both of us need to get out of the fight soon."

I glanced up at my partner. His face was tight, his jaw set. I tilted my head in the direction of the others and we continued.

The wind took my hair as soon as we made it outside. I looked around at the Naval vessels surrounding us. Their lights were trained on the ship, shining brightly in the dark night.

More groups of enemies came at us. Silver went after the closest one. Our escorts moved to cover us from the other side. "No!" I shouted. "Help him!" I pointed back at Silver.

"But ma'am..."

I held my staff at the ready, walking past them. "Just do it and then get him out of here!" I did not wait for a response. Using a burst of power, I took off at the other group approaching, slamming the end of my staff into the deck, creating another shockwave, sending a few flying off of the ship while others either hit walls or were sent several yards down the deck.

My power manifested itself in iridescent tendrils across my body. Tears appeared on my arms and legs, showing the power beneath. I could not burn it off fast enough. This would be my last stand. Hopefully it would be enough for the others to get to safety.

Bringing my hands up, my feet also left the deck as I conjured a large amount of water overhead before unleashing it in a tidal wave down the deck, stopping anyone from getting up and taking out the next wave of fighters.

"Ketayl!" Vince yelled.

I turned to see what I needed to deal with. Something sharp struck my shoulder, forcing me back from the impact. I pulled the dart out, staring at it for a moment before looking at Vince who held the rifle. The picture was wrong - I thought he was my ally. My feet touched the deck only a moment before my legs gave out and I dropped to my knees.

Two of the men with Vince ran at me and I swung my staff, missing completely. I swung again and they kept their distance. *"I'm not done!"* My voice boomed with power. I forced myself back up, one unsteady foot at a time.

Silver said something to Vince before running toward me. I pointed my staff at him, fire engulfing my weapon.

I took deep breaths to maintain the fragile control I had. The world became too blurry to make out details which meant I had little time left.

When my partner stopped, I took it as a sign I would be left to finish. No sooner had I turned away when strong arms grabbed me from behind. I recognized the feel of Silver's armored jacket against my skin. The adrenaline rush I rode suddenly left me and the arcane energy was being siphoned off.

"Stop! Let me go!" I pushed against him both physically and with my quickly draining power. Between whatever Silver was doing and the tranquilizer, I made no progress getting free.

"Kela," Silver whispered in my ear, "it's time to go home."

Those were the last words I heard before the world went black.

24

I floated in a golden-white light. It was familiar and comforting despite never having been here before. The light soothed my frayed nerves from the concentrated arcane energy.

Occasionally I heard voices, but ignored them. Whatever it was, it could wait.

After a long time the light faded and I could only see black. I heard the sound of gentle waves nearby and smelled the ocean. A light breeze wafted through.

I slid on slick fabric when I went to sit up. My arms responded sluggishly as I reached toward whatever was around my head.

Large rough hands wrapped around my shoulders and helped me sit up. "It's okay, Ketayl. You're safe," Silver said gently. He pulled me into a tight hug. "Thank the Gods you're awake." His necklace warmed against my chest.

I opened my mouth to ask questions, but my voice would not come. My power pushed at me as my mind raced to make sense of the current situation. I managed to get my hands to what was around my head. I could not figure out what my fingers told me it was. I started pushing it off.

Silver took my hands and made a soothing sound. "I know this is scary. They bandaged your eyes as a precaution. Let me get you some water."

I shook my head as he moved away and grabbed his arm.

"Here, hold this. I don't have to go far." Silver put something silky and woven in my hands.

I squeezed his braid tightly as I heard him pour liquid into a glass.

"They started talking about moving you somewhere else. It's been a few days." He took my hands and wrapped them around the glass.

I shook, spilling some of the water over my fingers. He steadied my hands and helped me guide it to my mouth. I tried to down it quickly, but he held the glass so I could only drink so much at a time.

"I know you're thirsty, but you need to take it slow."

It took what I believed to be hours to finish the small glass. Silver took it away, immediately replacing it with his braid.

When he came back to me he brushed my cheek with his thumb. "How are you feeling?"

Scared. Confused. Lost. "Fine."

Silver let out a short laugh. "I should know better than to ask that question. Anything hurt?"

I shook my head.

"Want me to take the bandage off?"

I nodded. I needed to know where I was and what was going on.

"Keep your eyes closed. It's night and I only have one light on in here so it shouldn't be too bad." Silver's hands moved around my head. "You certainly were a force of nature out there. Holding back on me again?"

"No," I said softly, "Couldn't burn off the energy from the ley line faster than I got more."

Silver let out a soft huff. "Well, either way, I underestimated exactly how angry you were." He tugged lightly at the tape to finish getting the bandages off. Then he gently pressed underneath my eyes. "Everything appears normal. Look at me?"

It took time to adjust to even the low light in the room, but I managed to do as he asked. Until I looked at him, I did not realize how much I needed to see him. To know he was alive and healthy. I reached up and touched his face to make sure this was real.

Something was off and it wasn't his lack of shirt. I searched his face for an answer.

His missing necklace was odd, but still not it.

The color of his eyes seemed off. Even in low light like this, it would be hard not to make out the bright blue, but now they appeared to have clouded over.

Silver put his hand over mine and turned his face into the touch, kissing the palm of my hand. "I think I'll wait until after sunrise to let them know you're awake."

I turned to our surroundings. "Where are we?"

"The resort we had been moved to. It's one of the cabins instead of the hotel."

"How long were we on the ship?"

"Three weeks. I heard Kitteren has been going ballistic being unable to reach you."

I let out a soft huff. I would need to deal with her soon, but not right now. Another question tugged at my attention. "Why did the Director shoot me?"

Silver sighed, threading his hands into my hair. "Because you were going to die if you weren't stopped."

I turned away from him. "I couldn't control it much longer. Figured I could make sure you got to safety and take the rest of them down with me. You shouldn't have stopped me."

My partner forced me to look at him. "Get this through your head now: you have made it clear you won't leave me and I sure as Hells am not leaving you."

I glared at him.

"Gods help me, you are infuriating sometimes."

"Good."

Silver laughed. "Okay, okay. What have I gotten myself into with you?"

I shrugged, looking out over the water outside of our cabin. "I guess I still owe you a couple of days on your proposal."

"I'll admit, this whole ordeal ruined it. For me at least."

I stared at my lap. How we saw things would be colored now. "Yeah..." I closed my eyes. My hands were as stained as his. I knew I should feel something other than satisfaction for the destruction I caused, but I simply could not. Perhaps when this all sunk in.

"I'd like to rebuild from the beginning. It would only be fair if I was more open with you. And preferably I'd like to do this without getting captured by pirates," Silver said.

I gave a short laugh. "Maybe."

Silence fell between us for several seconds. "Dawn is approaching. Come sit with me?" Silver asked.

"Yeah." I went to move, but my legs would not respond properly.

Silver simply picked me up and carried me outside to one of the lounge chairs on the deck. I shivered at the cool breeze off the ocean. The slip of a dress I wore gave me little protection.

My partner retreated into the cabin for a moment, coming back with a blanket he placed over me. He sat down in the next chair, taking my hand in his.

Silently we watched the sun rise and I soaked up the peace and calm coming from his morning ritual. I had not seen actual daylight for so long. My eyes watered at the sight. I had been prepared to not see it again. His pendant warmed and a desire to be closer to him washed over me.

I closed my eyes and separated myself from what I received from the pendant.

Silver knelt in front of me. "What's wrong?"

I picked up the pendant, staring at it for a moment before reaching behind me and undoing the clasp. "Thank you for lending me this."

"Ketayl..."

I took his hand and relinquished the item. "I can't have it influencing me. It's not fair to either of us."

"What?" Silver held up the pendant in front of him. "How could it influence you? It's just a piece of metal."

I bit my lower lip, unsure how to describe what I sensed.

"Actually, let's hold off on that conversation," Silver said, putting his necklace back on. "I have a feeling it'll be part of another. Let's get you inside and changed before breakfast. They brought us back our things. They also brought the new stuff if you feel like wearing a dress."

I scrunched my face up at the idea and Silver laughed softly.

I managed to coordinate my legs this time, but Silver insisted on helping me walk. My attention had been on making sure my feet moved correctly and looked up when my partner stopped inside the door.

Vince stood there with his arms crossed. "You were supposed to report immediately when she woke up. And also wait for a doctor before removing the bandages."

"Like Hells," Silver spat. "You expect me to follow your orders after you used us like that?"

"What?" It came out more as a breath.

"Are you going to tell her or should I?" Silver glared at Vince.

Vince raised an eyebrow at my partner before turning his attention to me. "While I was unaware of the plan until it had been executed, the responsibility does fall to me. The orb was stolen in transport and the previous team leader deemed it necessary to let the two of you be captured to track where they took it. Suffice to say he and those involved in bypassing protocols are not even on your security detail let alone this assignment."

Spotting a nearby chair, I separated myself from Silver to sit down. I leaned forward, hanging my head. "That's why help never came. Was that the reason Lockonis gave us the downtime? To make sure the orb was secured?"

"No. She wanted the two of you to take time-off. I tried to make it as soon as I heard what was going on, but I wasn't fast enough to stop it."

I sighed, too tired to deal with this.

"Ketayl, how can you be so calm?!" Silver asked angrily.

"Because it wouldn't have mattered how far we had gone. We would have been targets until the orb was out of enemy hands. However," I paused, taking a moment to muster the strength to continue and glared up at Vince, "We should have been informed so we could have gone in prepared." Granted, if he had not known until the plan was in action, there would have been no time to warn us.

"The team wasn't prepared for your fireworks either," Vince pointed out.

"I guess we're all guilty of withholding information," I snapped back.

"Lockonis trained you too well. We'll talk more during the debriefing." Vince turned and left.

I sighed and rubbed the bridge of my nose. It was hard to be angry when my own sister had done something similar to me several months earlier. Lately I kept finding myself on the darker side of the business.

When I looked up again, Silver sat on the edge of the bed. He held his pendant up to stare at it.

"Did I break it?" I asked.

Silver shook his head. "I've never sensed anything from it before."

"What is it?"

"I'm not sure. It's barely there, but I can sense power from it."

I tilted my head, considering what happened. "You touched the orb, right?"

"Yeah. It was a last ditch effort. I wasn't sure if touching the orb around your hands would allow me to use your connection to get in. Now I understand the draw of it. If you hadn't been there, I might not have wanted to leave."

I closed my eyes at what he put himself through. "There's a chance you have some residual effect from the connection. Whether it's from the orb or me, I don't know. It should fade in time."

He shrugged and dropped the pendant.

"Looks better on you anyway," I joked.

Silver smirked. "You'd just need a different chain. Something a little nicer and shorter."

"I don't care for gold."

"So does that mean you prefer 'Silver' instead?" he asked with a broad smile and gestured at himself.

I rolled my eyes. "That was horrible."

He snorted and we both broke down laughing at his bad joke. I wiped at my eyes as Silver knelt down in front of me, brushing my hair back. "I love hearing you laugh. Took so long to get you to and then... I really thought I was going to lose you so many times recently."

I turned my eyes to my lap. "Until that barrier broke, I needed to keep..."

Silver put a finger over my lips. "I know. I'm just glad we have the chance to share this now." He took my hand and put it over his pendant. "What do you feel from it?"

I raised an eyebrow at him. "I thought you wanted to hold off on this conversation."

"The questions I have about what happened, yes, but I want to know what you feel now."

Closing my eyes, I concentrated on the small object. "I can still feel the thrum of power I always have and it's warm." I did not feel Silver anymore from it, but I might not with it being around his neck.

Silver gave me a soft smile and kissed the back of my hand. "I've pestered you enough for now. You probably want to change into something you're more comfortable wearing before we figure out breakfast. You might want to consider a swimsuit. It's going to be a good day for it and you need to take it easy."

I slowly made my way over to my bags digging through for something to wear. How I acted on the ship during our escape bothered me. "I'm sorry you had to see me like that."

I stood up and turned around directly into Silver. When had he gotten behind me?

Silver pulled me into a tight hug, resting his chin on my head. "I'll admit, thinking back on it, the power you wielded was terrifyingly beautiful. I think we're even though - you saw me at my worst."

I dropped the clothes in my hands and held onto him, letting the reality of what happened to us sink in. Would we ever be able to fix what had been broken?

EPILOGUE

I STARED at the falling snow outside of my quarters. Sighing, I forced myself to return to my book. There was little for me to do outside of schoolwork until they took me off of medical leave.

If only they could give me an idea of when it might be. It had already been three weeks since we escaped the ship.

Silver occupied himself with physical training if he was not here keeping me company. He stayed quiet for the most part, often reading. I figured he was as tired of the meetings as I was. How many more times they wanted to hear the same information, I did not know.

Hearing my door unlock I knew Silver was back. They gave us access to each others quarters, but locked us out of anything related to work.

"Ket?"

I turned from where I sat on the floor in front of the short table, not expecting Kitteren's voice. I stretched to see her over the back of the couch and stared at her for a moment, unsure if what I saw was real.

The moment broke when she jumped the couch and nearly tackled me to the floor in a tight hug. She buried her face in my shoulder and shook. I held her, running my hand over her hair to comfort her, not knowing what she needed.

Once she calmed down, I asked, "What are you doing here?"

Kitteren wiped the tear tracks from her face. "Well, if you'd answer my calls you'd have known I was coming."

That would be a first. Normally she thought surprising me with her presence was a good idea. I turned back to what I had been working on, finding the slip of paper I used for a bookmark. I knew better than to ignore her, but I wanted to keep my work organized.

"Talk to me, Ket. Mom and Dad are really worried. They hoped you would have come down to visit by now."

I took a deep breath, coming up with a quick reason to hopefully satisfy her. "The weather hasn't been good to drive."

"Don't give me that crap. You're shutting me out. You're shutting everyone out - including the person who went through it with you."

I glanced at my sister out of the corner of my eye. What could she possibly know? "No, I'm not. Silver's here all the time."

"And you don't talk to him!"

I sat back and stared at my sister. Shaking my head I got up and stood in front of the large windows, watching the weather. It was better than facing her.

Kitteren grabbed my shoulder roughly and spun me around. The anger in her face was matched by a sharp sting in my cheek. I stared at her with wide-eyes and lightly touched where she slapped me.

"I'm not letting you revert to your old ways." She stormed away for a moment before turning back to me. "Do you realize exactly how many people watched and prayed you and Silver made it out of there alive? You had two full branch offices and the main office. And those were just the ones I know about. Not to mention the werewolves. I had Hells of a time convincing them not to send people."

I moved and dropped down onto the couch, having no energy for the fight Kitteren wanted to start. I hung my head. "It's not like I don't know. It takes me a long time to go through my messages everyday. It's just..."

"Ket," Kitteren said, taking a seat next to me. "You went through three weeks of torture on a level I don't think anyone can comprehend. And no one can try to understand if you don't talk."

"Silver..."

Kitteren cut me off. "Yes, Silver went through a few Hells as well. Especially with the intimacy he was forced into to keep you in one piece. The Gods only know how much it would have broken him if he had to do more not to mention what it would have done to you as well. I'm not sure he could have brought himself to do it. But the point I'm making is he wasn't forced into some psycho system over and over again."

I sighed. I should know how nosy she could get by now. "You know a lot already."

"Yeah, I do. I got a chance to look at the file. I watched you tear through waves of enemies like it was child's play. Though I'm told you were on an arcane high or something."

"We were near a concentrated ley line," I corrected.

"Whatever that means. I just know you were pissed and on a war path."

I cringed and clamped my hands together on my lap to keep from at least visibly shaking. "I had to get Silver out of there. I saw how much of a toll it took on him. I..." I paused, taking a deep breath. "I should feel horrible about all the death and destruction I caused, but I don't. Does that make me a monster?"

"No! Hells no. You paid them back for how they treated you. Both of you. Seems only fair. Actually, you should have done more."

"I wanted to, but they stopped me." No one knew how much I wished to continue.

"Because you were going to die."

I closed my eyes, clenching my jaw. I really had not wanted Kitteren to know, but I should have known she would find out no matter how much I hid it.

"Ugh!" Kitteren sat back, crossing her arms. "You're so damn calm about all of this and all I want is to find out who in the Hells came up with the plan to retrieve the orb and tear their head off myself."

Silence fell between us for a few minutes. Unused to my sister's quiet, I asked, "So, why are you at the main office?"

"Well, to start, I wanted to check in on you. Maybe see if I couldn't get through." She poked me in the side of the head and I swatted at her hand. "Also, I've got to clean out my quarters. I'm going to stay in Ocean's Edge. Run the training program and in between sessions I'll work with Savanas' team. Unless I'm needed for something else. And it doesn't hurt that things have been good with Rathal."

I forced a smile. "I'm glad it worked out for you."

"Hey," Kitteren said softly, wrapping her arm around my shoulders, "It could still work out for you too. You still have Silver. You just need to let him in. And I don't mean access to your quarters."

I rolled my eyes.

"Come on. Mom and dad are here and want to get everyone together for dinner."

I sighed and got up, heading for my bathroom so I could attempt to look somewhat presentable. "How did you get in here anyway?"

"Silver unlocked the door for me. Rathal has been keeping him busy while we talked." She took my brush from me. "Let me."

I stayed still while she brushed my hair. Silver took to the task after we escaped as I found little reason to care about my appearance. Especially if I had nowhere to go.

"Can I offer some advice?"

I rolled my eyes. "Since when do you ask?"

Kitteren tapped my head with the back of my brush before returning to her task. "Take small steps. One thing at a time and things will get back to normal. I'm here and so are others. Don't keep isolating yourself."

Right now I needed to figure out how to make it through dinner.

"So what was it like kissing him?"

"Kitteren!"

ACKNOWLEDGMENTS

Joshua Jackson, Brandi Burns, Amy Stoll, and many others I've met over this past year who continue to encourage me and keep me going.

My local critique groups: Kenneth Jorgenson, Loni Townsend, Jim Lambert, Danielle Parker, Troy Lambert and many others. A few of them also were subjected to being beta readers as well.

And all of my friends and family who have been cheering me along.

ABOUT THE AUTHOR

J.C. Jackson is originally from New England and currently lives in southwestern Idaho with her husband and daughter.

On top of writing, she enjoys gaming whether that is picking up a controller or throwing down some dice in a tabletop RPG (as well as other board games). She has also been a fan of science fiction and fantasy since she was little.

Blog: https://jeicjackson.wordpress.com/
Facebook: https://www.facebook.com/jeicjackson/
Twitter: https://twitter.com/JeiC
Instagram: https://www.instagram.com/jeicjackson/